I am, or wa̲s̲ ... o̲r̲ the Kontra, Moon Singer, leader of the little ones. I have been other things in the past, and am also now under bonds for a time.

What did we care for lord or Trader in that meeting in a tent at the fair of Yrjar? Neither were more to us than the dust of cities that stifle us with their dirt and greed and clamor, and the drab thoughts of those who will themselves into such confines. But it is not necessary now to speak of the Thassa and their beliefs and customs, only of how my life came to be pushed from one future to another only because I took no care for the acts of men. . . .

MOON OF THREE RINGS

MOON OF THREE RINGS

ANDRE NORTON

SF
ace books
A Division of Charter Communications Inc.
A GROSSET & DUNLAP COMPANY
51 Madison Avenue
New York, New York 10010

MOON OF THREE RINGS

Copyright © 1966 by Andre Norton
All rights reserved. No part of this book may be repro-
duced in any form or by any means, except for the inclu-
sion of brief quotations in a review, without permission in
writing from the publisher.

All characters in this book are fictitious. Any resemblance to actual persons, living or dead, is purely
coincidental.

An ACE Book

Published simultaneously in Canada

2 4 6 8 0 9 7 5 3
Manufactured in the United States of America

TO SYLVIA COCHRAN,
who guided so many "infant" pens

KRIP VORLUND

I

WHAT IS SPACE? It is a wilderness beyond any man's exploring, even if he had a hundred, a thousand life spans in which to prowl the lanes between solar systems and planets, to go questing, to seek ever new and newer knowledge of what may lie beyond the next sun, the next system. Yet to such seekers comes also the knowledge that there must be no boundaries to man's belief, but rather an acceptance of wonders which would leave the planet-bound, those who follow familiar trails, incredulous and refusing to accept the evidence of their own senses.

Those who do venture ever into the unknown— the First-in Scouts of Survey, the explorers, and not the least, the Free Traders who pluck a living from the fringes of the galaxy—to these it is a commonplace thing to discover that the legends and fantasies of one planet may be lightsome or grim truth on another world. For each new planet-fall brings its own mysteries and discoveries.

Which is perhaps too much of a pseudo-philosophic beginning for this account—save I know of no better, not being used to making more than trade reports for that repository of some very strange facts—the League of Free Traders. When a man tries to deal with the unbelievable, he finds it a fumbling business, in need of some introduction.

First-in Scouts, from their unending quest for new worlds and systems, turn in many weird and strange reports to Survey. But even the planets opened to human contact by their efforts can yield hidden secrets, after they have been pronounced favorable ports for wandering ships, or even for pioneer settlements.

The Free Traders who exist upon cross trade, having no fat plums to sustain them as do the Combines of the inner planets with their monopolies, face now and again things that even Survey does not know. Thus it was on Yiktor—in the time of the Moon of Three Rings. And who better can make this report than I, to whom this happened, though I was only assistant cargomaster of the *Lydis*, the last-signed member of her crew into the bargain.

Over the years the Free Traders, because of their way of life, have become almost a separate race in the galaxy. They own no one world home, nor do some ships possess a home port, but wander always.

So it is that among us the ship itself is our only planet, and we look upon all without its shell as alien. Although not in this sense are we xenophobic, for it is part of our nature that we have a strong bent toward exploration and acceptance of the outer.

Now we are born to the trade, for families live within the larger ships, it being decided long since that such was better for us than casual and transitory connections in ports which might lead to a man's losing his ship. The big space-borne ports are small cities in themselves, each operating as a central mart for a sector where large deals are carried out, where those who have a mate and children may enjoy a kind of home life between voyages.

But the *Lydis* was a bachelor ship of the D class, intended for risky rim trading where only men without ties would venture. And I, Krip Vorlund, was well content to so set my feet on the ladder of trade. For my father had not returned from his last voyage years back. And my mother, after the custom of the Traders, had married again within two years and followed her new mate elsewhere. So I had no one to speak up for me at the time of assignment.

Our captain was Urban Foss, well regarded as a coming man, though young and sometimes thought to be a shade reckless. But that suited his crew, who were willing to have a leader who might by some gamble advance them well into the ranks of those who had solid credit at the trade center. Juhel Lidj was the cargomaster, and my only quarrel with him, though he was no light taskmaster, was that he guarded some of his trade secrets jealously, leaving me to ferret hints for myself. But perhaps that was the best way of training, putting me ever on the alert when I was on duty, and giving me opportunity to think much when I was not being official.

We had made two good voyages before we landed on Yiktor, and undoubtedly we felt that we were perhaps better than we were. However, caution is never forgotten on a Free Trader. After we planeted, before we opened hatches, Foss had us all in to listen to the guide tape carrying all the warnings for this world.

The only port, such as it was—for this was truly a frontier world—lay outside Yrjar, a city as far as Yiktor knew cities, in the middle of a large northern land mass. We had timed our arrival carefully for the great trade fair, a meeting of merchants and populace from all over the entire planet, held at two-planet-years intervals at the end of the fall harvest season.

Like fairs on many other worlds, this gathering had once had, and still possessed as a pallid shadow, religious significance, being the supposed date when an ancient folk hero had met and vanquished some demoniacal enemy to save his people, died as a result of his exertions, and thereafter been entombed with pomp. The people still enacted a kind of play of this feat, followed by games in which the lords vied with one another, each backing his personal champions. The winners of each contest carried off enough awards and prestige—not for himself alone but also for his patron—to last until the next fair.

II

THE GOVERNMENT of Yiktor was at the feudal stage. Several times in its history kings and conquerors had risen to unite whole continents under their sway for perhaps their lifetimes. This unification sometimes extended into the following generation, or maybe two, but eventually fell apart through quarrels of the nobles. The pattern had held constant with no advancement. The priests, though, had vague traditions that there had been an earlier civilization which had risen to a position of greater stability and technical knowledge.

No one knew the reason for the stagnation at this step of civilization, and no native appeared to care, or to believe there could be another way of life. We had arrived during one of the periods of chaos wherein half a dozen lords snapped and snarled at one another. But none had the backing, audacity, luck, or whatever was demanded of a leader, to take over. Thus the existing balance of power was a delicate thing.

This meant for us Traders brain lock, weapon lock, nuisances though they were and much as we disliked them.

Far back in Free Trading, for their own protection against the power of the Patrol and the wrath of Control, the Traders themselves had realized the necessity of these two safeguards on primitive planets. Certain technical information was not an item to be traded, no matter how high the induce-

5

ment. Arms from off-world, or the knowledge of their manufacture, were set behind a barrier of No Sale. When we planeted on such a world, all weapons other than belt stunners were put into a lock stass which would not be released until the ship rose from that earth. We also passed a brain lock inhibiting any such information being won from us.

This might seem to make us unarmed prey for any ambitious lord who might wish to wring us hard for such facts. But the law of the fair gave us complete immunity from danger—as long as we stayed within the limits set by the priests on the first day.

For following almost universal galactic custom, one which appeared to be spontaneous and native to every world where such gatherings had existed for ages, the fair ground was both neutral territory and sanctuary. Deadly enemies could meet there and neither dared put hand to weapon. A crime could be committed elsewhere and, if the criminal reached the fair and was law-abiding therein, he was safe from pursuit or punishment as long as the fair continued. The gathering had its own laws and police, and any crime committed within was given speedy punishment. So that this meeting place was also a site for the cautious sounding out between lords for the settlement of feuds, and perhaps the making of new alliances. The penalty for any man breaking the peace of the fair was outlawry—the same as a sentence of death, but perhaps in its way, more torturous and lingering for the criminal.

This much we all knew, though we sat in patience as the guide tape told it over again. For on a Trader

one does not ever push aside any briefing as un-
necessary or time-wasting. Then Foss launched once
more into the apportioning of planetside duties.
These varied in rotation among us from world to
world. There was always a guard for the ship—but
the rest of us could explore in pairs in our free time.
From the morning gong until midafternoon we
would man our own booth for meeting with native
merchants. Foss had visited Yiktor once before, as
second in command of the *Coal Sack,* before he had
his own ship, and now drew upon his notes to refresh
his memory.

As is true on all Free Traders, though the cargomaster handles the main cargo and the business of
the ship at large, each member of the crew is expected to develop some special interest or speciality,
to keep his eyes open, and to suggest new products
which might add to the general prosperity of the
voyage. Thus we were encouraged to explore all
such marts in pairs and to take an interest in local
produce, sniffing out a need of the natives which we
might in the future supply, or picking up some
hitherto overlooked export.

The main cargo from Yrjar was Lidj's concern; it
was sprode, a thick juice pressed from certain
leaves, then hardened into blocks which could be
easily stored in our lowest hold after we had emptied
it of bales of murano, a shimmering, thick silk which
the Yiktor native weavers seized upon avidly. They
patiently unraveled its threads to combine with their
finest material, thus making a length go twice as far.
Sometimes a lord would pay a full season's land

tribute for a cloak length of unadulterated fabric. The sprode blocks, transferred at section base to another ship, would end up halfway across the galaxy, where they were made into a wine which the Zacathans declared heightened their mental powers and cured several diseases of that ancient lizard race. Though I can't imagine why a Zacathan needed his mental powers heightened—they already had quite a start on mankind in that direction!

But the sprode would not provide a full cargo, and it was up to us to discover odds and ends to fill in. Guesses did not always pay off. There were times when what seemed a treasure turned out to be a worthless burden, eventually to be space-dumped. But gambles had done so well in the past that we were certain they would pay off again for all of us.

Any Trader with a lucky choice behind him had a better chance for advancement, with hopes for not too long a time before he could ask for an owner's contract and a higher share in a venture. It meant keeping your eyes open, having a good memory for things recorded on past voyage tapes, and probably having something which our elders called flair and which was a natural gift and nothing learned by study, no matter how doggedly pursued.

Of course, there were always the easy, spectacular things—a new fabric, a gem stone—eye catchers. But these were usually right out in the open. And the fair steerer made very sure that the cargomaster saw them at the first sighting when the big merchants met. On such sales as these depended perhaps all a planet's lure for off-world Traders, and they were publicly hawked.

The others were "hiders," things you nosed out on spec, almost always an obscure product some native merchant had brought to the booths on spec himself—small items which could be made into luxury trade for off-world, light, easy to transport, to sell for perhaps a thousand times cost price to the dilettanti of the crowded inner planets, who were always in search of something new with which to impress their neighbors.

Foss had had a storied success on his second voyage with the Ispan carpets, masterpieces of weaving and color which could be folded into a package no longer than a man's arm, yet shaken out in silken splendor to cover a great-room floor, wearing well, with a flow of shade into shade which delighted and soothed the eyes. My immediate superior, Lidj, was responsible for the Crantax dalho discovery. So it was that a very insignificant-appearing, shriveled black fruit had now become an industry which made the League a goodly number of credits, put Lidj on secondary contract, and benefited a quarter of a struggling pioneer planet. One could not hope for such breaks at the start of course—though I think that deep down inside all of us apprentices did—but there were smaller triumphs to bring a commendation for one's E record.

I went with Lidj and the captain to the in-meeting on first day. It was held in the Great Booth, which was really a hall of no mean dimensions on a field beyond the walls of Yrjar, now the center of the fair. While most Yiktorian architecture tended toward the gloom and dark of buildings which must always be ready to serve as fortifications in time of siege, the

Great Booth, being free of such danger, was somewhat less grim. Its walls were of stone but only part way. Inside there was an open space almost the entire width, broken only by pillars which supported a sharply peaked roof, the eaves of which extended far out from the walls to afford good weather protection—though it was the dry season in which the fair was held and usually fine weather. The light thus given to the interior was far more than you could find in any building elsewhere on Yiktor.

We were the only Free Trader in port, though there was a licensed ship under Combine registry, carrying, by contract only, specified cargo which we did not dispute. This was one time when there was truce between off-worlders and no need for sharp maneuvering, our captains and cargo masters sharing the high seats of the senior merchants in amicability. The rest of us lesser fry were not so comfortably housed. We rated on a level with their second guildsmen and by rights would have had to stand in the outer aisles, save that we each bore, with a great deal of show, counting boards. These served the double duty of getting us inside with our officers, and impressing the native population that off-worlders were rather stupid and needed such aids for reckoning—always a beginning move in shrewd bargaining. We therefore squatted at the foot of the high-seat platform and took ostentatious notes of all the exhibits displayed and praised in the offering.

There were some furs from the north, a deep rich red with a ripple of golden light crossing them as they were turned in the hands of the merchant show-

10

ing them. Fabrics were brought out by the bolt and draped over small racks put up by subordinates. There was a great deal of metalwork, mostly in the form of weapons. Swords and spears appear to be a universal primitive armament in the galaxy, and these were undoubtedly forged by masters who knew their art. There was chainlink armor for the body, helmets, some of them crested with miniature beasts or feathered birds, and shields. And then a last merchant came up with the air of one about to top the show of war materials. Two of his guildsmen exhibited shooting at a mark with a new type of crossbow which, from the stir his demonstration provoked, must have been a vast improvement over the usual.

The arms display, which was a very large item in the local market, was more or less of a bore for us. Of course now and then one picked up a sword or dagger to sell to some collector. But that was the smallest of private ventures.

It was a long session. The Yiktorians broke it once for refreshments, passing around tankards of their bitter, and to us undrinkable, ale and a ''hasty meal'' made of a fruit-and-meat paste between flat grain cakes. But it was near to sunset before we were dismissed. By custom Captain Foss and Lidj were to go on to the official banquet given by the fair authorities, but we second men would return to our ships. The junior representative of the Combine Duffoldan who had been sharing the same uncomfortable board seat with me at the platform foot, stretched and grinned after he slammed his note board between his middle and his belt for safekeeping.

"Well, that's safely over," he said, stating the obvious. "You free to port crawl?"

Usually Free Traders and Combine men do not mix. There was too much trouble in the past history we share, though nowadays things are better policed than they used to be. The League has a weighty hand and the Combine leaders no longer try to elbow out a Trader who can call upon such support. In the old days a one-ship Trader had no hope of fighting back. But the feelings and memories stemming from those times still kept us apart, so I was no more cordial than mere civility when I answered.

"Not yet. Not until after report."

"Same here." If my coolness meant anything he did not show it. Instead he waited for me to stow away my own board, which I did slowly to give him a chance to go, though he did not take it. "I am Gauk Slafid."

"Krip Vorlund." Reluctantly I matched step with him. The exit was crowded by native merchants and guildsmen. And, as is wise for off-worlders, we did not push in among them. I saw him glance at my collar badge, and I returned that check. He was in cargo, but his disk was modified by two bars while mine bore only one. But then promotion in the Combine, while leading perhaps to greater wealth in the end, came more slowly.

One can never judge the planet age of those who spend most of their lives in space. Some of us cannot even tell the number of our years by that method. But I thought this Gauk Slafid might be somewhat older than I.

"Done your spec-looking yet?" That was a question I would have thought too brash for even a Combine man, arrogant as they were inclined to be. Yet when I stared at him, I believed he did not honestly realize that that was one of the questions one did *not* ask, save of a kinsman or blood comrade. Perhaps he had heard of Free Trader customs and was drawing on faulty knowledge to make conversation.

"We are not yet port free." No use taking offense if his question was an innocent one, though in bad form. One learns to put aside offense when dealing with aliens, and the Combine in the past had been more alien to those of my calling than many nonhuman contacts.

Perhaps he read something of my feeling, for he did not pursue that line; but as we came to a thronged side street he motioned at its gaudy flags and banners, each bearing the squiggles of local sign writing, and proclaiming a number of amusements, both innocent and bordering on the vicious. For, as the fair gathered sellers and buyers, priests and respectable people, so was it the focus for those who earn their livelihood by offering excitement for the mind and senses.

"There is plenty to see here—or are you ship-bound at night?" Was there or was there not a faint trace of patronage in that? I decided it was best not to explore beyond surface emotions. We were not engaged in any sale, and I was cautious.

"So I have heard. But I have not yet drawn my watch button."

He grinned again, raising his hand to his forehead in a gesture approximating a salute. "Fortune attend you then, Vorlund. We have already drawn and I have my night free. If you make it, look me up." Again he gestured, this time indicating a banner near the end of the line. It was not bright in color like those the wind tugged at around it, being an odd shade of gray, yet also shot with rose. Still, once you looked at it, your eyes kept returning, undeterred by the more garish lures surrounding it.

"That is something special," Slafid continued. "If you like beast shows."

A beast show? For the second time I was disconcerted. My mental picture of a Combine man suggested a far different taste in amusement— something closer to the sophisticated, almost decadent pleasures of the inner planets.

Then suspicion moved in me. I wondered if this Gauk Slafid was esper. For he had unerringly picked out the one entertainment which would draw me first, did I know of it. I allowed one of my mind-seek tendrils to uncurl, not actually to invade, naturally—that was the last thing I must do—but to seek delicately for any esper aura. There was none, and I was left a little chagrined at my suspicion.

"If I am fortunate," I answered him, "I will indeed follow your advice."

He was hailed then by a crewman wearing the insignia of his ship, and gave me that half salute once more before he joined his friend. But I stood for a moment or two watching that almost demurely colored banner, trying to figure out why it drew the eye

14

so steadily. Things such as that are important for Traders to learn. Was it only me that it could so influence, or was it the same for others? Somehow to know the answer became so important that I was determined to bring someone, the most cool-headed crew mate I could find to test it.

I was lucky to come away from the drawing with port leave for that night. The *Lydis* had so small a crew that only four of us were free, and it can be difficult for four pledged to go in pairs if they have very diversified ideas of amusement. Because of our junior status I went out with Griss Sharvan, the second engineer. Well, I had wanted a hardheaded companion to try my banner on, and in Griss fate had given me one. He is a born Trader, generations bred as all of us. But his first love is the ship and I do not believe that he ever, except when it was expected of him, searched for any trade. Luckily I remembered that the deep crimson banner of a swordsmith's display fencer flapped not too far from the beast show, and used that as a lure for Griss. Among our own kind Griss is a gambler, but that is another activity against which we are inhibited in an alien port. It can lead, as drinking, drugging, and eyeing the daughters of strangers, to trouble which would endanger the ship. Thus the desires for such amusements are blocked for us temporarily, and in our sober moments we agree that is wisdom.

At the end of the show street, now brilliant with lanterns, each as brightly colored as the banners above, each patterned with pictures through which light shone to advertise the fares within, I pointed out that of the fencer. The pink-gray flag was still there, but the lantern below it was a silver globe with no pattern breaking its pearl luster.

Griss pointed to it. "What's that?"

"I was told a beast show," I replied.

Living as we do mostly in space, Free Traders might be expected to have little contact or interest in animals. Long ago all ships carried felines for the protection of the cargo, since they hunted to rout out any pests stowing away. For centuries they were inseparable crew members. But their numbers grew less and less; they did not have as large or as many litters any more. We had forgotten where that animal had originated, so fresh stock could not be obtained to renew the breed. There were still a few at headquarters, highly prized, protected, tended, in hope that the breed might be reinstated. And we had all tried from time to time to replace them with various hunters from many worlds. One or two breeds had promise, but the majority could not adapt to ship life.

Perhaps this desire for companion animals gives us a strong pull toward alien beasts. I did not know about Griss, but I knew that I *must* visit the booth behind the moon globe. And it seemed that I would have no argument, for he came willingly with me.

From somewhere there was a dull, heavy gong note. The chatter, the laughter, the singing died down a little, the crowd paying tribute to a temple call. But the hush did not last, for while the fair had its religious side, that had faded with the passing of centuries.

We came under the shadow of the pink-gray banner into the halo of the moon lamp. I had expected some pictures of the animals to be strung up to entice an audience. But instead there was only a fabric screen bearing tangles of native scripts, and over the door flap a strange mask emblem, neither beast nor bird but combining the two. Griss gave a small exclamation as he looked up at that.

"What is it?"

His eager expression surprised me a little. I had seen such a look before only when he fronted a new and intricate machine.

"This is a real find."

"Find?" I thought of some piece of trade luck.

"A real sight," he corrected himself as if he knew my thought. "This is a Thassa show."

Like Captain Foss he had visited Yiktor before. But I could only repeat, "Thassa?" I believed I had studied the Yiktor tapes with close attention, but the meaning of this eluded me.

"Come!" Griss pulled me along to where a slender native in a silvery tunic and high red boots was accepting scale pieces for admittance. The native looked up and I was startled.

Around us was the crowd of Yiktorians born and bred—human as to form, with only slight differences between them and my own species. But this youth in his pale clothing seemed more alien to the world than we.

He had an appearance of fragility, almost as if the wind tugging at the sign banner over us could lap around him and carry him off. His skin was very smooth, with no sign that any beard had ever pricked through its surface, and very fair—little or no color in it. His features were human enough, except for the huge eyes, so dark one could not be certain of their color. His brows slanted so far up on the temples they actually joined with his hair, and the shade of that growth was silver-white.

I tried not to stare as Griss offered a token and the native lifted the tent flap for our entrance.

III

THERE WERE no seats, but several wide platforms raised in a series of steps at one end of the tent, such as might be easily dismantled when the show moved. These faced a larger stage which was now empty, but backed by draperies of the same pink-gray as the banner. A series of moon lanterns hung from the center pole overhead. The whole effect was somehow simple yet almost elegant, and to me not in keeping with any beast show.

We had come just in time, for a fold of the back drapery was lifted and the master trainer came to face the audience. Even though the hour was early, there were a goodly number of people, many of them children.

Master? No, the newcomer, though she wore tunic, breeches, and high boots similar to those of the doorkeeper, was clearly a woman. Her tunic was not collared tight to the throat, but fanned out behind her head in an arc of stiffened fabric that glinted along the edge with small sparks of ruby light, the color of which matched her boots and wide belt. She wore also a short, formfitting, sleeveless jacket of the same red-gold fur I had seen displayed in the Great Booth that morning.

She did not carry any whip such as most beast tamers flick about to enforce their commands, but a slender silver wand which could be no defense. It gleamed to match her hair, which was twisted into a high cone and made fast with pins headed by the sparkling ruby lights. In the triangular space between her long slanting eyebrows and the center of her hairline was an elaborate arabesque of silver and ruby which appeared fastened to her skin, for it did not shift with any turn or lift of her head. There was about her a sureness, a confidence that is a part of those who are masters of themselves and of some great art.

I heard a quick-drawn breath from Griss. "Moon Singer!" His exclamation held a tinge of awe, an emotion rare among the Traders. I would have demanded an explanation from him, save that she who stood on the platform made a gesture now with her wand and at once all hum of speech ended. The audience paid her far more respect than the crowd without had paid the temple gong.

"Freesha and Freesh"—her voice was low, a kind of croon, leaving one from the first word wanting to hear more—"give kindness now to my little people, who wish only to amuse you." She stepped to the end of the platform and made another wave of her wand. The drapery at the back rose just high enough to allow entrance to six small furred creatures. Their pelts were short-haired, but very thick and plushy, of a dazzling white. They scurried on hind feet, holding small ruby-colored drums to their rounded stomachs with forepaws which had a distinct resemblance to our human palms and fingers, save that their fingers were very long and thin. Their heads were round, and from them projected furless, slightly pointed ears. As with their mistress, their eyes appeared too large in proportion to the rest of their faces, which were wide-nosed and rounded of muzzle. Each carried in a loop over its back a bushy, silky-looking tail.

They trooped, one behind the other, to the opposite side of the stage from their trainer, and squatted on their haunches behind the drums on which they now rested their long-fingered paws. She must have given them some signal I missed, for they began to thump out, not ill-assorted bangs, but a definite rhythm.

Again the draperies arose and another set of actors came forth. These were larger than the drummers, and perhaps less quick in their movements. They were heavy of body for their size, but they tramped in time to the drumming, their coarsely furred bodies dark brown in shade, their huge, long ears and narrow, protruding snouts making them seem grotesque and truly alien. Now they swung their heads in time to the rhythm, their snouts flicking at the tips.

But they only served as mounts for yet another troop. Small heads of light cream, with big rings of darker fur about the eyes giving the faces an eternally inquiring look, were held high. Like the drummers these riders appeared to use their forepaws as we might our hands; they also carried cream-and dark-ringed tails pointing straight up.

The tapir-nosed mounts and their ring-featured riders paraded solemnly to the fore of the stage. And thereafter I witnessed sheer magic. I have seen many beast shows on many worlds, but nothing like unto this. There was no cracking of whip, no voiced orders from their mistress. They performed not as if they were doing learned tricks, but rather as though they were carrying out some ceremonies of their own, unwatched by those not of their species. And there was no sound from the audience, nothing save the different rhythms beat out by the furred musicians and the complicated series of cries the actors voiced now and again. The snouted beasts and their riders were only the first. I was too entranced to count all the acts. But when at last they paraded off-stage to a roar of applause, which they apparently did not hear, I thought we had seen at least ten different species.

She who was mistress came once more to the center of the platform and saluted us with her wand.

"My people are tired. If they have pleased you, Freesh, Freesha, they have had their reward. They will appear again tomorrow."

I looked to Griss. "Never have I—" I began when there was a touch on my shoulder and I turned my head to see the youth who had collected admissions.

"Gentle Homos," he spoke in Basic and not in the speech of Yrjar, "would you care to see the little ones more closely?"

Why such an invitation had been given us, I had no idea. But it was one which I was eager to accept. Then that caution ingrained in us asserted a warning, and I hesitated, looking to Griss. Since he appeared to know something of these Thassa (who or whatever they might be), I left the decision to him. But he seemed to have no doubts.

We drew apart from those who were reluctantly leaving and followed our guide to the stage and behind the draperies. There were strange scents here, those of animals, but clean and well-cared-for beasts, of bedding of vegetable matter, of food alien to our noses. The space fronting us was perhaps three times the size of the theater.

Lengths of wooden screen had been erected to enclose the area. Stationed alongside them were vans such as we had seen elsewhere for the transportation of wares. There was a line of picketed heavy draft animals, kasi, many of them now lying at ease chewing their cuds. Set in rows, almost in the form of a town with narrow streets, were a series of cages. At the end of the nearest of such rows was the woman. Woman—no—though I could not set age to her, she looked at this distance far more like a girl of few years. It was the elaborate coiling of her hair, the forehead decoration, and her vast assurance which gave the patina of years closer looks denied.

She still held the silver wand, slipping it back and forth between her pale fingers as if it were an anchor of sorts. Though why that thought crossed my mind I could not have said, for nothing else in her expres-

22

sion or manner would lead one to believe that she had ever known uneasiness of any kind.

"Welcome, Gentle Homos." Her basic was low-toned as the native speech she had used on stage. "I am Maelen."

"Krip Vorlund."

"Griss Sharvan."

"You are from the *Lydis*." No question, but a statement. We nodded in confirmation. "Malec," she spoke to the youth, "perhaps the Gentle Homos will take verfor with us."

He made no answer but walked rapidly down one of the cage streets to a lattice wall structure at the right of the picketed beasts. Maelen continued to study us and then she pointed with her wand to Griss.

"You have heard something of us." She swung that pointer to me. "But you have not. Griss Sharvan, what have you heard of us? And be no more silent about the ill than the good, if good there has been."

He was tanned darkly, as are all of us who live in space. Besides the fairness of this people he was almost black. And I was the same, but under that dark overlay he flushed now and I read self-consciousness.

"The Thassa are Moon Singers," he said.

She smiled. "Incorrect, Gentle Homo. Only some of us sing the Moon Power into use."

"But you are such a one."

She was silent and her smile was gone as if it had never been. Then she answered him. "That is the truth—as far as you know it, man of the Traders."

"All the Thassa are of another blood and kind. None of Yiktor, save perhaps themselves, know from whence and when they came. They are older than the lordships or temple-recorded time."

Maelen nodded. "That is the truth. What else?"

"The rest is all rumor—of powers for good and ill which mankind does not have. You can ill-luck a man into nothingness, and all his clan with him." He hesitated.

"Superstition?" she asked. "But there are so many ways of shadowing a man's life, Gentle Homo. Rumor always wears two faces, true and false, both at the same time. She must be harkened to and ignored. But I do not think that we can be accused of any over ill-wishing by any now living on this world. It is true that we are an old people and one content to live in our own fashion, troubling no one. What do you think of our little people?" Abruptly she swung from Griss to me.

"That I have never seen their equal on any world."

"Do you think other worlds would welcome them?"

"You mean—take the show into space? But that would be chancy, Gentle Fem. The transportation of animals needing diverse foods, special care—some cannot adapt to space flight at all. There is a way of putting them into freeze between landings. But that has a high risk and some might die. I think, Gentle Fem, it would take much planning and perhaps a specially built and equipped ship which would—''

''Cost a fortune,'' she finished for me. ''Yes, so many dreams shatter on that rock, do they not? But if not the whole show, perhaps some of the main attractions might travel. Come, see my people—you will find this an experience to remember.''

She was very right. We discovered as she led us up one of the cage streets and down another that these were not places of confinement but rather, as she pointed out, places of safety to protect her people from the harm which might come from human curiosity. The inhabitants were at the front of their dwellings as she stopped before each one and formally introduced us to them. And the feeling grew in me that these were indeed ''people'' with minds and feelings, strange to but approaching my own. There rose in me a great longing to have one for a ship comrade, though prudence argued against such recklessness.

We were near to the end of the last street when someone came running. He was one of the ragged ''odd boys'' who haunted the fair, picking up tokens by message running, and perhaps by less legal means. Now he danced from one bare foot to the other as if he had a message of import yet feared to disturb the Thassa girl. But she cut short her speech and looked to him.

''Freesha, the beast seller. It is as you asked me to discover—he has a furred one in torment.''

Her face seemed to narrow, her lips drew taut against her teeth. She was even more alien for an instant, and it seemed to me that she expelled her breath in a feline hiss of anger. Then her calm mask was once more in place and she spoke to us.

"It would seem that one has need of me, Gentle Homos. Malec will entertain you. I shall not be gone long."

What impulse then moved me I did not understand, but I said quickly, "Gentle Fem, may I go with you?"

There was no reason to believe that this was not her business alone. And I think she might have said so. Again her expression altered and she nodded.

"As you wish, Gentle Homo."

Griss looked from one to the other, but he did not offer to accompany us. He made his way to the living quarters with Malec as we followed the messenger. The late hour had filled the street here, though it was the rule that selling and buying, for the protection of the customer, must be done only in the bright light of day when all defects in the merchandise would be plain to see. It was the night hours that drew men and women to the amusements, and through that part of the fair we now made our way. I noted that when the natives saw the identity of my companion they made way for her, some watching her pass with a kind of apprehension or awe, such as might be given to a priestess. But she paid no heed to them.

Nor did she break the silence between us. It was as if, having agreed to my coming, she had then pushed me from her mind, to concentrate on a matter of greater importance.

We reached the end of the straggling collection of

amusen at places and found a rather pretentious tent of raw carlet splashed with eye-torturing green, from v ich came the calls of gambling games. The clamo sounded as if such games depended less upon menta skill than upon uproar, though I caught a glimpse of one table near the open door where they were playing the galaxy-wide Star and Comet. And seated there was my acquaintance of the afternoon, Gauk Slafid. Apparently his ship did not keep the strict discipline of the Free Traders, for he had a pile of counters before him that towered higher than those of his neighbors who, by their dress, were at least the close kinsmen of lords, though they appeared too young to be feudal rulers in their own right.

He raised his head as we passed and there was surprise in his glance, a glance which became a stare. He half raised his hand as if he would either wave or beckon to me, then his eyes dropped to the action on the table. One of the lordlings was also staring, and continued to watch us, with so intent and measuring a gaze that I fell a step or two behind Maelen and returned that scrutiny steadily. Nor did he then drop his eyes, but met mine, whether in challenge or mere curiosity, I could not read. And I dared not loose esper in that time and place to find out.

Beyond the gambling tent there was a place of small shelters—the living quarters, I presumed, for those working in the various amusement places. An odor of strange cooking, of sickly scents, and lesser and worse smells hung there. We turned again, picking our way around the huddle of huts to a quieter area where there were parked the wains, or carts, of the small merchants.

And thus we came to another tent from which the smell was vile and nose-twisting. I thought I again heard that hiss of anger from Maelen as she thrust forth her silver wand, using its tip to raise the entrance flap as if she refused to touch the fabric with her fingers. Within evil stenches warred mightily with one another, to raise a choking cloud, and there was also a clamor of barks, growls, raucous snarls, and sputterings. We stood in a small open space in the midst of cages which were not cherished living quarters, but rather places of imprisonment for their occupants, and wretched they were.

A beast dealer who cared for naught save quick profit and many sales owned them. The man himself came out of the shadows, his lips stretched in a smile which never reached his eyes in the way of greeting. But when he saw Maelen that smile was wiped away as if it had never been, and the coldness in his eyes was lighted by a spark which I read for hate— tempered by a wariness of the powers of the one he hated.

"Where is the barsk?" Maelen wasted no greeting on him, her tone was one of outright command.

"Barsk, Freesha? Who in possession of his full bag of wits would do aught with a barsk save slay it? It is a devil, a demon of the moonless dark as all know."

There was a listening look about her as if among all that clamor of unhappiness she could detect a single note and was now engaged in tracing it to its source. She paid no more attention to him but walked forward. I saw hate burn away his fear, so that he prepared to take a stand. His hand went to his belt and my seeking thought was a beam of light, showing me the weapon there, a curious, secret, and very deadly thing, unlike honest steel. This was small enough to be near swallowed up in a closed palm, fashioned not as a blade but a hooked claw, and it was green-smeared with what would be more deadly than its bite.

Whether he would have used it, even eaten as he was by rage and hate for the moment, I do not know. But he had no chance. The stunner in my hold, set to low ray, froze his fingers as they grasped the hidden fang. He stumbled back against one of his smelly cages and then cried out as the creature within, only a dark shadow, flung itself in a frenzy against the bars, striving to reach him. Maelen glanced around and then pointed her wand. The man reeled back and down, crouched on the floor with his useless hand doubled against him, now slobbering with a rage that choked him so he could not speak.

Maelen surveyed him coldly. "Fool, twice fool! Would you have me accuse you of peace breaking?"

She might well have dashed a bucket of icy water into his face, so quickly were the flames of anger gone. Fear replaced hate in his eyes. The thing she threatened meant outlawry. And on Yiktor that is the ultimate in punishment.

He scrambled on hands and knees back into the

shadows. But I thought it prudent to stand guard, and told her so.

She shook her head. "There is no need to fear this one. The Thassa are not to be befooled—as you will know—nather!" She did not speak scornfully as she addressed him with the name for worthless-hanger-on, but rather as one who states a fact.

So we went beyond a dividing curtain into a place of more cages and even worse smells. She hurried to one prison set apart by itself. What was housed there lay inert and, I thought, dead, until I saw the bone-creased hide rise and fall in long-spaced breaths.

"The cart there—" She was on her knees before the cage, staring intently at its occupant, but her wand indicated a board balanced on four wheels, and I pushed that forward.

Together we lifted the cage onto the cart and then pushed it to the outer portion of the tent. Maelen paused and took from her belt purse two tokens, tossing them to the top of one of the other cages.

"For one barsk, five scales and two fourthers," she said to the man still crouching in the shadows. "Agreed?"

Mind-seek told me he wanted us out. But a spark of greed had awakened behind his fear.

"A barsk is rare," he half whined.

"This barsk is near dead and worth nothing, not even the hide, you have so starved it. If you agree not, petition the price judge in open hearing."

"Enough!"

I caught her amusement. We pushed our burden into the open. The lad who had guided us hither came out of the dark and with him one of his fellows. Between them they took over management of the cart and cage. We took another route in return, one which brought us through a swinging panel in the lattice wall. As the cage was trundled by the line of the burden beasts, they snorted, and several rose to their feet, their nostrils wide, their heads tossing.

Maelen stood before them, her wand weaving from side to side, her voice raised in a low, comforting croon which restored their peace. The boys pushed the cage to the far end of the line and stood by it, waiting. Malec and Griss came out of the booth and the Thassa youth stooped to peer into the cage. Shaking his head, he paid the boys.

"It is hopeless for this one," he told Maelen as she came from the now quiet kasi. "Not even you can reach it, Singer."

She stood looking at the cage with a brooding stare, her wand in one hand while, with the other, she stroked the fur of her short jacket as if it was a beloved pet animal, alive and breathing.

"Perhaps you are right," she agreed. "Yet perhaps its fate is not yet written in the Second Book of Molaster. If it must go on the White Road, then it shall begin that journey in peace and without pain. For now it is too worn out to fight us. Let the cage for the sick hold it."

Together they loosed the fastening of the cage and lifted the creature within to wider, freer quarters in one of their own places, a soft litter spread to support the bone rack of body. It was larger, I saw, than any of the animals that had been on the stage this night;

standing, I would judge, if it could rise upon its feet, about as high as my lower ribs. The coat was dusty, befouled, dull, and ragged, but in color it was the red of Maelen's jacket.

In form it was an oddly proportioned animal, for the body was small and the legs very long and thin, as if the limbs meant for one beast had been fitted wrongly to another. The tail ended in a fan tuft, while from between the pointed ears, down the neck, and across the shoulders was a growth of longer hair of a much lighter shade, forming a brush of mane. The nose was long and sharp, showing strong teeth beneath black lips. All in all, had the thing not been so outworn, I would have said it was dangerous.

It aroused enough to snap feebly as they lowered it onto the bedding in the new cage. Then Maelen used her wand with a light touch, drawing it caressingly down between its eyes to the point of its nose, and its head ceased to move. Malec returned from the living quarters with a bowl from which he dipped liquid, dribbling it from his fingers onto the creature's head, and then down the belly, finishing by getting a small measure of it between the jaws and into the encrusted mouth from which a blackened tongue lolled.

Maelen stood up. ''For the present that is all we can do. The rest—'' Her wand drew a symbol in the air. Then she turned to us. ''Gentle Homos, the hour grows late and this poor one will need me.''

''Thank you for your graciousness, Gentle Fem.'' I found her open dismissal abrupt. It was as if she had once had some reason to seek us out, but it was no longer of importance. And somehow I disliked that thought, which might or might not be rooted in fact.

"And you for your aid, Gentle Homo. You will return." And that was no question, and not quite an order, but a statement of fact in which we both agreed.

On the way back to the *Lydis*, Griss and I did not talk together much, though I told him of what had happened in the tent of the beast seller and received his advice that I note it in my report, lest there be some future trouble.

"What is a barsk?" I asked.

"You saw. They provided the fur displayed this morning, that which Maelen wears as a jacket. They have the reputation for being cunning, intelligent, and dangerous. And they are sometimes killed, but I do not believe very often trapped alive. More than that—" He shrugged.

We were passing the port guards when all of a sudden I caught it—not the hatred of the beast seller alone, but that coupled with a strong and driving purpose. So joined with the emotions they struck the mind as keenly as one of the spears we had seen displayed by the armorers would tear into the body. I halted and swung around to face that mind-stroke only to see nothing but shadows and darkness. And then Griss was beside me, a drawn stunner in his hand. I knew that he, too, had felt it.

"What—?"

"The beast dealer, but also another—" Not for the first time in my life did I wish for the full inner power to read esper. As it was, sometimes a warning could cripple instead of armor a man.

33

Griss stared at me. "Take care, Krip. He may not dare to go against a Thassa, but he may deem that you are in his reach. This must go to the captain."

He was right, of course, though I hated to admit it. Urban Foss might restrict me to the *Lydis* until lift-off. Caution was a Trader's shield in strange places, but if a man always clung too tightly to his shield he might well miss the sword stroke which would free him from all danger. And I was young enough to wish to fight my own battles, not sit under cover waiting for the storm to sweep me by. Also, that thrust had been born of two wills and not one. I could understand the beast seller's enmity, but who had coupled that with another assault and for what reason? What other enemy had I made on Yiktor, and by what means?

MAELEN

IV

TALLA, TALLA, by the will and heart of Molaster and the power of the Third Ring, do I begin my part of this tale thus as would any Deed Singer of some upcountry lordling?

I am, or was, Maelen of the Kontra, Moon Singer, leader of little ones. I have been other things in the past, and am also now under bonds for a time.

What did we care for lord or Trader in that meeting in a tent at the fair of Yrjar? Neither were more to us than the dust of the cities that stifle us with their dirt and greed and clamor, and the drab thoughts of those who will themselves into such confines. But it is not necessary now to speak of the Thassa and their beliefs and customs, only of how my own life came to be pushed from one future to another, because I took no care for the acts of men, overlooked them—something I would not do with the little ones I respect.

Osokun came to me at the mid-point of day, sending to me firstly his shieldbearer. I think that he held me so much in awe that he would not treat me as one less than his own rank, though the plainsmen profess to believe the Thassa wanderers and vagabonds, not saying so to our faces however. He craved speech with me, said this young cub of the forts. And I was curious, for Osokun I knew by repute—and that repute clouded.

It is of the nature of the lords that power among them shifts often. This one or that rises to draw under him or remove all rivals, to become for a space the High King. So it has been many times in the past, an endless parade of mountains and plains in their history. Under one man a kind of uneasy peace holds, then straightway does it fall again. And for a space of many twelves of years now there has been no paramount lord, only many quarreling among themselves.

Osokun, son of Oskold, had in him the fire for great things, that will to power which, when blended with luck and skill, can bring a man successfully to the high seat. But when it is not so companied it torments the one who contains it, consuming him utterly. And I did not believe that Osokun had more than ambition to arm him. Such men are a danger not only to themselves but to their kind.

Perhaps it is not well to be aloof as are the Thassa,

looking upon others' quarrels with amusement or indifference. For this disarms wisdom and fore-knowledge.

I did not refuse Osokun's coming, though I knew that Malec did not agree that in this I moved with any wisdom. I confess that I had a certain curiosity as to why he sought contact with the Thassa, since he professed to consider us beneath his notice.

Though he had sent his sword-sworn to arrange the meeting, he came himself with no escort, but rather with an off-worlder, a young man with an easy smile and fair words on his tongue, but darker things unsaid in the mind behind his searching eyes, whom Osokun named Gauk Slafid.

They gave formal greetings and we gave them a just due at our table. But that impatience which would bring Osokun and all his plans to naught plunged him quickly into a business which was indeed perilous—though more for him, should it be detected, than for me, as the laws which bound him were not the Standing Words of my people.

It was more or less this: Osokun wanted special knowledge of the superior weapons of other planets. With this and such arms in the hands of his sword-sworns, he could straightway set up as the war lord of all the land and be such a high king here as generations had not known.

Malec and I smiled inwardly. I schooled my voice not to betray my laughter at what seemed to me to be his childish simplicity as I made him an answer which was courteous enough:

"Freesh Osokun, is it not well known that by their

arts all off-worlders hide such knowledge before they set boot sole upon Yiktor soil? And that they put also such safeguards upon their ships as locks not to be broken?''

He scowled, but then his face smoothed again. ''There is an answer for both bars to what I must have. With your aid—''

''Our aid? Oh, we have ancient learning, Freesh Osokun, but none to avail you in this circumstance.'' And I thought then that sometimes our reputation among the plainsmen could be a disadvantage. Perhaps Thassa power *could* break off-world barrier, but it would never be so turned.

But that was not what he wanted from us. Instead he hurried on, his thoughts and desires so urgent that his words tumbled from his lips in a race like unto the current of a mountain stream.

''It is the Free Trader we must pillage,'' he said. ''This Freesh—he indicated the off-worlder who was with him—''has furnished us with information.'' He then took from his belt pouch well-scribbled parchment from which he read and then expounded. And all the while the off-worlder smiled, nodded, and strove to mind-search us and what lay about us. But I held to the second level of thought and he gained naught that would do him any good.

Osokun's plan was simple enough, but there are times when simplicity backed by audacity works, and this might be such a time. Men from Free Traders are encouraged to seek out new products. Thus Osokun need only entice some crewman of a Trader outside the boundary of fair law and take him captive. If he could not wring the information he needed from his prisoner, he could bargain with the ship's captain for his return.

To this Slafid agreed. "It is a point of honor among these Free Traders that they care for their own. Let one be taken and they will buy his release."

"And how do we fit into your plan—if we choose?" Malec asked.

"Why, you provide the bait." Slafid told us. "The beast show will draw some of them, for they are forbidden to drink, gamble, or seek out women on strange worlds. In fact they could not if they would, being conditioned to such a state. Therefore we cannot tempt them by ordinary means. But let them come to one of your shows, invite them farther into your life, interest them as much as you can. Then, make a pretext that for some reason you must move for a space outside the fair. Draw one of them to visit you again—and your part shall be over."

"And just why should we do so?" Malec allowed some hostility to creep into his voice.

Osokun looked at us both directly. "There are threats I could make—"

I laughed then. "To the Thassa? Freesh, you are a brave, brave man! I see no reason why we should play your game. Get you other bait, and such fortune as you deserve attend you." And I reached out my hand to reverse the guest goblet standing on the table between us.

He went very red and his hand was on his sword

hilt. But the off-worlder lay his fingers on his arm. Though Osokun shot a look of anger at him also, yet he got to his feet and went with the other, saying no farewell. Slafid, smiling again, gave due courtesy, having about him the air of one not defeated but merely willing to try another path to his goal.

When they were well away, Malec laughed. "Why do they deem us fools?"

But I turned the guest goblet around and around on the smooth green board of the table and my question was:

"What made them think we would be their tools?"

Malec nodded slowly. "Yes, why that? What gain or threat did they believe so powerful as to in a manner wand-bind us from our powers?"

"Which makes me believe that perhaps I was not wise to dismiss them so quickly." I was irritated that I had done so with such lack of subtlety. "Also— why is one off-worlder ready to entrap another? Osokun would deal very unhappily with any prisoner he took."

"That much I can guess," Malec replied. "There is an ancient feud, though not much returned to in these days, between the men of the sealed cargo ships and the Free Traders. Perhaps that is now revived for some reason. But that is their affair, not ours. However"—he rose from his stool, his hands hooked in his belt—"we should let the Old Ones know of this."

I neither agreed nor disagreed. In those days I had some ill feeling toward certain ones in authority among us, but that was a matter private to me, not affecting any but my own house clan.

Our little people performed their own magic in the afternoon and the pleasure they gave was great. My pride in them flowered as the lallang blossoms under the moon. Also I did as I had in other fair years, set out scale pieces for these odd boys who trace down animals for me. For I have this private service to Molaster, that I bring out of bondage where and when I can such of the furred ones as suffer from the ill treatment of those who dare to call themselves men.

That evening, when the moon globes were lit and we set things ready for the evening performance, I said to Malec:

"Perhaps there is a way we can learn more of this matter. Should any of these Traders arrive to watch the show, and should they appear to you to be harmless men, do you offer to bring them here thereafter and let me talk with them. All we can learn will be food for the Old Ones for their understanding."

"Best not to meddle farther—" he began and then hesitated.

"It will go no farther," I promised, not knowing then how quickly such a promise can become a dawn web, vanquished by sun rays.

In this much was Slafid right. There were Traders, two of them, at the performance. I cannot read off-worlders' ages aright, but I believed them young, and neither wore many service bands on his tunic. Their skin was very dark, as comes from space, and their hair, clipped close to the skull for the better

wearing of their helmets, was dark also. They did not
smile ever as had Slafid, nor did they speak much
with each other. But when my little people showed
their talents, they were as Slafid, nor did they speak
much with each other. But when my little people
showed their talents, they were as enrapt as children,
and I thought we might be half friends, were they of
Yiktor.

As I had suggested, Malec brought them behind
when the show was over. And when I looked at them
closely I knew they were not as Gauk Slafid. Perhaps
they were simple men as we Thassa judge most other
races to be, but it was a good simplicity, not that of
ignorance which can be made crooked by malice or
ambition. And I was moved to speak to the one
calling himself Krip Vorlund concerning my old
dream of seeking other worlds with my little people.

In him I read a kindred interest, though he was
quick to point out to me the many dangers which
would hedge about my desire, and the fact that it
could be accomplished only if one had vast treasure
to draw upon. Deep in me sparked the thought that
perhaps I, too, had a price. But that quickly vanished.

As his kind is judged, this off-worlder was good to
look upon, not as tall as Osokun, but rather slender
and wiry. And I think that, were he matched weapon-
less to Oskold's son, the latter would have a surprise
in the struggle. My little people enchanted him, and
they liked him also—which warmed me to him. For
animals such as ours can read the spirit. Fafan, who
is very timid in strange company, laid her hand paw

in his at first advance and called after him when he went from her, so that he returned and spoke softly as one does in soothing a child.

I would have explored farther this man and his comrade, only Otjan, one of the run boys, came then with his tale of a barsk in harsh imprisonment and I had to go. This Vorlund asked to go with me and to that I agreed, I know not why, save that I wanted to know more of him.

And in the end it was his quickness which saved me trouble, for that torturer of fur people, Othelm of Ylt, would have used a snik-claw knife. But Vorlund used his off-world weapon, which cannot kill nor greatly harm, merely deter a would-be attacker, giving me time to wand-wish that nather. With his aid we brought back the barsk and saw to its housing. But then I knew that I could not be two-minded while I nursed that hopeless one, and I dismissed the Traders with what courtesy my impatience would allow.

When they were gone I wrought with the barsk as best I could, using all the skill of Molaster's servant. I thought that the body might be healed, but so dampened with pain and terror was the mind that never might I establish contact. Yet neither could I find it in me to send it along the White Road now. I left it in a sleep without dreams, to heal its limbs and body, to take away the pain of its thoughts.

"There is no use," Malec told me near drawn. "You will have to keep it in dream or make the sleep complete."

"Perhaps, but let us wait awhile. There is something—" I sat by the table, drooping with that fatigue which makes one's muscles and bones leaden and slow to answer to an equally slow mind. "There is something—" But the burden of my weariness kept me from probing then. Instead I stumbled to my couch and truly slept.

The Thassa can dream true, but only under controlled conditions. What I pictured then in the depths of sleep was a return of memory which flowed on to be mingled grotesquely with the present, to give birth to a possible future. For first I held in my arms one who cried herself into a bleak despair for which there was no comfort. And I looked upon another who, in the fair and unblemished body of youth, was empty of all reason, to whom no power could return. Then I walked with the young Trader, not as I had through the fair this night, but rather in a mountain place, which I knew with sorrow and dread.

But man shrank into animal, and beside me paced the barsk who turned now and again and looked upon me with cold eyes full of menace, which became entreaty, then hatred. But I walked without fear, not because of a wand—which I no longer held—but because I had that which tied the animal to me in a bondage it could not break.

And in that dream all was clear and had much meaning. Only when I awoke, with a dull pain behind my eyes and no refreshment of body, the meaning was gone, I held only scraps of haunting memory.

But now I know that dreaming planted in the depths of my mind, or awoke there, purpose that grew within me until it influenced clear thought. Nor did I shrink from that purpose when the moment came to put it into action, because it had grown to fill my being.

The barsk still lived, and inner seeing told me that its body mended. But we left it in deep sleep, which was the best we could now do for it. As I dropped the curtain across its cage, I heard that metallic ring which had come to mean space boots to my ears, and I turned somewhat eagerly, thinking that mayhap the Trader—Only it was Slafid who walked there alone.

"Dawn light fair to you, Freesha." He gave greeting in the town tongue as one who was entirely sure of his welcome here. And, needing to learn the reason for his persistence, I gave greeting in return.

"I see," he said, looking about him, "that all is well."

"Why should it be otherwise?" Malec came from the kasi lines to ask.

"There was no disturbance here, but elsewhere last night—" Slafid looked from one to the other. And when we stood blank-faced to his gaze, he continued, "One Othelm of Ylt has made formal complaint against you, Freesha, and one he terms an off-worlder."

"So?"

"Use of an off-world weapon, theft of valuable property. Both are black crimes in fair law. At best you may be embroiled with the court, at worst expelled and fined."

"True," I agreed. I had no fears of Othelm's complaint myself, but the Trader's case was another matter. Osokun—was there any way he could turn

45

this to his advantage? By port law the Traders had a right to wear body weapons, since the effects of those were relatively harmless. In fact they were less dangerous than the swords and daggers no lord or sword-sworn would move without. And Vorlund had used his in my defense, against a weapon that was outlawed and the very possession of which could condemn Othelm to greater penalties than I believed he would care to think upon. Only, any embroilment with fair law could set the Trader's superiors against him. We all knew of the strictness of their code on alien planets.

"Osokun's kinsman-by-the-third, Ocorr, is chief guard today."

"What would you say?" Malec fronted this Salfid, his impatience sharp in his tone.

"That perhaps you have done Osokun's will in this matter after all, Freesh." Slafid smiled his slow smile. "I think you might be wise to claim credit for it, even if you did not intend to have this result."

Now I could not bite back the question, "Why?"

Still he smiled as he leaned against a cage. "The Thassa are above and beyond plains law. But what if there be new laws, Freesha? And what if the Thassa legend be mostly that, legend only, with little in the way of deeds to back it should it be challenged? Are you now a great people? Rumor says not—if you ever were. So far you have kept aloof from the affairs of the plainsmen, you who are not men as they are men, nor women as they are women. How do you run under the Three Rings, Freesha, on two feet or four—or do you sail on wings?"

I took that as a warrior might take a sword in his vitals. For such words and what lay behind them were a sword, a weapon which, if used rightly, could cut down all of my clan and blood. So—this was the threat Osokun could bring to force us, or try to do so, under his hand. But I was proud that neither of us, Malec nor I, showed the effects of the blow he dealt us.

"You speak in riddles, Gentle Homo," I answered him in the off-world speech.

"Riddles others will begin to ask and solve," he replied. "If you have your safe places, Freesha, it would be best to gather there in days to come. You may have let war pass you by, as the occupation of lesser species. Now it seeks you out, unless you make alliances."

"No one speaks for many, unless he is sent under the talk-shield," Malec observed. "Do you speak for Osokun, Gentle Homo? If not, for whom? What has an off-worlder to do with Yiktor? What war threatens?"

"What is Yiktor?" Slafid laughed. "One small world of backward peoples who cannot begin to conceive of the wealth, the power, the weapons of others. It can be chewed and swallowed as one bites and swallows a thack berry. And with no more interest to the swallower than an instant of tart juice taste on the tongue, too small an incident for memory."

"So now we represent a thack berry to be swallowed?" I allowed myself laughter in return. ":Ah, Gentle Homo, mayhap you are right. But a thack berry taken before the day of ripeness, or only slightly past that hour, can cause a vast tumult and discomfort in one's middle. We are a small and backward world to be sure, and now I begin to wonder what treasure lies here that great ones from beyond the stars are seriously mindful of us.''

I did not expect to trap him so easily, and I did not. But neither did he, I think, learn aught from us—at least no great fact such as he had revealed when he had aimed that blow meant to rock us so we would be easy prey for his questions.

"We thank you for your warning." Malec's thoughts marched with mine. "For this court we shall have our answer. And now—"

"And now you have tasks which can better be performed in my absence," the off-worlder assented cheerfully. "I shall be off and leave you to them. You need not reverse the cup this time, Gentle Fem."

When he was gone I looked to Malec. "Does it seem to you, kinsman, that he went pleased with himself?"

"Yes. What he spoke of—" But even between ourselves, within the hearing of only our little people who might neither tattle nor betray aught their ears caught, he did not put more into words.

"The Old Ones—"

"Yes," Malec agreed to my thought. "Tonight the moon waxes."

My wand slipped through my fingers, not cool to the touch, but warm with the life my thoughts relayed to it. To do so, in the very heart of what might

48

now be enemy territory was an act of possible danger. Only Malec was right, the need was greater than the risk. He read my assent in my eyes and we went to our routine of setting up the show.

Twice during the day did I visit the barsk, each time mind-probing. Its hurts continued to heal, but not yet would I lift the rest-slumber and try to touch its mind. There was no time for such experimentation with this other thing pressing us.

We drew good crowds as always, having to turn some away. And my little people were happy and content in their acts, both of us being careful to shield our minds so that our apprehension would not distress them. I looked to see the Traders, if not the two who had visited us before, then others. For, if Vorlund had reported what had happened in Othelm's tent, then surely some of them would come to us about the matter. But none did.

At nooning Malec sent Otjan to see who dealt with customers in the booth that belonged to the *Lydis*. He reported that he saw neither Vorlund nor Sharvan there. But they were doing a brisk trade and there was evidence they might be sold out and gone before the end of the fair.

"Which would be wise for them," Malec observed. "And the less we now see of them the better. What quarrel these off-worlders have among themselves, or what Osokun would do with them is none of our concern. If possible we should also be packed and away this day."

But that we could not do. One could sense it in the air, the feeling of being spied upon. And by afternoon that uneasiness reached the little people, in spite of my efforts at maintaining a mind-guard to protect them. Twice I had to use the wand to wipe fears from their minds and I put out the high-power globes that night to blank-out the show tent. Yet on the surface there was naught. The fair guard had not summoned me to answer to Othelm's charge. I began to believe it might have been wiser had I made a countercharge first.

We caged the little people and I put the moon lamps at the four corners of their homes, setting up the middle power to protect them during the hours of dark. Together Malec and I inspected the barsk, and then went to take our messenger from its place.

The large winged form stirred uneasily as Malec set it gently on the table of our living quarters, half mantling its strong wings, blinking as if awaking from sleep.

I burned the powder and let it drink in the fumes, its beak half open, its thread of tongue flicking back and forth in increasing rapidity. Then Malec held its head steady between his palms so that I might fix my eyes upon the red ones set in its narrow skull. I sang, not aloud as was the usual custom, but with the hidden voice that no others might hear.

To that singing I put much effort, holding the wand between my two palms until it burned fire-hot, yet still I held it steady that the power might be channeled through me into our messenger. And when I had done, my head fell back and I had strength only to sit upon the stool and not tumble to the floor. But Malec looked now into the messenger's eyes and he spoke in short, sharp whispers, laying in its mind the words it would repeat precisely as he said them in the far place to which it would fly.

Having done this he took up his cloak and drew it about him and the bird he held to his breast. He went out into the dark of very early morning, to seek the open field where our beasts sometimes foraged, well outside the place of tents and booths.

I did not have the energy to rise and leave that seat now hard to my flesh and bones. Rather did I fall forward, my arms stretched across the table, my head resting on the board. I was wearied to the edge of faintness but I did not sleep. My thoughts were too alert, running hither and thither beyond my control. And memory pricked through the present need for sane and careful planning.

Once more mind-pictures came to me, and in these the face of a dark Trader fitted over one I knew much better, and both were erased in turn by the snarling mask of an aroused animal. It seemed to me that all this had a meaning, but one beyond my reading.

There rose then in me the desire to beam-read—though I knew the concentration needed for it was now far beyond my power. But I promised myself that this I would do. Do we beam-read the future, or only its possible path? Once having beam-read, do we then unconsciously turn our feet into the way that sight has opened? I have heard this debated learnedly many times. And the half belief that it does influence the choice of one's future leads it to be looked upon with distaste by many of us. We can be called to account for its use by the Old Ones. But now this I must do, when my strength returned. So having made my decision, I slept, my body cramped and stiffening, my thoughts at last leaving me in a fleeting peace.

KRIP VORLUND

V

THE LAW OF cause and effect is not one which our species, or any other I have ever heard of, has been able to repeal. One can hope for the best, but must be prepared to face the worst, so accepting ship restrict was now my portion and logically I had no quarrel with it. I was lucky, I supposed, that Captain Foss did not add to this relatively minor punishment a black check on my E record. Some commanders would have. I had the persona tape we all carried in our belts to give the true account of the fracas in the beast dealer's tent. And, to my credit, my hostile move there had been made in defense of a native of Yiktor, not merely to save my own skin. Also Foss knew more of the Thassa and their standing than I did.

Much as he would have liked to make my restrict entire, our limited crew prevented total imprisonment. I had to attend the ship's booth during some selling hours. But I was left with no doubt that the slightest infringement of orders on my part would end in complete disaster for one Krip Vorlund. And he told me that he awaited now some complaint on the part of the fair authorities. He would be my defender in any such trial and the tape would be my best argument.

Most of the morning in the booth was routine. I would have no further chance to go hunting on my own; I had forfeited that privilege on Yiktor. But I kept thinking in my free moments of Maelen's dream of a traveling beast show in space. As far as I knew, such had never been seen before. All the difficulties I had listed for her were only too true. Animals were not always adaptable, our tough species being one of the exceptions. Some cannot thrive away from their native worlds and can eat only highly specialized foods which cannot be transported, or they cannot stand the strains of shipboard life. But supposing a species that could overcome all such difficulties could be located, trained, taken out to roam the stars—would such a venture be profitable? A Trader's mind always turns first to that question, just as he is willing to leap beyond the next sun if the answer may be yes.

There I could judge only by my own reaction to the performance of the night before—and personal judgments were chancy. We had been long trained to use our own enthusiasm only to spark initial interest, beyond that to test and retest before committing a fortune to any venture.

I wondered about the barsk, why Maelen had been so determined to rescue it. There had been other ill-housed and presumably ill-treated beasts in that selling tent. But only the barsk had interested her. It was a rare animal, yes, and one seldom seen in confinement. But why?

"Freesh—"

A pluck at my sleeve brought me around. I had been standing at the open front of the booth and now I looked down at the ragged boy, shifting from one bare, grimy foot to the other, his hands clasped together over his middle as he bobbed his head up and down in a "salute-to-superior." I recognized him as the one who had guided us last night.

"What wish you?"

"Freesh, the Freesha asks that you come to her. There is that which she has to say with her own lips."

It says much for discipline that I hesitated in my refusal for less than a second. "Give to the Freesha," I dropped into the speech of formal Yiktorian politeness, "that I bide under the word of my liege lord and so cannot do as she desires. It is with sorrow that I must say this, by the Rings of the True Moon and the Flowering of the Hress."

He did not go. Then I drew a small scale token from my pocket and held it out.

"Drink sweet water on me, runner."

He took the token, but still did not go.

"Freesh, the Freesha wishes this very much."

"Does the sword-sworn go about his own desire when he is under orders from his lord?" I countered. "Say to her as I have said, I have no choice in this matter."

He did go then, but with a kind of reluctance which puzzled me. For the excuse I had given him was sound and acceptable anywhere on Yiktor. A follower was bound to his lord, and his commander's whim must be set above, far above, any personal desires, even above his own life. Why had Maelen sent for me, an out-worlder who had no connection with her save that we had shared a small adventure last night? Prudence dictated that it was better to keep well away from the tent of the Thassa, from the little people, from all that had to do with them.

Still, I kept remembering her silver-and-ruby trappings, herself as she had stood, not outwardly directing her animals but as if she, too, watched them. I thought of her concern over the barsk, her remote contempt which had frozen the beast dealer as her wand had bound him. Strange powers were allotted to the Thassa by rumor, and there seemed to be some truth at the roots of rumor, at least Maelen gave one the suspicion it was so.

But there was little time for dreaming over puzzles, for two of the high merchants from the north swept into the booth as the boy departed. They were not dealers in sprode, but offered other wares to make up our light cargo, small luxury items which could be packed in the ship's treasure room and so realize good return for small bulk. Captain Foss greeted them, they being his own customers, enticed here not by our regular cargo but our own light wares. These were the true aristocrats of the merchant class, men who had founded their fortunes securely and now speculated in things to pull wealth from the belt purses of the high nobility.

I produced the talk cups, plasta-crystal of Farn, reflecting light with diamond brilliance, yet so light in the hand that they appeared to be water bubbles. A man could stamp a magnetic-plated space boot on their rounded bowls and slender stems, and they would emerge unshattered.

Foss poured the wine of Arcturus into them, that deep crimson liquid which made them shine as the rubies on Maelen's collar. Maelen—I put her sternly out of mind and stood respectfully, waiting to show whatever Foss or Lidj would signal for, needfully alert to unvoiced orders.

The four bearers the merchants had brought with them, all senior servers, took their places across the booth, the small chests they had carried hither before them. In spite of the peace of the fair they demonstrated the worth of their burdens by the fact they were all wearing, not the daggers of custom but, swords of defense.

But I was never to see what they guarded so closely. For there came a shrill whistle at the open front of the booth, and all the surge of noise to which we had become accustomed during the hours died away to a silence so complete one could hear the faint jangle of armor, the scrape of sword which heralded the arrival of a squad of fair justiciars. There were four of them, armed as if about to go against a fortified tower. Leading them was a man in a long robe that was half white (though marked with dust), half black, to signify the two sides of justice. He went unhelmed, a wilted wreath of Hress leaves sitting slightly crooked on his head, so that we knew him for a priest who had temporary duty thus, to remind, if only faintly, that there had once been a sacred meaning for this assembly.

"Hark and give heed." His voice was high-pitched, specially trained in the sacerdotal style of delivery. "This be the justice of the Moon of Rings, by the favor of Domtatoper, by whose will we run and walk, live and breathe, think and do! Let he stand forth who Domtatoper calls—even the off-worlder who drew weapon within the bonds of the Fair of the Moon of Rings!"

Captain Foss fronted the priest in one quick movement.

"Upon whose complaint does Domtatoper's sword-sworn summon my liegeman?" He made the conventional reply to the summons.

"Upon the complaint of Othelm, sworn on the altar and before witnesses. There must be answer made."

"There shall be," Foss returned. I caught the slight movement of his eyes and went to join him. He had my persona tape in his tunic pocket. It would be enough to justify my use of the stunner. But how soon we could get a hearing before the mixed tribunal of priests and merchants was another matter, and I knew that this present conference between the captain and the northern men was an important one.

"Let me go," I said in Basic. "If they propose to try me at once, I can send a message—"

Foss did not answer but called into the booth. "Lalfarns!"

Alfec Lalfarns, tube man, had no regular booth duties save to lend a hand in unpacking and stowing goods.

"This man," Foss said to the priest, "goes as my eyes and ears. If my sword-sworn comes to trial, he will inform me. This is permitted?"

The priest looked to Lalfarns and after a moment nodded. "It is permitted. Let this one," he turned to me, "lay aside his weapon."

He held out his hand for the stunner in my holster. But Foss's fingers had already closed about its butt and the captain drew it.

"His weapon is no longer his. It remains here—as is custom."

I thought for a moment that the priest was going to protest, but by custom the captain was right. For, by Yiktor reckoning, all weapons worn by an underling were legally the property of the lord and could be reclaimed at any time, especially if the lord considered that his sword-sworn had transgressed some ruling.

So without any means of defense I stepped forward and took my place between the guards, Lalfarns following a few short paces behind. While a stunner was no blaster, I had worn one for most of my life, hardly knowing that it hung at my belt. Now I had an odd naked feeling and a sudden wariness of all around me. I tried to believe that this was merely reaction to my disarming, to the fact that I was, for the moment at least, at the mercy of alien law on a world strange to me. Only my uneasiness grew, until I knew it for one of the forewarnings that come with even the slightest gift of esper most of us in the space-borne communities have. I glanced back at Lalfarns just in time to see that he, too, was looking over his shoulder, his hand going to the grip of his stunner and then falling away again, as he realized that gesture might be misinterpreted.

It was then that I took better notice of the way in which my guards were going. By right we should have been heading for the Great Booth wherein the court sat during the ten days of the fair. I could see the wide-eaved roof above the tents and booths ahead, but well to the left. We were edging toward the fringe of the fair, to the space which held the ornamented tents of the nobles who could not be housed in Yrjar.

"Follower of All Light." I raised my voice to catch the ear of the white-and-black-clad priest, who had quickened step so we must lengthen stride to keep the proper distance in his wake. "Where do we go? The court lies—"

He did not turn his head, or give any evidence that he heard me. And I saw now that we were turning from the last line of merchant booths in among the tents of the lords. There were no crowds here, only a servant or two in sight.

"Hallie, Hallie, Hal!"

They came out of hiding, that swirl of men, stampeding into our small part with their mounts trained to rear and smash at footmen with their heavy hoofs. I heard Lalfarns shout angrily. Then the guard to my right gave me a shove which sent me skidding, trying to keep my balance, between two tents.

There was a sharp pain in my head and that was an end to it for a time.

Pain sent me into darkness, and the throb of pain brought me out of it, or accompanied me on a reluctant journey into consciousness once again. For some moments I could not understand the sensations that racked my body. Finally I came to guess, and then to know for a certainty that I lay face-down across the back of a burden kas, bound there, and jolted painfully by every heavy-footed step the beast took. Around me I heard a jangle, the murmur of men, so that I knew I was carried in the company of more than one rider. But their speech was not of Yrjar and the few words I caught I could not understand.

I do not know how long the nightmare continued, for I slipped in and out of consciousness more times than my painful head noted. And after a while I prayed that I would not return from the welcoming dark the next time it engulfed me.

A body made tough by a whole life of space voyaging, a body inured to all the stress and strain and dangers, does not easily yield to ill treatment, as I was painfully to discover in days to come. I was forcibly dismounted from the kas by the easy method of cutting my bonds and allowing me to fall to a very hard pavement.

About was the flicker of torch and lamplight, but

my vision was so fogged I distinguished my captors only as vague figures moving about. Then I was lifted by my shoulder, dragged along, and with a last push sent tumbling down a steep incline into a wanly lighted place.

More of the speech I could not understand and a figure clumped down after me. There was the full force of some liquid dashed into my face and I lay gasping. Water was good on my parched lips, though, and I put forth a feverish tongue to lick off the small moisture. A grip in my hair, which tore at the roots, jerked my head up, and more water was poured into my mouth, half strangling me until I made some shift to swallow.

It was not enough, but it was some small alleviation. The hand in my hair released me before I had more than a swallow or two, and my head thumped back on the floor, with enough to send me off again.

When I blinked out of that swoon or sleep, or both, there was a darkness which was frightening. I blinked and blinked, trying to clear my vision—until I realized that not my sight, but the area in which I lay was at fault. With infinite effort I managed at last to brace myself up on one elbow so that I could better see the place of my confinement.

There was no furnishing save a bench, and that rude work. The floor was littered with ill-smelling straw. In fact there was an evil odor about the place which grew stronger the longer I sniffed it. A window slit, tall as my body, made a vertical cut in one wall. It was no wider than a couple of hand spans, but through it came a grayish light which did not master the corner shadows. On the bench, as my bleary eyes focused there, I saw an earthen jug, and suddenly that became the sole interest in my world.

It was impossible to get to my feet. Even sitting up left me so giddy that I had to close my eyes and remain so for a space. In the end I reached that promise of water by a worm's progress, mostly on my belly, across the cold pavement of the floor.

There was liquid in the jug, my hope and fear concerning which had warred all during my crawl. It was not water alone, for it had a sharp, sour taste which drew mouth tissues. But I drank, for I would have lapped up far worse and thought it wine at the moment.

Though I tried to limit myself sanely once the water was on my tongue, easing the dry torment of my mouth and throat, it took all my will power to put the jug aside while liquid still sloshed in it.

My head was clearing and, after a short time, I was able to move without bringing on a giddy attack. Perhaps the odd taste in the water had been that of a drug or stimulant. Finally I lurched along the wall to the slit of window, to see what lay without.

There was sun there, though its rays reached me only as a kind of twilight. And my field of vision was exceedingly narrow. Some distance away was a gray reach of solid wall that resembled any fortress of Yiktor. There was nothing else, save pavement which must run from the base of the building in which I was imprisoned to that wall.

Then a man passed across my slip of outer world. He did not linger, but I glimpsed enough to know that he was a sword-sworn of some lord, for he went in mail and helm and had a surcoat of yellow bearing a black device. I could not see the manner of that device, nor would I have been able to read it, the intricate heraldry of Yiktor not being one of the matters of Trader concern.

Yet—yellow and black—I had seen that combination of colors before. I leaned against the wall and tried to remember where and when. Color . . . the last time I had thought about color—silver and ruby—Maelen's costume—the pink-gray of her banner which had exerted such an odd influence—the banners of the other amusement places—Amusement places—the searing red and green of the gambling tent that had done more than beckon—it had screamed!

The gambling tent! Half memory sharpened into a mental picture . . . Gauk Slafid at the table, the piles of counters heaped into small towers of luck, and to his left the young noble who had watched me so intently as I passed with Maelen. He had worn a surcoat, too, glistening half silk of a forceful yellow—and the breast of it had borne a house badge outlined and stitched in black. But the bits and pieces I now held could not be fitted into any recognizable pattern.

Any quarrel with a native of Yiktor was with Othelm, not with the young man in black and yellow. I could not see a logical alliance between two such widely separated people. The beast seller would have no call upon a lord's protection. My knowledge of Yiktorian customs was as complete as

Trader tapes could make it, but no one could absorb the fine nuances of social life and custom on an alien world without years of intensive study. It might well be that the brush with Othelm *had* led to my present predicament.

Wherever I now was, it was not within the boundaries of the fair. That was astonishing. I could remember part of a journey by kas back which meant, I was sure, that I had not been taken into Yrjar. But I had been forcibly removed from the jurisdiction of the fair court, which was so bald a refutation of all we knew of custom that it was hard to believe it had happened. Those who had so snatched me, as well as he who gave the order for it and any who conspired with him to bring it about, were to be outlawed without question as soon as the fact of my disappearance was known.

What made me worth such a desperate price? Only time and my captors could supply the answer. But it would seem that they were in no hurry, for the hours crept by and no one came near me. I was hungry, very hungry, and though I tried to ration what remained of the water I finished it and then knew thirst again. The dim light went with the day, and the night washed in, to drown me in waves of shadow.

I sat with my back against the wall, facing the ramp down which I had been pushed, trying to make my ears supply information. Now and again some sound, distorted and muffled, reached from beyond the slit window. Then came the call of a horn, perhaps announcing some arrival. I got to my feet again and felt my way back to the window. There was the beam of a lantern flashing across the outer wall, and I heard voices. Then a body of men crossed my line of vision, one wearing the cloak of a noble a step or two in advance of the other three.

Not too long afterward there was the sound of metal striking metal at the top of the ramp. Hearing it, some ill-defined need sent me back along the wall to my old position facing the upper door. Light thrust down, powerful enough to blind me, to hide those behind it. Only when they came down into my cell could I see a little through the glare.

It was the same party that had passed by the window. Now I was also able to identify the noble as the young man from the gambling tent.

There is a trick, so old as to be threadbare, but I held to it now. Remain silent, let your opponent speak first. So I did not burst out with any demand for an explanation, only studied them carefully as well as I could see them, determined to outwait their patience.

Two of the men hurried to draw the bench away from the wall, and the lord sat down as one to whom ease of body was his just due. The third follower hung the lantern on a wall hook to my left, and from that position it gave equal light to us all.

"You!" I do not know whether my silence had surprised the lord or not, but I thought I read irritation in his tone. "Know you who I am?"

This was the classic opening between Yiktorian rivals, a chanting of names and titles intended to impress a possible enemy with the weight of one's reputation.

When I did not answer he scowled, leaning forward, his fists planted on his knees, his elbows angled out.

"This is the Lord Osokun, first son to the Lord Oskold, Shield of Yenlade and Yuxisome." The man who still stood beneath the lantern chanted in the voice of a professional battle herald.

The names, son or father, meant nothing to me, even the lands they represented were unknown. I remained silent. And I did not see any gesture from Osokun, nor did he give any order. But one of his bully boys leaped at me and slapped my face with his open hand, sending my head thumping back against the wall with a pain so intense that I almost fainted. Only will kept me swaying on my feet, and by will I tried to hold to a halfway clear mind. So it was going to be that way? Whatever they wanted of me they were prepared to gain by force.

And what they wanted Osokun made clear in a rush of words.

"You have weapons, knowledge, off-world skulker. Both you will give to me, if not one way, then another."

For the first time I made answer, my lips swelling from the blow.

"Did you find such arms on me?" I gave him no title of courtesy.

He laughed. "No, your captain was too clever. But you have the knowledge. And if he would see you again, we shall have the weapons also, within a short time."

"If you know anything about the Traders, you

also know that we are mind-locked against such disclosures planetside.''

His smile grew wider. ''So I have heard. But each world has its own secrets, as you must also be aware. We have a few keys to open such locks. If they do not work, a pity. But your captain has a bargain to consider, which he shall be doing shortly. As for the rest—get to it!'' His last order had the snap of a riding whip.

I do not want to remember what happened thereafter in that stone-walled room. Those who took part in the questioning were indeed experts in their line. I do not know whether Osokun really believed that I could, if I would, reveal what he wanted to know, or if some monstrous compulsion drove him to enjoy such an occupation for its own sake. Much of it was afterward gone from me, past recalling. An esper, even to the smaller degree, can shut off parts of consciousness to save the balance of one's mind.

They could not have learned anything to their value. And they were expert enough in their dirty employment not to maim me permanently. But I was not aware of their going, nor of anything else for a period of time. And when pain again roused me, there was once more wan day beyond the window. The bench was back against the wall, and on it sat once again the jug, and this time with it a plate bearing a mass of something congealed in cold fat.

I crawled to that sustenance. I drank and felt the restorative of the bitter water, but I sat for a long space before I could make myself try the food. Only the knowledge that I must have strength of body for

the future made me choke it down, nauseous as it
was.

This much I knew: I had been kidnapped by Osokun, who hoped to exchange me for weapons and
information—doubtless that he might use both in a
bid for a kingdom. The boldness of this act meant
that he either had backing so powerful as to set aside
the laws of the fair, or else that he hoped to make his
bid with such rapidity that the authorities would not
have time to move against him. The recklessness of
his act was so near the borderline of utter folly that I
could not believe he meant it. Yet I had only the past
hours here to realize that he had already far overstepped all bounds and could only keep on the same
dangerous way. There was no turning back.

That Captain Foss would buy me with the price
Osokun asked was impossible. Though the Traders
were close knit, and one of their main rules was
loyalty to one another, the *Lydis*, her crew, and the
whole good fame of the Free Traders could not and
would not be risked for the life of a single man. All
Foss could do would be to turn to the machinery of
the Yiktorian law.

Did he know where I was? What had the raiders
done with Lalfarns? If our tube man had escaped,
Foss must have already learned that I had been taken,
and could have set in action all countermoves.

But I must depend not on vain hope but on my own
efforts now. I had to think and think clearly.

VI

Now was I driven to loose a mind-search, exhausting as that could be. For this was the place and time in which only desperate methods were left. Since thought-seek operates differently between races and species, I could not hope for any open message, perhaps nothing at all. It was as if I tried to monitor a band of communication so high or so low that my pickup caught only an indistinct pattern. No words, no clear thoughts, but what did come was fear. So sharp at times was that emotion that I believed those who broadcast it did so in peril.

Prick here, prick there, perhaps each prick signaled the emotions of a different defender of this fort. I raised my head to look at the pale window slit, then I crept to it to listen. But there were no sounds without. I pulled myself up to peer through. Day, yes, even a small strip of sunlight on the other wall. All was very quiet.

Again I closed my eyes to the light, strove to thought-seek, to fasten on one of those fear-pricks enough to read the source of that unease. Most of them still swam in and out beyond my catching. I found one near to the very door which guarded my prison, however, or so I thought. And into that I probed with all the effort I could summon.

It was as if I tried to read a fogged tape which was not only overexposed but also composed of alien symbols. Emotion, yes, one could feel that, for basic emotions remain the same from species to species.

All living creatures know fear, hate, happiness—
though the sources or reason for these feelings may
be very different. And of the common emotions fear
and hate are the strongest, the easiest to pick up.

The fear that rode minds here was growing, and
intermingled with it was anger. But the anger was
weak, much overborne by the fear. Why? What?

My teeth closed upon my underlip, I gave all my
remaining strength to the need for discovery. Fear
. . . of something . . . someone . . . no present
. . . coming? Need . . . need to get rid . . . rid
of me! That breakthrough came so sharply that I
straightened as if to meet a physical blow.. Yet there
was no one there to deliver it. But I knew as well as if
it had been shouted aloud that my presence here was
the cause of fear. Osokun? No, I did not believe that
the lord who had tried to impress his will in this cell
had had such a forceful change of attitude.

Prick, prick . . . I readied my mind, pushed aside
amazement, went back to the patient mining of those
incomprehensible thoughts. Prisoner—danger—
Not my present danger, no—but as a prisoner here I
was a danger to the thinker. Perhaps Osokun had so
overstepped the laws of Yiktor that those who aided
him, or obeyed his orders, had every reason to fear
future consequences.

Dared I try a countersuggestion? Fear pushed too
far erupts in violence in many men. If I added to that
fear in the mind I had tapped and concentrated upon,
I might well bring a sword to my own end. I weighed
one thing against another while holding the link
between us.

What I decided upon was perhaps so thin a chance that it already lay under the shadow of failure. For I attempted to set in that wavery mind-pattern the thought that with the prisoner gone there would be no fear, and that the prisoner must fare forth alive not dead. In the simplest pattern I could devise, and the most emphatic, I sent that thought-beam along the linkage.

At the same time I edged along the wall to the ramp which gave entrance to this place. I stopped only to pick up the jug, drank the remainder of its contents, and then grasped it tightly in my hand. I tried to remember how the door above opened, though my eyes had been dazzled when Osokun had come that way. Outward—surely outward!

Now I was halfway up the ramp, braced, waiting

. . .

Free the prisoner . . . no more fear . . . free the prisoner . . .

Stronger—he must be moving toward me! Now—the rest would depend upon fortune alone. And when one sets his life on such scales it is a fearsome thing.

I heard the click of metal against metal—the door—I raised the jug— Now!

The door swung back and I threw outward not only the water container but also a blast of fear, directed down the link between mind and mind. I heard a cry from the figure silhouetted against the light. The jug struck against his head and he staggered back.

I scrambled up, putting all my weakening force

into that dash, reaching and passing the door. The light was dazzling even in this inner corridor, but the man who had unlocked the door was slumped against the opposite wall, his hands to his face, and between his fingers trickled blood. He was moaning.

My first thought was for his sword. I staggered to him, making his weapon mine. Even to have an unfamiliar weapon in hand bolstered my confidence. He did not fight me. I thought afterward that the blast of fear had struck his mind a far greater and incapacitating blow than the shattered jug had inflicted on his body.

With a roll of shoulder, a thrust of arm, I sent him down into the pit from which I had climbed. He had most thoughtfully left the lock rod still in the door and that I turned swiftly and withdrew to take along.

So much I did before I looked around. The light here, while stinging my dark-oriented eyes, was, I thought, after a moment or two of blinking adjustment, perhaps that of late afternoon. How long I had lain below I did not know, the passing of days and nights had escaped me.

But for the moment, at least, the hall in which I stood was empty. I had made no plans beyond this instant. All I could do was try to reach the open, though I might not have such good fortune in another meeting with any member of the garrison. Mind-seek was too thin to use for scouting. I had tried my esper talent to the full when I had drawn upon it to unlock my cell. What I did now must be accomplished largely by physical means alone, and the weapon I carried was strange to me.

I staggered along the corridor, ever listening for any sound which might herald the coming of another. There was a sharp bend where another narrow window slit gave light. I paused there to look out. Again I saw a small piece of courtyard bounded by a wall. And this showed me a portion of gate, now shut—such a portal as would serve a large party. If that was the only way out of this place, I tasted defeat indeed.

At the jog in the corridor the way turned left. Doors opened along it and for the first time I heard voices. However, there was no other way out save this. With my shoulder against the wall, a bared untried sword in my hand, I began my journey.

The first two doors, recessed in the thickness of the wall, were closed, for which I would have given devout thanks had I been able to spare any relaxation of concentration. Though I knew my esper was at a very low ebb, I tried to use its remnants to feel out any life ahead.

So faint a flickering. I already knew from the sound of voices that there were at least two in one of those rooms, and mind-seek confirmed this. But there could be a dozen more and I would not pick them up now. I shuffled along. The voices grew louder, I could make out separate words, but in another tongue. By the sharpness of the tone I thought they were quarreling.

Brighter light, cutting from a half-open door across the corridor. I halted to study the door. Like that of the cell, it opened outward and it was more than half closed. The lock looked the same as that of

the prison, some inner system which was made secure by a rod inserted in a hole and turned. My left
hand went to the one I carried. Could it be that the
same one might be used successfully here?

First, could the door be entirely closed without
arousing those within? I dared not show myself in the
open space to see what or who were there. But the
voices had reached close to the shouting point, and I
hoped they were so engrossed that my next move
would go unnoticed.

I put the sword in my belt, took the rod in my right
hand. The left I placed palm-flat against the surface
of the door and gave it a gentle push. But no such
easy touch would work with this ponderous slab, I
discovered. It needed shoulder muscles to move it. I
waited tensely for some betraying creak, some lull in
the conversation, to tell me that I had made the
wrong choice.

Move it did at last, inch by inch, until finally it
fitted into its frame. Within the voices continued as I
fumbled, my fingers slick with sweat, to push the rod
into the hole. It resisted a little and I was ready to
leave it. Then it clicked into place and I thrust it up
and down as I had seen such rods used before. My
faint hope paid off—the rod locked.

From the continued noise within, they had not yet
discovered they were prisoners. Twice now I had
succeeded, but I must not take too much confidence
from that, for such luck was too good to last.

There was another turn in the corridor with a
window where once more I paused to look out. My
guess as to the time of day was proven, the glow of

sunset lay on the pavement and wall out there. And night is ever the friend of the fugitive. As yet I had no thought as to what I would do when I was out of Osokun's stronghold, free in an unknown countryside. One step at a time was all my mind and will could encompass.

Before me was another door wide open on the courtyard. I could still hear the muffled quarreling behind, but now I tried to pick up sounds ahead. There was a sharp, high noise which I recognized as the squeal of a kas—but no man's voice.

I gained the deep recess of this door and peered out, sword once more in hand. To my left was a roofed space in which kasi were stabled, their triangular heads with the stiff, upstanding stocks of black hair tossed now and then. But there were ragged bits of leaves hanging from their jaws and I thought they had just been given their fodder.

For a moment I debated the chance of securing one of those mounts, but regretfully decided against it. Mind-seek worked better with animals, even with alien species, than with humanoids, that was true. But to concentrate upon controlling a beast which might be unruly would require too much of me now. I would be safer, I was sure, depending upon myself.

The bulk of the building from which I had come cast a long shadow ahead. I could not see the outer gate, but I tried to reach a place in deeper shadows between two bales of kasi fodder and succeeded.

Now my field of vision was far better. To my right was the wide gate, well barred. Above that was a kind of cage and in it I detected movement which

lattened me low against the bales. There was a
entry there. I waited for the shout, perhaps a
rossbow bolt to find me, some sign I had been
ighted. For I could not believe that I had escaped
otice. When moments passed and no discovery
ame, I began to think that the sentry on duty there
ad eyes only for what lay outside these walls, not
vhat chanced within.

I planned out a route which took me well along,
irst the bales of fodder, and then the end of the stable
etween me and that lookout. I moved slowly,
hough every nerve in me screamed for speed, feel-
ng that a scurry might attract attention where creep-
ng would keep me one with the concealing
hadows. I counted the beasts in the stable as I
assed, hoping to get some inkling as to the size of
he present garrison. There were seven riding beasts,
our of them used for burden. But that did not help,
or this place might have a permanent unmounted
garrison. However, the small number of mounts in a
table manifestly built to hold three, maybe four
imes that number suggested that there might only be
a skeleton force in residence. And it also suggested
hat Osokun and his sword-sworn might well have
gone.

There were two more of the high-placed sentry
osts. But, though I watched them carefully, I
:aught no sign that they were manned. Then I
lucked behind a half wall as tramping boots sounded
oudly on the stones. A man came along. Though he
vore the scale jerkin of a foot fighter, his head was
are of helm and he had a yoke across his shoulders

supporting slopping buckets of water which h‹ emptied into a stone trough that ran the length of th‹ kasi stalls.

He went out with the yoke and empty buckets. Bu‹ in my hiding place I fought down a sudden soar o‹ spirit. For in those moments he had been ridden by s‹ strong a desire that it reached me as a distinct mes‹ sage. Fear in him had given way to determination, ‹ determination to act that was so strong I had bee‹ able to read it. Perhaps he also varied from hi‹ fellows in some quirk of mind which had laid hin‹ better open to my esper, for such variations exist, a‹ we well know. And this was the third boom fortun‹ granted me that day.

He was acting a part, I was sure, going about hi‹ duties but using them as a screen for his purpose‹ And the moment had come when immediate actio‹ was demanded if he would succeed. Carrying hi‹ yoke and the empty buckets, he strode openly along while I slunk behind him, for what he wanted wa‹ my own wish.

There was a well in the yard beyond, and from th‹ center core building extended a wing at a sharp angl‹ about it as if the stone blocks threw out an arm t‹ shelter the source of valued water. In the wing wer‹ more of the narrow slit windows and a door. Th‹ man I followed did not stop at the well. He gave quick glance to right and left as he neared it. Appar ently reassured, he sped straight to the door of th‹ wing. I gave him a moment or two for lead and the‹ followed.

This was a combination armory and storeroom‹

78

Weapon racks on the walls, gear piled in neat heaps, and the distinctive smell of grain and other food for man and beast. Behind one of the piles of supplies I saw the abandoned yoke and buckets. As I kept on the trail the mingled fear and will of my guide was a cord pulling at me. I came to another door half hidden behind a pile of grain bags, and that gave on a narrow stair, steep enough to make a man giddy to look down. There I paused for a space as I heard the boots of the one ahead, lest my own footgear make a noise he could hear. Wild with impatience I had to wait until all sounds had died away. And then I went slowly, aching with the effort of placing each foot, afraid my weakened body would betray me. Luckily that descent was not a long one.

At the bottom was a passage which ran only in one direction. Dark here, and I saw no gleam of light ahead to suggest that my guide used a lantern or torch. It must have been a way he knew well.

Nor could I hear him any longer. Then, along our mind link there was a burst of relief, as bright in my brain as a lantern would have been in my eyes. He had reached his goal, he was free of the fort to find what he believed to be safety. And I did not think he would linger at that exit.

So I put on what speed I could, staggering on at a half run to find the same gate. In the dark, I came up hard against sharp projections. But I did not fall, and was able after a moment to put out my hands to serve as eyes. Before me, according to touch, was another flight of steep steps, and up these I crawled on hands and knees, not certain I might take them otherwise.

I paused now and then to feel above my head for any sign of exit. At last I found a trap door which gave to my push. There was still not much light as I came out in a cave, or rather a heaping of rocks I did not believe to be natural, cleverly made to resemble nature as a cover for this door. In a land so constantly riven by petty wars such a burrow must have been necessary for each fort. To my mind this was less concealed at the other end than one might have thought needful.

For the time being my full concern was for getting out of sight of any wall sentry. The rocks covering the exit of the passage were, I saw as I edged along belly flat to the ground, only one such outcrop. And I thought I could trace a pattern in them as if they marked the site of a much older and ruined fortress.

There was no sign of the deserter who had preceded me through the bolt hole, but I continued to move with caution. At last I took cover behind what could be the end of the ruins, much earth sunken and tumbled, and for the first time I surveyed the back trail.

The sky blazed with the particular wild color with which sunset was painted on this planet, sometimes so brilliantly that one dared not closely observe those strident sweeps of clashing shades. Under it the fort was a dark blot, already closed in by shadows which accented its grim aspect. It consisted of one inner building and the outer wall, and was even smaller than it had seemed when I was making my way out. I did not believe it was any holding, but rather a border post, a defense for the land it guarded. For one thing there were no dwellings or any cultivated fields ringing it. This was a camp for soldiers, not a place of refuge for farmers and townsfolk as any main castle keep would be.

There was a road by its main entrance, coming from a notch between two lines of hills, extending into the unknown level land. That road must tie it to both the center of the domain and the outer world, perhaps even Yrjar. And it was my guide.

My journey here had been such that I might just as well have been blindfolded all the way. I had no idea whether the port lay north or south from here, but it was certainly to the west. But I could not travel on the road. For the first time I began to think that all my good fortune in winning free from Osokun's keep had ended. I had the sword I had taken, but water, food, protection against any storm were lacking. And the energy which my will had fathered and which had sustained my ill-used body so far, was fast ebbing. Whether I *could* pull myself on was a question I was afraid to ask myself, because the answer was so plain.

Both the fort and the place of ruins where I emerged crested small hills. The passage which had brought me hither must have run under the gap of low ground between. Once I had put that high ground between me and the sentry post, I was in the clear. Then I got to my feet, determined to keep putting one before the other as long as I could, then to crawl, wriggle, do anything I could to keep moving.

Time became a phantom thing without measurement, save that which comes between one step and the next. I was favored by this much, the methods Osokun's questioners had used had caused great pain but had left muscle and body unimpaired for the effort I must now put forth. But I lapsed into a kind of stupor in which another portion of my mind took control, one which did not consciously know, plan, or live, but lay deep below all that.

Twice I roused enough to discover that I had wandered down to heel and toe along the smoother surface of the road, some hidden warning signal flashing possible danger. Both times I was able to stagger up again into the rough land where bushes and rocks gave me cover. Once I believe I was trailed for a space by some hunter of the night. But if that unseen creature was intrigued by me to considering me prey, it decided again and was gone.

The moon was bright, so bright its Rings were shining fire in the Sotrath, that moon, held always two rings about it. But in a regular cycle of years came a time of three, which was a great portent for the natives. I did not look up to that wonder, and I was only thankful for the rays which made it possible to see the worst of the possible stumbling blocks before me.

It was near dawn when I passed through the gap between the hills, needing there to take to the road. My mouth was dry as if filled with ashes, acrid ashes which burned the tissues of tongue and inner check. Only my well-worn will kept me moving, for I feared that if I rested I could not possibly find my feet again, or even crawl. Somehow I must get past this place where the road was the only exit, into the open western country. Then, then promised my body, I would rest in the first hole I could find.

Somehow I made it, the hills were behind me. I wavered off the open surface into the brush, pushing on until I knew I was indeed finished. There I fell to my knees with a last forward thrust that plunged my scratched and whipped body between two thick bushes. Then I lay still and what occurred immediately after I do not remember.

A river, a precious river of water wetting me, giving my parched body new life. But there was the thunder, the beat of rapids in the river. I dared not allow myself to drift on into a wild stretch of water, be beaten against rocks— Water—thunder—

I was not in any stream, rather did I rest on a hard surface which was secure and unmoving under me. I was wet, but the moisture came from above, falling in fierce curtains of rain. And thunder cracked indeed, but in the sky.

When I levered myself up from the ground, my tongue licking at the rain which spattered my face, I saw the flash of lightning along the hill crowns. It must be day again, but so dark a day that there was hardly more visibility than existed at twilight. For the moment I only raised my face to the rain, opened my mouth to it, sought to drink it in.

A thunderous rumble reached across the curtained sky, a wild split of lightning, almost as bright as a ship's tail flames—I looked through a small opening in the bushes at a party of mounted men riding as if driven by some storm whip eastward. They were cloaked and hooded and strung well out, with the mounts of the laggers laboring, threads of foam strung from their jaws. The whole aspect of the company was one of some overwhelming need for speed. As they passed my hiding place emotion washed over me from them—fear, anger, desperation—so strong that it was a blow for an esper mind. Under the muffling cloaks I could not see color or heraldic design, nor did any lord's travel banner crack over their heads. But I was certain this was Osokun riding to his den. And if it were not already, now the hunt would be up for me.

So stiff and sore was my body that I could barely get to my feet. My first wavering steps racked and pained me. I had thought that I was tough and so honed by the life of a Free Trader that I was not to be easily worn by bodily discomfort. But now I moved again in a haze which wrapped me as close as if I were caught in the hunting web of a Tiditi spider-crab.

The storm creviced the ground with runnels of fast-running water, as if so much rain now fell from the skies that it could not sink into the soil but spun away on the surface. From these I drank from time to time, far past caring if they carried any alien element to injure me. But if I had water I lacked food, and the memory of the greasy mess I had so reluctantly eaten—when? a night ago, two nights?—haunted me, to assume the proportions of an Awakiian banquet with all the five-and-twenty dishes of ceremony. After a while I pulled leaves from the bushes and chewed upon them, spitting forth their pulp.

Time again had no meaning. How much of the day lay behind, I neither knew nor cared. The fury of the rain slackened. There was some slight clearing of sky, but not enough to dim the light—

Light? Suddenly I was aware that I marched steadfastly toward a light. Not the yellow of the lanterns I had seen in the fort or in Yrjar—no—

Moon globe—silver—beckoning— Once before there had been such a globe. A last whisp of warning in my mind faded quickly—moon globe . . .

MAELEN

VII

BY THE WILL OF Molaster I have Singer's power, and having it so am I also bound to other things—the far sight, the long sight, the spinning of the Rings. And these be hard things to live with at times since the will within one can be set crosswise to all of them, and if that is done then the will of Maelen is always the loser. I, who desired only to remain at the great fair with my little people, rose from the first sleep of night knowing that a call had come, though I did not reckon the why and the wherefore. And in the cages I heard the whimpering cries of my little people, who are sensitive to the power, for its compulsion strongly touched also upon them, bringing uneasiness and fear.

My first thought was of them, putting my cloak about me, going to walk wand in hand up and down so that they could look upon me and forget fear. But when I came to the place wherein we had put the barsk, I saw that beast on its feet, with head down a little as if to spring, while its eyes were yellow fire and in them dwelt madness.

"There is a sending—" Malec came to me.

"There is a sending," I agreed. "But not from the tongues or the minds of the Old Ones. Unless they have called upon the power and that has answered not them but me!"

He looked to me gravely and made a gesture which in part denied my words. We are blood kin, though not to the second closeness, and Malec does not always see as I see. He acts many times to keep me from what he believes folly.

However, he could not deny a Singer who says she has caught a sending. So now he waited. And I took my wand between my hands and turned it slowly. For, now that my little people were soothed and their fear rose, no more as a wall to bar the waves of power, I could so direct it. North, west, south—the wand did not move in my light grasp. But as I wheeled to the east did it right itself, pointing straight outward. In my fingers it was warm, demanding, so that I said to Malec:

"This is a debt-sending, and for me. Payment is required."

At a debt-sending one does not hesitate, for giving and taking must even be equal on the scales of Molaster. This is even more true for a Singer than others, for only so is the power nourished and kept flaring bright.

Then I asked of him, "What of the off-worlder? And of Osokun, who has been planning plans of darkness?"

Malec shifted his feet upon the ground before he spoke. "Osokun can claim blood-kin to the second degree with Oslaph who—"

"Who has been chosen by temple lot this year to represent the lords upon the tribunal of the fair. And also, did not the off-worlder Slafid say his other kin, Ocorr, captains the guard. But surely neither can break all law and custom."

Then my certainty faded, for Malec did not speedily agree with me. I saw that he was troubled, though his eyes did not fall from mine, for he is of the Thassa and between us always there is truth and open dealing. So that I now said:

"There is that I do not know."

"There is. Shortly after midday gong the guards took the off-worlder, Krip Vorlund, to answer the claims of Othelm, the beast dealer. And the party were set upon by mounted men from beyond the boundary. When the skirmish was over the off-worlder was gone. It is believed that he is back with his kin, and the chief priest has ordered their trade booth closed and the Traders to remove themselves."

"You did not tell me this?" I was not angry, save with myself for believing that Osokun dared not move. For I should have read better in him that he was one to dare greatly without thinking overlong about the future consequences of any impulsive act.

"It was more rational to believe in his escape to his ship," Malec returned. "For it is very well known that the Free Traders care for their own. And they might not trust the justice of the court."

"Also that this was no concern of ours," I said a little sharply. "Perhaps it is not—of the Thassa. I know we are oath-bound not to interfere in the matters of the plainsmen. But this is a debt personal to me. And of you I ask one thing, by blood right, that you seek out the captain of the *Lydis*. And if it is true Krip Vorlund is not safe among his crew, you tell him all that has passed."

"We have not had an answer from the Old Ones," he objected.

"I take it upon me, by the scales of Molaster, the responsibility for this." And I breathed upon my wand so it shone silver-bright.

"And what will you do?" he asked, but I knew that he had already guessed my answer.

"I will go seeking what I must seek. But also it must be done with an excuse to cover my going. For now I do not doubt there will be eyes watching, ears listening, marking our coming and going. Thus—" I turned slowly and looked along the lines of cages, "we shall put up the van cart and in it I shall take Borba, Vors, Tantacka, Simmle, and"—I laid hand upon the barsk cage—"this one. Our excuse shall be that these ail and I fear they may spread some sickness among the others of our company, so it is best to withdraw them for a time beyond the crowded life here."

"Why this one?" he pointed to the barsk.

"For him that reason may be the truth. In the open country perhaps his mind will be at rest and he may be reached. Whereas here there is much to remind him of past torment."

I saw a shadow smile about Malec's lips. "Ahy, ahy, Maelen, ever do you hold to a wish, do you not? So still you think that you shall be the one, the first one, to add a barsk to your company?"

And I met his smile with my own. "I am patient, I am one with a strong will. And this I know, not guess, blood kin, I *shall* be the one to command a barsk. If not this, then another, someday, somehow."

I know that he thought this folly. But no one argues with another on whom a sending has been set, if that sending be one of debt payment. So he put the kasi to the wagon yokes and aided me to place those of our company I had chosen in the van, putting the barsk cage apart and screened. Weak as that creature was, still it continued to watch us and snarl whenever we approached, nor could my thought meet aught within its skull but the churning of madness.

We broke our fast together and summoned Otjan, the odd boy, to bring a priest who would take charge of our booth for an hour or so while Malec went on his errand to the *Lydis* and I turned east. Malec urged me to wait for his return, but in me swelled a feeling of urgency and I knew I could not do this, but must be on the move. For already I was sure in my mind that the off-worlder was not safely among his friends, but rather in dire danger elsewhere, or the debt by sending would not have come to burden me so sharply and without warning.

The van could not move swiftly, and moreover I must keep to its slowest pace while still in sight of the fair by reason of my excuse. For to tumble ailing animals would have been suspicious to any watcher. Thus, when all inside me urged speed and yet more speed, I set the kasi to an amble as I passed beyond the last line of fringe tents. I had believed that some-one might question my going, though I had taken care to give my reasons to the priest and Otjan.

Those I had chosen to accompany me on this mission, though they now rode caged, were the keenest of mind, and the most aggressive of all our company. Borba and Vors were glassia of the moun-tain forests. They were in length the span of four hands placed end to end, and had long slender tails as long again as their bodies, their fur as black as a night of storm and no stars. They each had long paws with very sharp claws which they carried sheathed, but were like a sword blade to be used when the occasion demanded. Their heads were crowned with a tuft of gray-white stiff hair and this they flattened to their skulls when going into battle. By nature they were curious and fearless, willing to face enemies much larger than themselves—and oft-times they won such battles too. They were seldom seen in the low-lands and thus could pass for animals we dared not lose.

Tantacka looked more dangerous than she was, though once roused her ire was a dogged, smolder-ing emotion which lasted long and made her more cunning in attack than her appearance suggested. She was plump of body, with a blunt-nosed face and small rounded ears, the merest stump of tail which she usually carried plastered down to her haunches. Twice as large as the glassia, she had power in her shoulders, for her favorite food in the wild was found only under rocks of size which her kind must uproot before dining. Her yellowish fur was so coarse that it resembled quills rather than hair. She was not a beautiful animal, rather clumsy, grotesque in appearance, but that added to her appeal when she gave her part of the show, for those watching marveled that such an apparently clumsy animal could do such clever things.

Simmle was of the same general species as the barsk, though her body hair was very short and tight to the skin. At a distance she looked to be not furred at all, but with a naked hide oddly marked, for across the even cream of her lower back and haunches were stripes of dark brown. Her tail was round and very thin, like the last of a whip, her legs seemingly skin laid over bone with little flesh between, and the like upon her head, so that one could plainly see the ridges of her skull. Like Tantacka she was no beauty, but instead of clumsiness she gave the impression of speed and wiry endurance. And that was truth, for the venzese have long been used in the high plains for the coursing of game.

As I drove I felt their eager inquiry, their wonder at the meaning of our journey. To them I relayed my sense of danger, the need for wariness, to which they responded each in his own way. And, once well beyond sight of the fair, I brought each in turn out of the cage to sit beside me for a space, to look upon the country, to use his own senses for guide. For they had eyes to see what man's eyes do not, noses to lift from the breeze messages we do not note, ears to hear what we remain ignorant of—and these were in my service.

Simmle was uneasy, not because of what she sensed as she sat quietly beside me in the sunlight of the morning, but because of the barsk. To the rest he was no kin, near or far. And since they knew he was not free to harm them, they ignored his presence. But to Simmle he was enough like her own clan that she was even aware of him, and I had to ease her fear, for madness is something so alien it breeds panic in those who come in contact with it.

On Yiktor there is madness, the brain does not think along smooth paths but slips out of pattern into chaos. And the mad man, the woman so afflicted, are deemed touched by Umphra, a primeval power. No one will harm such. When discovered they are put under restraint of the priests and taken high in the mountain to a certain Valley. And from memories of that Valley my mind ever flinches. To harm or kill the mad is to take into one's own body, believe the plainsmen, that illness which twisted awry its victim.

But animals that go mad are killed, and I think they are the more kindly used, being loosed so on the White Road where suffering and sorrow are naught, drawn so into Molaster's great pattern and keeping. I feared that I must deal so with the barsk, though still

I was loath to take that final step. For as Malec had said, it had long been my wish to add this very rare and independent rover to our company. Perhaps I was vain of my own power and desired to add to the small frame I already had of one who worked well with the little people.

We forded the river, meeting with none other on the outward road from Yrjar than some belated fair-goers. And tō the greetings of these I replied as one who had cares, twice saying that illness among my beasts drove me to this departure. But after midday I turned from the open road into a side trail which still led eastward, lest some passer-by would begin to wonder why I needs must go so far in my search for peace and quiet for my ill ones.

Before sunset we came to a meadow place by a stream, and there I made camp, loosing the kasi for grazing, my other ones to explore and enjoy their freedom. They relished this ability to nose about and lap from the stream, though none of them wandered far from the van, and in that the barsk remained curtained and alone.

After my companions were fed and bedded for the night and all was well, I looked upon the moon at its rising. Already the Third Ring was better defined. Another night or two and it would be bright—to be visible for sometime after. In my hands the wand caught its light and made it dazzle the eyes. I longed fiercely to try beam-reading, but since I was alone, and he who reads thus must in a manner of speaking depart from the body, lie entranced so that he may not easily awaken, I did not dare. But it was a hunger eating in me and I must rise and pace back and forth to quiet my nerves. Though I did dare again the use of the wand, it pointed firmly to the east.

At last I realized I must use the Qu'lak Song to summon slumber since the body must never be over-ridden by the mind, unless the need is very great. A Singer early learns that the temptation to forget the body is a strong one, and must ever be resisted. So I sang the four words and the five tones and opened my mind to rest.

There were twitterings and squeakings in the grass and I looked upon the mists of early morning. I released my little people once again while I prepared our food and put the kasi to the yoke. I fed the barsk and he lay quiet on his bedding. To the mind-touch he was weaker, growing lethargic as if the frenzy which had eaten him the day before had bruised and injured what contained it. And I wondered if this weakness was a good thing, to afford me a way of reassuring and perhaps leading those impulses back to stability. But my probe showed me that the time, if it would ever come, was not yet.

Once more we set out, though the trail we fol-lowed grew rougher and I feared I might reach a point the van could not pass and I would have to retrace my steps and seek out a side way. There was a kind of tension in the air which we all shared. I knew it for what it was, no warning of ill but rather the foreshadowing of what the Three Rings would bring to all who opened their minds rightly to the power. For at this time there was little limit on what might be assayed by the bold—though boldness is never enough when dealing with the power.

We were going into the hills and though this was

not a country I was much familiar with, I knew that in this direction lay the holdings of Oskold. But I wondered at Osokun's rashness at bringing any captive here, unless the very boldness of such a move would, in a way, cover his tracks. None would believe that he would take a secret prisoner into the heart of his father's domain. But was Oskold himself a party to this? That set another design on the loom. For Oskold was seemingly a man of some intelligence and cunning. And if he were ready to defy law and custom, it would mean he held a mighty weapon in reserve with which to confound his enemies.

I remembered the half threat the off-worlder Slafid had made—that more was known about the Thassa than was right or safe for us. I hoped that our warning would stir the Old Ones into such countersteps as they could beam-read into taking. Rumor has always made much of us among the plainsmen. It is true that we are older in this land than they, that we were once great as they consider greatness, before we learned other ways to measure power and growth. We, too, built cities, of which only scattered stones abide in lonely places, knew rises and falls in history. Men progress, however, or they destroy themselves and sink back to their dim beginnings. By the will of Molaster did we progress beyond such matters. And to us now the quarrels and strivings of these newcomers were as the clamor of the little people, save that the little people are moved by simpler needs and go about their ways in more honest openness.

All through the day did the Abiding Influence of

the Third Ring act upon us. From time to time my little people gave vent to their rising excitement with yells or barks, or whatever manner of sound was their normal speech. Once I heard the barsk, too, give tongue, but in a mournful, echoing howl full of mind-pain, which sent the rest of them dumb. I sent a sleep-wish to quiet him. Simmle gave me warning near midday of something coming, and I stopped the van to alight and followed her on foot through the yet frost-unkilled weeds and leafed brush to the top of a rise from which we could see the road east. A party came along it at a determined trot and their leader was Osokun. He did not ride in ordinary state, but headed a small squad with no display of banners, no way horn—as if he would pass through this wilderness with as little note as possible.

I watched them well out of sight before I returned to the van. My kasi were not meant for burst of speed, but only an unvarying pace. In a long haul they could beat and leave behind such swifter mounts as those of Osokun's men, but no spurt was in them and I must abide by that.

That night we reached the hills and I hid the van, went ahead to find a pass. But there was only one cut I could find which would take the passage of the van, where the road ran. I was very loath to return to that. Too open, the sort of place where any lord but the most foolish would have sentry posts. I loosed Simmle and she quickly found two—surely manned by guards selected for keenness of eye.

Here I could give when challenged no reason for my wayfaring. Danger or no, this night I must summon the power, for to run on headlong would be the sheerest folly.

I brought out Borba and Vors and sent them to seek what we needed, safety and solitude, not too far from the road. They were back well before twilight, patterning in from different directions. Borba had what was wanted. The van must remain some distance away from the spot, but there was concealment in a thicket of luk weed, which could be pulled and tangled about to hide it.

The kasi I freed to graze in the dell Borba led us to, setting upon them a no-stray thought, for there was plenty of water in a pool fed by a small falls, and fresh plaken growing knee-high in clumps. I could not shift the barsk cage, so I set the sleep thought deep for its inhabitant and took the others with me.

We ate of the supplies I had brought, for strength of body must back strength of mind in what I must do at moon-rise. Then I said "guard" to my little people and they melted into the shadows to obey.

I fed rest thoughts to my mind as best I could, though the Rings worked against such a pattern. Still, that would heighten my putting forth when the hour came. And when the moon found our hillside pocket I was ready.

With the wand I traced out the shield and go design in the level sand beside the pool, using white stones from the gravel of its bed to point the ends of the three curves. And the moon globe, mounted on a flat stone so that its rays shone over that area, gave all the light I needed. I began the Shield Song and sang it, watching the spiraling upward of the visible power from my stones. And then I came to the Go Plea and closed my eyes upon the outer world that I might better see the inner.

When one evokes the power with as little conscious guide as now I did, one accepts what is shown without hold or selection, thus learning in bits and pieces what must afterward be fitted together. So it was with me—for I was as if suspended in the air some distance above a small fort, no more than a portal sentry place. I looked down into that with the eyes of the mind, not those of the body.

Osokun I saw there, and also the off-worlder Krip Vorlund. And I saw what was done to the off-worlder by the orders of Osokun. Then there came a messenger riding, and Osokun and his men mounted and went forth in the dawn light.

The off-worlder I could not reach. Between us stood a barrier I might have breached with effort, but I felt that I had neither time at this moment nor dared I waste the strength such effort would cost me. I could see the spirit which dwelt within him and that it was strong and not easily vanquished. What I could do for him I could, moving certain forces this way and that so that he would be favored by fortune rather than hindered, though all initial effort must be his own.

Then I returned from that place which was not wholly one with Yiktor but shared it only in part. The dawn was very bright and my moon globe pale and wan. For the present I had my answer, not to go on, but wait where I was. And ofttimes waiting is by far the greater burden.

There passed a long day. We slept by turns, my little people and I. I longed to know how well I had wrought for him who lay in that fort across the land. But, though I be singer, I am not of the Old Ones who can aim their sight at command around half the world if the need arises.

I went to the van and tended the barsk. It awoke and ate of food, lapped at water, but only because my will held it to that nourishment. It was no longer savagely twisted of mind, but now apathetic. It would not care for its own needs had I not set it to such action. Malec was right, I thought sorrowfully, there was naught to do save set it free on the White Road—yet I could not bring myself to that. It was as if some command I could not understand had been laid upon me.

Night came, but past its middle the moon was veiled, dark clouds gathered and spun wide nets to choke the stars, those suns that nourish worlds we cannot see. And I thought again of what it would mean to walk alien worlds, see strange animals and people, learn ever more about all the wonders which are the gem-dreams of Molaster. And I sang a little, not one of the great power songs, but such words as lift the heart, strengthen the will, give meat and drink to the spirit. My little ones came to me in the darkness of the night, and I eased their hearts and turned outward their thoughts.

There was a storm threatening before dawn, so no real dawn broke the dismal hold upon the hills. We found a small place in the wall of our dell where we could wait under an overhang of stone, and huddled there together while thunder strode drumming from height to height, the lash of lightning urging it on. I have seen such storms in the uplands of the Thassa, but not heretofore so close to the plains.

In such torments of the sky, time and man are lost, the power to think grows dim. There was the warmth of furred bodies close about me, and I crooned to soothe them. For so much I was glad, that I could busy myself so to put aside my own unease.

At length the worst of that assault from sky upon earth died away. I was moved then by a message of the power, not a clear sending, just a suggestion weaving in and out of mind-pattern. With my little ones I went to the poolside and there rescued the moon globe from a stone now encircled by rising water. I went down the dale to a place where the grass was less thick and there were outcrops of stone. On one of these I set up the moon globe, alight once more as if it could serve as a beacon. But for what, or whom, I was not yet sure. The belief grew in me that he whom I sought would be so drawn, providing such fortune as I had spun for him had been of tight enough thread.

Simmle growled and rose to her feet, showing her teeth in a snarl. Borba and Vors lifted their heads, crests flattened, ready to do battle, while Tantacka shifted her weight from left to right and back again on her broad pawed forefeet, rumbling deep in her throat so her warning was more vibration than audible sound.

Down the slope wavered a figure, pulling itself onward by grasping bush and sapling, going to the knees, yet always rising doggedly to advance, until at last it fell and slid limply down into the circle of moon-globe radiance, mud encasing much of its length. I stooped and gripped a shoulder, exerted my strength to turn over that flaccid body.

The face was mud-splattered, cut, bruised, swollen, yet the one I had expected to see. The offworlder had won out of Osokun's hold and through the hills. Now I was ready to repay my debt—but how? For it was well like he had come from one danger into another equally as great. We stood on the border of Oskold's land where none would gainsay his orders—or rather I stood, and Krip Vorlund lay in a swound now so deep that I could not probe it. Like the barsk, he slept and perhaps was the better for fleeing the here and now. And so passed much of that day.

KRIP VORLUND

VIII

THERE WAS A SINGING, low and sweet, a croon which sounded in my ears as the wind which the space-borne so seldom feel on their bodies. And from whatever place Krip Vorlund had gone into hiding, I was pulled back to be one again, body and spirit locked together. When I opened my eyes to look about me, it was upon a strange company. Still, their strangeness did not truly amaze me; it was as if I had expected to see each and every one of them—girl's face with silver hair escaping about it from the hood of a cloak, furred muzzles with bright animal eyes glistening inquisitively about them.

"You are—Maelen—" My voice surprised me, for it was a hoarse croaking.

She of the hood nodded. "I am Maelen." But she spoke absently and her head turned as if she stared beyond in search of something she feared to see. All the other heads swung also, and from them came snarls and growls, low and rumbling, each differently pitched. My drowsy content vanished, apprehension awoke.

Her hand lifted and light glowed along that which she held between her fingers, the wand. She put this with care on the flattened palm of her other hand. I saw, though she did not touch it, the rod stir of itself and turn to point in the same direction her eyes sought.

As if by a signal, the furred ones vanished into the gloom beyond the borders of the lamplight in which I lay. Now Maelen took up again the wand and pointed with it to the moon globe, which died into nothingness. She leaned closer over me, her weather cloak out in wide wings tenting us both.

"Quiet!" Her order was a mere puff of breath.

I found I was listening, straining to hear whatever her ears also sought. There was the sighing of the wind, the splashing of water not too far away, other sounds of the open—nothing more—save the rising pound of my own blood in my ears.

So we waited for a space I could not measure, save it seemed very long. Then once more she spoke, perhaps to me, perhaps only voicing her thought.

"So—they hunt."

"Me?" I whispered.

"You." I did not need confirmation of that.

"Listen now," she continued swiftly. "There are

more than just Osokun's sword-sworn—these come from before and behind. And—'' she hesitated, ''I do not see how we can get through the net they weave for our taking.''

''It is not your trouble—''

Her finger tips pressed upon my lips, cool and strong. ''Mine the debt, man of the star lanes, mine the payment, so say the scales of Molaster—the scales of Molaster,'' she repeated. Then after a pause, she whispered again, ''should I give you another skin, Krip Vorlund, for the undoing of the enemy?''

''What do you mean?'' It seemed to me, although the cloak about us cast a dark pool of shadow, I could see her two eyes a little above me as sparks of frosty light, much as a beast's eyes will shine in the night if caught by a torch's ray.

''To my mind has come the answer of Molaster.'' She sounded bewildered, the confidence I had always seen in her shaken. ''But you are not Thassa—not Thassa—'' Her voice trailed away into a moment of silence. Then she spoke with her old assurance. ''So be it, if you choose, so be it! Hark well now, off-worlder. I do not think we have a chance to elude those who search these hills. By their thought-throws I read they would have your death and that speedily if they come upon you.''

''That I can believe,'' I told her dryly. ''Have you time to get away? I may not be a trained swordsman but—''

I think she found that amusing, the sound she gave might have been a tiny laugh. ''Brave, oh, brave star rover! But we have not come to such straits yet. There is another path, though a very strange one, and you may think being cut down by the blades of Osokun's men better than the walking of it.''

Perhaps I read challenge into what was only warning, but I reacted stubbornly to her words. ''Show me this path, if you think it means escape.''

''There is this, you may change bodies—''

''What!'' I struggled to sit up, pushed her so that we both overbalanced and struck the ground.

''I am not the enemy!'' Her hands thrust against my chest, punishing old bruises and making me wince. ''Another body is what I said, and what I meant, Krip Vorlund.''

''And this body I now wear?'' I could not believe that she was serious.

''Let Osokun's men take it and welcome.''

''Thank you!'' I retorted. ''Either I lose my life in my body, or they kill my body and leave me outside somewhere.'' The utter folly of what I said made me laugh a little hysterically.

''No!'' Maelen retorted. She had pulled her cloak away and we sat facing each other in the twilight. I could see her face, but it was hard to read her expression, though I believed she was in earnest and meant exactly what she said.

''They will not harm your body, once you have gone from it. They will believe you under the cloak of Umphra.''

''So they would let my body go?'' I decided to humor her. My mind was in an odd state, nothing about this adventure had any reality by the standards

I knew. I began to think it was one of those vivid dreams which now and then visit a sleeper, plunging him into an inner state of awareness so that he believes he is awake, not sleeping, as he undertakes impossible feats. It was beginning to seem, in this real dream, that perhaps all things were possible.

"Your body would not be tenantless, for two spirits will pass from one housing to another. For a space only need this be, as we can then retake your body and once more exchange."

"Because they would leave it here?" I continued, willing to go along with the fantasy.

"No, they would take it to the Temple of Umphra. And we would have to follow, even to the Valley of the Forgotten." Her head turned away and I had a feeling that what she said had some meaning for her which had nothing to do with me.

"And where would I be while we went hunting my body?"

"In another body, perhaps even better fashioned for what might have to be done."

This was a dream, of course. I no longer questioned that it might be anything else. Perhaps it was all a dream—my escape from the fort which had been so oddly favored by fortune, the nightmare journey through the hills and the storm, my coming here. Perhaps the dream extended even further—I had never been kidnaped from the fair, I lay safely now in my ship bunk and dreamed all this. And an odd curiosity awoke in me. I wanted to know how far this dream would take me and what new and weird action would come next.

"Let it be as you wish," I said, and I laughed, for I knew that neither this, nor the waking hours of my life were real.

She looked at me again. Once more I fancied I saw those sparks in her eyes.

"Truly you come of a strong race, star rover. Perhaps, though, seeing much along the space lanes leaves one with a loss of astonishment and a capacity for accepting what may or must come. But it is not because I wish it so, this must be *your* desire."

"Then it is." I humored her in my dream.

"Stay you here and rest." Her hands on my shoulders pushed me back to lie as I had when first aroused to this part of my dream. I lay there wondering what would come next. Would I be waking in my bunk on the *Lydis*? One's dreams are boring to listeners, but this was so strange a one that if I could remember it once I roused I would tell it. Still I rested on the grass and saw sky above, smelled woodland scents and heard wind and the splash of water.

I closed my eyes and willed myself to wake. But it was an art beyond me, for the dream continued as vividly as ever. Something stirred beside me, I turned my head and opened my eyes. There was a furred head there, eyes peering at me intently. The fur was dark save for a crest of gray which stood erect, giving the animal the appearance of wearing a helm of dark metal surmounted by a standing plume, not unlike those of the sea rovers of Rankini.

Sea rovers of Rankini . . . my mind strayed, floated . . . but surely they had not been part of a dream, this or any other. I *had* stood with Lidj on one of their floating trade rafts and exchanged steel harpoon points for Aadaa perls. Rankini, Tyr, Gorth—worlds I had known. I strung them from memory as one would slip beads along a string. Now they were spinning around those worlds . . . whirling . . . whirling . . . No, I was whirling dizzily, memory fled, and close after it all awareness.

> "Ayee, Ayee—run on four feet.
> Scent well the wind's messages—
> Be wise and be fleet—
> Strong and fair.
> Arise and greet the moon.
> By Molaster, and the Law of Qu'eeth,
> By two power, into four power.
> Up, runner of the high places!
> Greet the sun after night,
> For this be the dawn of your birthing!"

I opened my eyes. Then I screamed, for the world I looked upon was distorted, a matter of odd shapes, shades—so altered that terror walked there for me. But no scream did my ears record, rather a howl with naked fear in it.

"Fear not, the change is good, good! I had hoped only, but it is good! In all parts did you travel and arrive."

Did I hear that with my ears, or did it form only in my brain?

"No—no!" I tried to shriek, which I had not done when Osokun's men had worked to bring cries from me. But again came only a kind of barking.

"Why do you fear?" The voice sounded puzzled, even annoyed. "I tell you, it is even as I have said, the exchange went well. And just in time. Simmle says that they come. Lie you still."

Lie still? Exchange? I tried to put my hand to my head which still whirled. But no hand moved, though flesh and muscle obeyed the commands of my brain. I looked again. There was a paw covered with red fur, attached to a long thin leg, and that leg to a body—and the body—I was in that body! But no, this was not true, it could not be! I struggled wildly as in a nightmare. Awake, just let me awake! A man could go mad in such a dream. Awake!

"Let me out!" I might have been a child shut into a terrifying dark cupboard. But no words, only a yipping came from my jaws. I realized dimly that this panic was indeed driving me into a darkness from which there might not be any return at all. I fought then, as I have never had reason to fight before—not any outward enemy, but the terror which was imprisoned with me in this alien body.

I felt a touch on my head and jerked away, looked into animal eyes set in a cream-tan animal face. From sharply pointed jaws a tongue issued to lick me.

Reassurance was relayed by my heightened senses from that touch. And somehow it drew me back from the brink of madness. I blinked, tried the better to see the face of my companion, and found that this small concentration did make a difference. The distortion was fading, adjusting. I could see clearer with every second. The licking went on and the comfort soaked into me.

Stand up—I wanted to stand up. I wavered, staggered. To rise to four feet was not the same as standing upon two. I lifted my head. Scents, my nose drowned in scents; so thickly did they assault my nostrils that it was as if all possible odors had been sprayed into one ship's cabin and I was locked therein. I choked, thought that I could not breathe. But I did and the scents began to carry messages which I only partially understood. I tried to creep as a man would go on all fours, and tottered a step or two. The animal that had licked my head shouldered against me in support until I managed to stand without wavering. To look about me from this new angle was another thing to be learned, and I had by no means mastered it when there was a disturbance behind me.

The animal at my shoulder snarled, and I heard answering rumbles from the bushes a little beyond. Menace and danger read so sharply in those growls that I pushed around and raised my head to the highest to see who came.

Distortion remained, changes in size bewildered me. Again the scents were overpowering. But I was able to make out Maelen, her back to us, the long folds of her cloak sweeping the ground, confronting a group of men. Two were mounted and held the reins of riderless kasi, three advanced on foot, swords sharp and bright in their hands.

I felt lips wrinkle back from the teeth now mine, an unconscious reaction to the odor of men. For I now discovered that emotions were part of some scents, and here were to be felt anger, cruel triumph, and danger. The snarl of the animal that flanked me grew louder.

"—come for him—"

What had been a gargle of meaningless sounds sorted out into words. Or was it that I read those words as they filtered through the mind of Maelen, who displayed no surprise or dismay.

"What you have made of him, that is here."

She turned her head as if to point out what they sought with her eyes. Someone sat, or rather lolled, upon the ground. Slack lips hung loose with a thread of spittle spinning from the lower. I blinked, closed my eyes tight, and willed not to see what was there. But when I opened them again, it remained the same.

How many men ever looked upon themselves, not in a mirror's surface, but as if their bodies had a life apart from their intelligence—their essence? To my belief such was impossible. Yet I stood now on four legs and looked through alien eyes to see and scent what was—*me*!

Maelen went to that sprawling body, put her hands to its shoulders, urged it up. But it seemed that my husk was just that, a husk which had naught left to animate it. It lived, yes, for I could see the breast through the ragged tunic rise and fall with great shuddering breaths. As she pulled and tugged to get it up it moaned and whined. I howled and one of the sword-bearers started, swung around to eye me.

"Be quiet, Jorth!" Maelen's words were in my head, and I guessed she spoke to me, not to the shambling thing which she had at last standing, though she had to support it, for it appeared to want to drop to earth again.

Her order was enforced by the beast beside me, who nipped delicately at my ear and from whom came a telepathic warning.

Maelen led the body—somehow I could no longer think of it as *my* body—a few stumbling steps forward. And the men stared at the drooling, witless thing, stirring uneasily.

"Your work, sword-sworn?" Maelen demanded of them. "So did this one come to me, and you know who I am."

It would seem that they did, with awe and a little more than awe—fear. I saw two of them make gestures toward her as if to ward off ill fortune.

"Thus do I lay upon you your debt, men of—of—" she looked at them intently "Oskold. This one is under the cloak of Umphra, do you deny it?"

One by one, if reluctantly, they shook their heads. Those with the bared swords sheathed them.

"Then do you with him what must be done."

I thought, from the looks they shared, that they would object. But if they were so inclined her manner quelled such protests. One of them led out a kas and between them they got the thing that was no longer a man up on the beast's back and there made fast. Then they turned and rode away into the very early sun, which came from behind a cloud to illumine the dell.

"Why? What?" Yaps from my mouth, but she must have read my thoughts, for once they were gone she came swiftly and knelt before me, putting her hands out to hold my head firmly while she looked into my eyes.

"Our plan is working, Krip Vorlund. Now, give them a small lead, and we follow!"

"What have you done to me and why?"

Now she stared again into my eyes, her attitude one of puzzlement. "I have done as you desired, star rover, given you a new body and taken care to save the old, that you might not bubble forth your life's blood from rents their swords would make. So—" she shook her head slowly, "you did not believe that this could be done, even when you said aye to the doing! But it is done and lies now on the scales of Molaster."

"My—that body—can I get it back? And—what—what am I now?"

She answered my second question first. There was a small overflow of pool like unto a shallow plate of water. To this I was guided by her hand on the nape of my neck. Over it she passed her wand, and the water was still and calm so that I looked into it as I might a mirror. I saw an animal head, with a thick mane between the ears and running down the shoulders; red fur with a golden note—

"The barsk!"

"Yes, the barsk," she said. "And the body—they will take it, as they must or else face certain darkness now and ever after, to a place of refuge. We will follow and, once in the Valley of Forgetting, we shall be safe from Oskold. For those were Oskold's men, which means that much of this country is a

114

death trap, or would be if you still abode in your former shell. Safe from Oskold you may once more be yourself and then move as you see fit."

She spoke the truth as she knew it. I had one last lingering thread of hope.

"This is a dream," I said to myself, not to her.

Again her eyes met mine and in them, as well as in the words she spoke, was that which cut the threat for me.

"No dream, star rover, no dream."

"And now," she rose. "We shall go, but not too fast on their heels lest suspicion be roused. Oskold is no fool and I think that Osokun has plunged his father, through his recklessness, into deep folly. I have saved you by the only method I knew, Krip Vorlund, however ill it may be to your eyes."

So I followed her out of the dell in the guise of an animal who owed her allegiance. For now I discovered that though the barsk body held the essence of a man, yet also was I now attuned in a new way to the form I wore, and more than just in the way I faced the world. Those four who trotted with me were not a company of servants following a mistress, but something more—companions of varied natures allied with another species who understood them and in whom they placed supreme trust.

We came to one of the vans such as I had seen in the yard of the show, the interior of which held cages. My companions went confidently forward and jumped in, pawed open the unfastened doors of the cages and settled themselves therein. But I stayed on the ground, growls rumbling in my throat.

Cage—I was in that moment far more man than beast, and I had had enough of cages in Osokun's keep.

Maelen laughed softly. "Well enough, Jorth—so I have named you. For that means in the ancient tongue 'One-who-is-more-than-he-seems,' and was once granted as a battle name to Mimber of Yitha-men when he went up against the Night Valks. Share my seat if you will, and I shall tell you of your name-hero and how he wrought."

There was nothing farther from my mind at that moment than the desire to listen to the folklore of Yiktor while riding blindly into a future which yet seemed so beyond belief that only by determined will could I consider it. Yet I mounted the seat beside Maelen and there sat upon my haunches, studying the world through eyes which still gave me strange reports.

But I began to see that there was more than the wish to beguile me out of considering my plight which moved Maelen to tell her tale. For as she continued to speak mind to mind, her powers to communicate and mine to receive were heightened and strengthened. Perhaps the esper I had used in my human body still worked in my favor. And, too, I found her story of value. Through its fabric was interwoven such of Yiktor—not the present, but an older, far more complex civilization which had once rooted here and of which the Thassa were the last survivors. There was much she said beyond my understanding, references to events and people un-known, such hints only making me wishful to go through the doors they represented and see what lay on the far side.

The van followed no path, taking the most open way across a wilderness country. We were on the eastern slopes of a range of hills forming a barrier between Oskold's holdings and the plains of Yrjar. But to return to the port in my present guise was the last thing I wished. Maelen continued to reassure me that our eventual goal was the mysterious place of refuge in the higher hills to which my body was being escorted. She explained that the natives believed mental disorders to be a visitation of certain powers, and those harboring them were sacred, to be placed as speedily as possible in the custody of priests trained in such care. But we dared not follow too closely to this place, she warned me several times over, lest they suspect some trickery.

"How did you—how did you make me thus?" I asked at last.

She was silent for a space and when she replied, her thoughts were guarded and remote.

"I did that which I long ago took oath not to do. For this I shall answer in another time and place to those who have the right to demand it of me."

"Why did you?"

"I was debt-laid," she replied still more remotely. "It was through me that you came into this misfortune, thus I must level the scales."

"But you did nothing—that small matter of the beast seller—"

"That, but also this. I knew that you had an enemy, perhaps more than one, and I did not warn

you. Rather did I say that as Thassa the concerns of
others were naught, save where they touched me.
And for this I must also answer.''

''Enemy?''

''Yes.'' And she told me of how Osokun had
come to her with the man from the Combine ship,
Gauk Slafid, and how they had suggested she attract
a Free Trader into a net they would set. Although she
had not done openly as they wished, she now believed that she had served their purpose because of
curiosity. Thus had she begun the chain of events
which had led to my kidnaping.

''That is not true. It was chance only until—''

''Until I made the moon-weave for you?'' she
interrupted. ''Ah, that seems to you now the greatest
of interference. But perhaps you will discover it the
least as the future opens before us, then passes behind us. What I have done is a thing private to the
Thassa.'' Then she stopped and I felt her thoughts
withdraw and I could not touch her, for a barrier
grew between us. Her body sat there, but her eyes
were really turned inward and she had gone where I
could not follow.

But the kasi forged onward as if she had set some
direction in their minds and they kept on as a
navigator would hold to his chart, at a speed which
might be slow but which held steady. Above us the
sun was warm and bright. Then I set myself to
learning my new body, that I might inhabit it compe-
tently as long as I must—though still I could not rid
myself of the belief that this was a long dream
haunting the mind of one safe in his own place and
person.

IX

Two DAYS we traveled so, camping at night in hidden thickets. I became more and more a part of the body I wore, and I learned that there are some compensations, lessons to be learned, by one who travels four-footed and looks upon the world through animal eyes. Maelen fell into moods of abstraction now and then, but between these she talked much, either relating legends or else pointing out features of the country and speaking of her own life as a wanderer there. But, I came to note, she did not often mention her people in the here and now, only as they were in the past. Also there were questions I asked that she adroitly avoided answering. I came to make it something of a business to try to trap her and I think she knew what I would do and as cunningly slipped past me.

On the morning of the third day as we climbed into the van she was frowning slightly.

"From here," she said, "we come into the land of villages and men. And to cloak our purpose we shall call upon the skills of the little people."

"You mean—give shows?"

"Yes. The road to the Valley is such that there are no side ways. Also we may learn of those who have gone before us."

It was almost a shock to think of my body having ridden this road ahead, a sensation difficult to put into words. Maelen continued to promise me that those escorting that mindless thing would be careful to keep the spark of life within it, that, according to their superstitions, any neglect would result in a fate such as they would avoid at all costs.

"And I will be part of your entertainment?"

She smiled slowly. "If you wish. A very great part if you agree. For to my knowledge, and I assure you that is not small, no one has ever shown a barsk before."

"But you had hoped to."

"Yes, I had hoped to."

"What happened to—to—"

"The spirit who wore your present body? It was failing. Another day, perhaps two, and I would have out of compassion sent it on the White Road."

"But in my body—now?"

"It is a feeble tenant. It does not suffer, only lingers for a time to keep the lamp lit until you return."

I had come out boldly with what I had tried to discover earlier. She looked at me.

"To each his own secrets, Krip Vorlund. I told you—this burden is mine, you will not be called to account for what has happened."

"But you will?"

"I will. Now let us consider what lies before us, not what may exist behind a mountain range or two. By midday we shall arrive at Yim-Sin, the road to it lies there—" We were coming down a bank to a road into which the kasi turned, heading upward from the plains.

"In Yim-Sin there is a temple of Umphra," Maelen continued. "There we shall be quartered and, if possible, learn of Oskold's men—though they may have taken the other road on the eastern side of the mountains. This night we shall give a performance. So now let us study what a barsk may do to astound the world."

I was willing to fall in with her plans, for this was the case of depending upon a navigator in the deeps. To the one with the proper knowledge one leaves the ordering of the ship. Together we set up a performance, suggesting the act of a well-trained animal. When we came to a place where terraced fields, now mainly cleared by harvest, made steps on the hillsides, Maelen paused and I withdrew from my usual seat beside her to the traveling cage like the rest of the four-footed company.

They drowsed, for two of their species were nocturnal in normal life, and the other, Tantacka, was a lazy animal when well fed with no need to forage. I found that my new body had habits, too, which were emerging. And I curled up nose to tail and slept a little as the van trundled along.

The scents of the open gave way to other odors, acrid, nose-tickling. I heard voices as if people were gathering around the van, running beside it—high shrill voices of children. Maelen must be bringing us into Yim-Sin. It was, she had told me, a farming village, with the addition of two inns and a temple for the accommodation of those bound for the Valley. Oftentimes those who had relatives there made the journey to look upon them. It was also true that the priests of Umphra sometimes wrought miracles and cured certain of their charges, so not all who went there were hopelessly lost.

While the fields of this up-and-down country were not wide or rich, yet they rooted a vine-grown crop which produced wine favored in the cities. The villagers were prosperous enough, at least their overlords were. But hereabouts there were absentee landlords and there would be only bailiffs and overseers in the two castle holdings along the road we traveled.

I tried to understand the cries, but the words were of a country dialect, not the speech of the Yrjar merchants. Yrjar—suddenly I wondered what had happened there after my kidnaping. Had Captain Foss taken his case to the fair authorities? Some of those authorities or their subordinates must have conspired in my disappearance for it to have happened at all. Had they taken Lalfarns too, or killed him?

Why had I been so important to risk so much on my capture? Surely Osokun must have known I could not give him what he wanted. Nor might Foss have traded the price demanded for me. Maelen had provided one small clue to what might be a greater coil—the part Gauk Slafid played. But the life-and-death struggle between Free Trader and Combine had been all in the past. Why this move now? I had read all the tapes of the old days and the struggle had been a bitter one, carried from planet to planet. Now the Combines dealt mainly with the inner-system worlds and sometimes dabbled in politics on those, to their hurt or gain. What could possibly interest them on Yiktor?

The van came to a halt and the smell of the town—or better described for barsk nostrils—the stench of the town was thick. I longed to peer through the curtains and see our surroundings. But I now wore a skin around which far too many legends of peril and death had been woven.

Borba and Vors uncurled from fur balls and came to peer out of their cages. Simmle whined a greeting to which my barsk vocal cords responded at a lower pitch. Their thoughts reached me as broken bits of expression.

"March-march—"

"Thump-thump—" That was Tantacka.

"Up and down."

So did they foresee their parts in the coming performance. They appeared to look upon their stage appearances as amusement to be anticipated and enjoyed.

"Many smells," I tried my own return.

Simmle barked. "Man smell—many men."

"March-march," chorused the glassia, "good—good!"

"Food," grunted Tantacka, "under rocks—food." She snorted and went back to doze.

"Run." Simmle was wistful. "Run out in the fields—good! Hunt—good! Together—we hunt—"

Instinct of my body answered her. "Hunt—good!" I agreed.

Maelen opened the back flap of the van and climbed in. A man of the plainspeople, wearing a black robe which was crosshatched on back and breast with white and yellow, came with her. He was smiling and chatting in the village dialect, but, through Maelen, the sense of his words filtered to me.

"We are indeed fortunate, Freesha, that you have

chosen this season for your return! The harvest has been good and the people plan a festival for thanksgiving. The Elder Brother wishes to make a happy time for all. He will open the west court for you and will pay all fees, so that your little people may give joy to all with their cleverness.''

"The Elder Brother is indeed a maker of happiness and a force for good in this so-blessed village.'' Her reply sounded formal. "Does he permit that I loose my little people that they may stretch their legs in freedom?''

"But certainly, Freesha. Aught you may need is at your call—the third-rank brothers will serve you.'' He raised his hand. Fastened to thumb and forefinger were two flat pieces of wood and these he clicked loudly together. Two more heads crowded into view at the tail of the van. The closely clipped hair, the Hand of Umphra branded into their foreheads, marked them as priests, though they were only boys.

They were smiling broadly, and apparently well pleased to serve as Maelen's assistants. She opened Simmle's cage and the cream-coated venzese came out, swinging her tail eagerly, while Maelen fitted her with a show collar flashing small gems. Borba and Vors were so accoutered and loosed, and then Tantacka, to whose collar was added a kind of frontlet of richly embroidered red cloth, pointed forward between her ears. It would seem that the animals were old friends as the young priests greeted each by name, but with a gravity which suggested that Maelen's little people were far more than mere animals. Then she put her hand to the latch of my cage and the senior priest leaned forward as if to see me better.

"You have a new friend-in-fur, Freesha?"

"I have indeed. Come forth, Jorth."

As I passed around the door she opened, the priest's eyes went wide and his breath hissed between his teeth. "A barsk!"

Maelen was busy putting about my neck the collar she had sewn at our last camp, a strip of black with mirrorlike stars glittering in a scattered trail along it.

"A barsk," she agreed.

"But—" His astonishment had become half protest.

Maelen straightened, her hand still resting lightly on my head.

"You know me, Elder Brother, and my little ones. This is a barsk in truth, but Jorth is no longer a flesh eater and haunter of trails, but our comrade-in-fur, as all others who travel in my shadow."

He looked from her to me and then back again. "Truly you are one who accomplishes strange things, Freesha. But this is yet the strangest of all— that a barsk should come to your call, suffer you to lay hand upon his head, that you should name him and make him of your company. But if you so speak—that it will not give way to the evils of its kind—then shall man believe you. For the gifts of the Thassa are like unto the laws of Umphra, fixed and unchanging."

Then he stood aside and I went with Maelen, leaping down from the tail of the van. The young priests hesitated and drew a bit apart, their amazement more open even than that of their superior.

They allowed us to precede them. The other animals came to join us, Simmle beside me, aiming a quick lick at my cheek as I fell into step with her. We went out of the courtyard in which the van had halted into another walled space through a double-leafed gate, only one half of which was open for us. The inner area was paved with black stone veined with yellow, and empty, save along the walls where trained vines and trees grew from beds of earth bordered by fitted stone. At the far left was a fountain, the water boiling out of a stonehead into a pool.

One of the animals headed for the pool and lapped from its bounty. The water was cool, tasting good. Tantacka dipped in not only her blunt muzzle but also forepaws, flipping them up to send showers of drops flying in all directions.

I sat back on my haunches to look around. At the other end of the area were three broad steps which led to a columned porch, and in that was another door, intricately carved with a sprawling design I could not figure out. That gave entrance to a building which I thought must be the center portion of the temple. There were no windows to break the sweep of wall, only more carved panels, in alternating white and yellow stone, to pattern the black of the walls.

Maelen directed the boy priests who carried some boxes from the van to set them along the steps, and I noted that they continued to glance at me with some awe. When they had done, Maelen dismissed them

with thanks and sat down on the lowest step. I lost no
time in joining her.

"Well?" There was only one thing I wanted to
know—had she gained any news of Oskold's men
and that which they were transporting.

"They have not passed this way," she answered
me. "Nor was I sure they would. If they needed to
appraise their lord of what had happened they would
have gone eastward and thus come on the other road
which leads to the Valley."

"You seem very sure they want to get to this
Valley."

Maelen put her hands to either side of my barsk
head and raised it so she could better look into my
eyes.

"Accept this, star rover: of the ways of the people
of Yiktor I do know much. They are set to patterns
which they do not break, not when there is naught to
endanger them. Rest assured Oskold or his men will
not alter *this* pattern. One way or another they shall
bring that which belongs to you to the Valley."

"Ah, Freesha, so it is true:"

The voice behind us rang in my ears as if Maelen
spoke and I was startled, for this was the first time I
had "heard" so as to understand except through her
intermediacy. I jerked out of her hold and snarled
involuntarily as I looked up the steps.

A man in priestly robes stood there. He was old,
bent a little, leaning on a support which was more
staff of office than cane, for it was almost as tall as
his age-bared skull. His face was open, yet that of a
man who had seen so much of sorrow that he would

be colored with its gray wash to the end of his days.
Only now he smiled, and in his smile was the sweet-
ness of one to whom compassion was the greatest of
virtues.

"You have brought a marvel indeed." He came
down a step and in turn Maelen sped to join him,
setting her arm under his in support. That aloofness
which stood always between her and the plainsmen
vanished and there was respect in her tone as she
made answer.

"I bring a barsk, yes, Eldest Brother. Jorth, show
your manners!"

Thus the first of the tricks we had worked out
together was shown to the guardian of the temple as I
bowed my head thrice and then barked my deepest.
And gently, with the same smile, the priest inclined
his head to me in answer.

"Go with the love and care of Umphra, brother of
the upper ways," he said.

The beliefs of the Free Traders are few, and we
seldom express them, even among ourselves. At
ship's swearing, or when taking a permanent life
companion, or when accepting a foster child into
one's household—yes, we have oaths and powers
we call upon as witness. I think that all living things
with intelligence recognize THAT WHICH LIES ABOVE
AND BEYOND. They must or be ever lost and driven by
their inner fears and doubts beyond the endurance of
their spirit. We give respect to gods of other worlds,
for they are but man-distorted images of that which
stands ever behind such faulty windows into the
unknown. Now, in this man who had given his life to

the service of such a god, I saw one who walked closely to the Great Truth as he saw it, and perhaps it was indeed a truth, if not one in which my people believed. Thus, forgetting the skin which covered me, I bowed my head as I would to those who have my respect.

And when I raised it to look once more in his face, I saw that his smile was gone; rather did he look at me very intently, as one might view some new thing which caught the full attention.

"What we know of the barsk," he said as if he spoke to himself, "is very little, and most of that, ill, having been sifted through the screen of fear. Perhaps there is much we should learn."

"My little people are not quite like those of their wild kin." Maelen spoke swiftly and I read both unease and warning in the half-thought she shot at me, a warning that this was one who had some of the inner sight and whose suspicions must not be aroused.

Thus I barked and snapped at an insect buzzing overhead and then went to join the others at the pool, hoping I had done my best to cover any lapse I had unwittingly made.

Maelen lingered with the priest and they spoke together in a murmur which did not reach my ears. Also she had shut off mind-communication with me and this I did not like. But I dared not try to listen in that manner either.

In the early evening we gave our show to all the villagers who could crowd into the court, repeating it twice so that all could see, using the porch of the temple for our stage, the boy priests helping Maelen arrange the few properties we used. They did this with such practiced skill that I guessed this was not the first time this had happened, though why Maelen would have come this way before, I did not know.

The acts were less elaborate than those which her other troop had presented at the fair. Now Tantacka sat on her haunches and thumped a drum to which Borba and Vors danced and marched. Simmle leaped over a series of ascending bars, prancing on her hind legs, answered questions from the audience with barks, played a small musical instrument by pressing on large keys with her forepaws. And I sat up, bowed, and did the other small tricks we had planned. I think my appearance alone would have been enough, for the villagers were startled. I wondered more and more at the fearsome reputation my host body held in this country.

When we had done we went back to our cages, and for once I did not demur at being so housed. I was as thoroughly weary as if I had labored man-fashion throughout a day.

But I had discovered that a barsk's sleep was not like that of a man. It did not last the night through, but was a series of short naps, between which I lay awake and alert, keenly aware through nose and ear of all that went on outside the curtains of the van. During one such wakeful spell I heard a stir in the fore part where Maelen had a couch she used in bad weather or when it was not possible to sleep in the open.

Light, so thin it seemed only a very pallid and

weak reflection of her moon globe, filtered through a curtain slit. The latch of my cage had not been dropped. I was free to come and go, though I knew the danger of doing so in the village. Now I nosed open the door and moved to set my eyes to that slit.

On her bed place Maelen sat cross-legged, her eyes closed. One might have thought she slept, but her body moved from the waist slowly back and forth, as if in time to music I could not hear. Nor could I reach her mind, for when I strove to do so, I came against a tight barrier with the force of one running headlong into a fort wall.

Her lips were slightly parted and I caught a sound, the faintest whisper of sound issuing from them. She was singing—or was she? I could not be sure whether it was song, or some muttered invocation, even some plaint. Her hands rested on her knees, but between forefinger and forefinger her silver rod made a taut bridge, and it was from that the faint light beamed.

Around me, as I watched, the air held a kind of electric charge. My mane roughened and raised, there was a tingling along my hide, a prickling in my nose. We men of the ships have our kind of power and energies, but we never deny the fact that there are others elsewhere whom we do not understand and cannot control. For the art of controlling such may be a matter of birth and not of learning.

This was power, but whether she called it to her or whether she sent it forth, I did not know. And in that moment of my watching I was strongly aware she was alien, far more alien than I had believed.

She was silent after a space, and the tingling in the air began to ebb. Then with a sigh her head fell forward, and she jerked as one awakening, to place the now dim rod under her head as she stretched herself on the couch. The light was gone and I was sure she slept.

In the morning we left Yim-Sin, with the villagers cheering us out, shouting their desire for our return. We took a road which climbed and climbed. These were not hills we faced now, but rather mountains. The air was chill and Maelen wore her cloak, but when I took my place beside her on the seat I found my thick pelt needed no cover. The scents here were exciting and I found awaking in me time and again the strong desire to leap from my perch and run to the timbered slopes, in search of I know not what.

"We come now into barsk country," she told me with a laugh. "But I would not advise you to take advantage of your wish to see it better, Jorth. For, though some part of you is native here, you would speedily be at a disadvantage."

"Why do all look upon a barsk in your company as so strange and rare?" I asked.

"Because, though the barsk is known, in another way it is not. If that sounds to be a riddle, perhaps it is. Men of the high slopes, of whom there are few—though the Thassa haunt the mountain-caught clouds by choice—have slain the barsk, which in turn hunts them with cunning and patience. There are many legends about the barsk, Jorth, and it is credited with almost as much power as men set into the hands of the Thassa. Many lords have coveted a caged barsk, only to discover—if they are able to find one—it either gains its freedom and then takes dire vengeance upon man and herd, or else it wills itself to death. For it does not accept any curtailment of its freedom. The spirit which wore your body was so willing itself when the exchange was made."

I shivered. "And if that will succeeds?" I demanded.

Maelen hastened to reassure me. "It will not, there was a limit set upon it in exchange. Your body will not die, Krip Vorlund—it will not be a discarded husk when you find it."

"Now," she shifted to another subject, "there is the watch post of Yultravan. But most of the people must be in harvest on the slopes. We shall not stop. But before the sentries see you, it would be well for you to be caged."

Reluctantly I climbed back and found my cage. Maelen exchanged greetings with two armored men who came from a small shelter beside the road. One of them lifted the curtain at the tail of the van to glance within, so I kept well in the back of the cage to escape notice. Again I thought they knew her as if she had made this journey before.

That night we camped in the open once more, and Maelen brewed a pot of liquid which gave forth such enticing odor that we all gathered around the fire to sniff longingly. I admit that I gulped my portion with no more manners than the real barsk might have displayed under the circumstances. Anticipation had ridden me during the day's journeying, for I knew that we were very close to our goal. But when I settled in my cage that night—Maelen deeming it safer for some reason that we all rest inside the van—I went immediately to sleep and this time did not waken.

We roused in the first of the dawn light and broke our fast on some crumbled cakes which were a mingling of grain and dried bits of meat. Then once more the van started upward. This time the slope was steeper, so that the kasi bent their shoulders to the yoke with visible effort. We stopped now and then to let them breathe, Maelen putting small weights she carried to block the backward roll of the wheels.

But we did not pause for a regular nooning, again sharing out cakes and lapping from bowls filled from Maelen's water bottle. It was midafternoon when we reached the top of the grade. Now the road descended through a cut between two heights. But what lay below was veiled by drifting mists, which only now and then parted to give a blurred hint of the depths.

"The Valley," Maelen said, and her voice was flat, wrung dry of emotion. "Stay with the van, we must keep strictly to the road. There are barriers and safeguards here which cannot be seen."

She gave the command to the kasi, and the van crawled on down into that place of mists and mystery.

MAELEN

X

"Look with unclouded eyes upon your own desires," say the Old Ones when they speak among the Thassa. But one may believe all his thoughts clear, his motives open, and yet be moved by some hidden compulsion, as my little ones obey my wand when there is need for me to raise its power. Was my hidden desire awakened when I left Yrjar, virtuously telling myself and Malec that I went only to obey the law of the scales? If it was, then it was indeed deeply hidden.

Or did it spring to life after I had broken oath and sent the off-worlder from his own body into that of the barsk, that act sowing the seed? Or do any of us move, save by some design of Molaster's far beyond our understanding? To the Old Ones such an argu ment as that is blasphemy, for they hold that each i: answerable for his own acts—though they some times take into consideration the motivation fo those acts, when it is a strong one.

But the thought was already near to fruition in Yim-Sin, so that I was knowing and yet denying it When the priest Okyen had speech with me private ly, he had ill news and left me with despair and futile anger to chew upon. So when we traveled on, com ing ever nearer the Valley where many hopes are buried, I was constantly under assault by temptation even though I could not believe that naught but il might come of it.

It was very difficult for me to occupy my mind with the plight of Krip Vorlund during those hours and I determined that once we found what he sought I would make the exchange speedily to lay thi: temptation. Nor would I trust myself to think upon the one who abode there and whose days were surely numbered.

We came down from the lip of the Valley, through the chill mists which cloud it, into that portion which is allowed to those from outside. I answered the off-worlder's questions as shortly as I could, still wrestling with myself. It was near sundown when we pulled into the outer court of the great temple, tha which is for visitors. The guard priest came to gree us. I knew his face, but I could not set name to it—there is a kind of merciful forgetting allowed one at times—and this was the man who had greeted me here on a different occasion I tried not to recall.

asked to speak with Orkamor, only to be told he was busy and could not receive me. We took the van into the second courtyard and I released the kasi and fed and watered my little people. But Krip Vorlund asked me questions by mind-touch and some I could not answer.

We had lighted the moon globes by the van when a third-rank priest came to say Orkamor would see me. Krip Vorlund wished to go with me. He was impatient with all save finding and being united with his body. But I had to tell him that I must prepare Orkamor for what would happen and explain carefully, lest our story be thought wild raving. This he could accept.

Did it move stronger in me then, the belief that I need only act and much of the burden I had carried so long would be resolved? If it did, I still had the courage to resist.

Okramor is not a young man and the burdens on him are a weighty load which grow heavier with the years, not lighter. Nor is he like the Thassa with their stronger, longer-lived bodies. So that each time I meet him, he seems to me even more shrunken, wasted, shadowy. Yet in him burns so strong a flame of will, and the need to answer need, that the spirit waxes while the fleshy envelope which holds it shrivels. After the first moments one sees only the spirit and not the man form that wears it.

"Welcome, sister." His voice was tired that night, thin and fluting as if it, too, had been used too much and too long.

I bowed my head above my wand. There are few

the Thassa give full reverence to, besides their own Old Ones. But Orkamor deserves greatly of all Yiktor.

"Eldest Brother, peace and good." I made the Three Signs with my wand.

"Peace and good," he returned, and this time his voice was stronger, deeper, as if he battled away weariness with his will. "But we need no soothwords between us, sister. I cannot tell you all is well."

"I know. I came through Yim-Sin."

"Was it well to come, sister? There is naught you can do, and sometimes surveying a wreck sorrows the heart past ever lifting of the cloud. It is better to remember a loved one walking in pride, than without pride or even manhood left."

My hands tightened on my wand, and I knew he saw me do that, but with Orkamor I did not care; he has seen worse self-betrayal in his time.

"I have come on another matter." Resolutely I thrust aside what he confirmed, and continued. "This—"

Quickly I turned to the matter of the off-worlder, telling the story to Orkamor simply. I could do this because he was who and what he was and would not read aught into my actions to make him think me more or less than himself. The priests of Umphra and the Thassa are not so un-kin as we are with others who dwell in the plains. When I was done he stared at me, but there was no great astonishment in his face.

"The way of the Thassa is not the way of mankind," he said.

"Tell me something I do not already know!" All that I had borne since Yim-Sin flared out in my sharp speech. And then, when I would have asked pardon, he waved it aside.

"Yes, you must have thought of the cost before you did this, sister. Those of your calling do not move lightly. This off-worlder was worth that much to you?"

"There was a debt."

"Which, if he knew all the consequences, he would not have demanded any payment from you. Now I must also say—there has been no charge brought hither by the men of Oskold."

I was not greatly disturbed. "If they returned to seek Oskold's leave— We came by the fore road, and though the van moves slowly that path is shorter."

"What if he is not brought, sister?"

I looked to the wand I twirled in my fingers. "They cannot—"

"You hope that they will not," he corrected me, and now there was sharpness in his voice. By all you have told me, Osokun broke fair law in taking this man. He involved his father when he imprisoned the captive in a border fort. It was a man wearing Oskold's livery who came hunting him to the death in your camp. It may be that they think to kill him, hide his body, and leave it to their enemies to prove their crime. Would you not think thus, were you Oskold at this hour?"

"Being Oskold, with a plainsman's mind, perhaps I would. But not one who was—"

"Who was under Umphra's cloak?" Orkamor did

not need to read my mind to follow my thoughts. "Having broken one law, it is always easier to break another."

"They broke man's law at the fair, but would they dare to break Umphra's law?"

"You are thinking as a Thassa." He sounded more gentle now, as one who must reason with an alien. "You have few Standing Words, and your mortal precepts are so secure that they are seldom threatened. But, sister, what of your own actions under the Moon of Three Rings?"

"I have broken law, yes, and I will answer for it. Perhaps the reason for the deed will outweigh the deed. You know the judgment of my people."

"Yet you broke it with open eyes, though not in fear for yourself. Fear is the great lash the powers of darkness use to torment all men. If fear be great enough, then no law of man or god can stand against it. I have heard of Oskold. He is a strong man, though hard. He has but one heir, Osokun, and this has been that youth's bane. For his father favors him too greatly. Do you think that Oskold will tamely accept the outlawry of his son?"

"But how could he hope to conceal—"

"What men may say they know, and what they are able to prove are two different matters. And the full proof of Osokun's ill doing is the body of the offworlder."

"No!" I should have seen this, of course. Why had I been so blind to logic.

"My sister, what did you really want?" Again Orkamor reached into my mind and sought what I did not want to see light.

"I swear—by the breath of Molaster, I swear—I did not—" I broke then, heard myself babbling, and strove to win control once more.

Orkamor looked at me steadily and made the truth, or what was now the truth, plain to both of us.

"And did you think, sister, that such could be? I tell you, it is not the body that makes a man, but what dwells within it. You cannot fill an empty frame and expect the past to come alive and all be as it once was. The Thassa can do much, but they cannot so give life to the dead."

"I did not mean it so!" I denied that once-hidden thought, now open in my mind. "I saved the off-worlder's life—they would have cut him down without mercy."

"And which would he have chosen, had all been made plain to him?"

"Life. It is a part of most to cling to life at that final Question."

"And now you will offer him life again, under new terms?"

I could, it would be so easy. Krip Vorlund had been in shock when he realized he was Jorth. Offered a human body again, would he hesitate—if it were proven his own body was beyond recall? Beyond recall—I stiffened against temptation.

"I will make no offers until I am sure that all has gone so awry." I promised.

"But you will tell him this now?"

"Only that his body has not yet reached the Valley. For that may be the truth, may it not?"

"We can always lean upon the mercy of Umphra. I shall send a messenger down the western road. If they are on the way, we shall be prepared. If not, there may be some news—"

"Thank you, Eldest Brother. Is it permitted that I—I—?"

"Do you really wish this, sister?" Kindness, great compassion, once more warmed his voice.

For the moment I could not decide. Was Orkamor right—that I should not see the one in the inner chamber, harrow my heart by looking upon—I shrank from that journey which was only a few steps, yet for me marked a distance like that between the stars which Krip Vorlund knew. Krip Vorlund—if I saw, then could I hold to my resolve, put aside desire?

"Not now," I whispered.

Orkamor held up his hand in blessing. "You are right, sister. And may Umphra arm you with his strength. I shall dispatch the messenger, do you have dreamless sleep."

Dreamless sleep! A kind wish, but not for me this night, I thought as I returned to the van. The off-worlder would want news. A part of the truth was all I had to offer him. Truth—perhaps the rest was not truth but surmise, perhaps Orkamor's messenger would meet the party we sought and all would come right after all—for Krip Vorlund. There are many rights in any world, and some may stand for others' wrongs. I must push away such thoughts.

I was right about the off-worlder and his questions. He was distraught when I said that the party from Oskold had not yet arrived, only small part reassured by the idea of the messenger sent down the western road. I dared not use mind-talk too much, lest I reveal in some way my new knowledge of myself. So I pleaded great weariness and went to my couch, lying there for half the night, hearing him shift and turn in his cage.

Morning came with the dawn call of the priest from the peak of the temple tower. I listened to those singing notes which, though not of the power of Thassa, yet had in them power of their own kind. For in this place where sorrow and despair could so well lay a black blanket over all, yet Umphra's servant sang of hope and peace, and compassion. And by so little was my own day lightened.

I brought out the little people and let them free in the courtyard, while two of the third-rank priests, who were hardly more than children, came gladly to bring us food and water. Krip Vorlund sat close to me, and ever as I looked up I found his eyes watching my every move, as if by such close surveillance he could trap me.

Why had I thought that? Such ideas out of nowhere sometimes carry the germ of truth.

"Krip Vorlund—" To use the name Jorth now, I believed, would add to his suspicion. He must continue to think of himself as a man only temporarily dwelling in a barsk body. "Today perhaps—"

"Today!" he assented eagerly. "You have been here before?"

"Twice." What was it that loosened my tongue then, made me tell him the truth? "There is one abiding here who is claim-kin to me."

"Thassa!" He seemed surprised, and I read that he looked upon my race with some of the awe which the plainsmen feel toward the Thassa.

"The Thassa," I said bitterly, "share much of the troubles of all men. We bleed if one raises sword or knife against our flesh, we die, we suffer many ills. Do you think we are impervious to that which ails others?"

"Perhaps in a way I did," he admitted. "Though I should have known it was not so. But what I have seen of the Thassa led me to think they were not akin to the rest of Yiktor in much."

"There are perils which are ours alone, perhaps, just as you have those which are peculiar to your people also. What are the dangers faced by space rovers?"

"More than I have now time to tell," he returned. "But your kin—the one who shelters here—is there nothing which can be done—"

"No!" I cut him short. To explain the why and wherefore of he who dwelt in the hall of Umphra, I could not. It hovered too close to his own present plight.

Among us those who would become Singers must undergo certain tests which reveal whether or not they have the proper gifts. And Maquad had been struck down during that time, not through any fault of his own, but because of one of those fell chances which are random shot by fate. We had surrendered what still lived into the hands of Umphra, not because we feared what he had become, as most of the plainsmen fear the deranged, but because we knew that here what life was left to his husk would be gently tended. For the Thassa no longer have fixed homes.

Once we had our halls, our cities, our rooted places. Then we chose another road and it was no longer necessary for any of us to claim a certain place for kin-clan being. There are old sites in hidden places, where we gather when there is need for council or on one of the Days of Remembering. We wander as we will, living in our vans. And thus to care for such as Maquad now was something we could not easily do. He was not the first we surrendered unto Umphra, though those had luckily been few.

"When will we know about—"

I roused out of my thoughts. "As soon as the messenger returns. Now, come, I would have you meet Orkamor."

"Does he know?"

"I have told him as was necessary."

But the man in the barsk body did not rise to follow as I stood, and to my surprise I read in him an emotion which I could not understand—shame. So strange was this to any Thassa that my amazement grew.

"Why do you feel thus?"

"I am a man, not a barsk. You have seen me as a man, this priest has not."

I could not yet understand. It was one of those times when two who seem to have put aside the alien separation of their backgrounds are pulled sharply apart by their pasts.

"To some men on Yiktor this would matter, to Orkamor it does not."

"Why?"

"Do you believe that you are the only one on this world ever to put on hide, run on four feet, test the air with a long nose?"

"You—this has been done before?"

"I—yes—also others. Listen, Krip Vorlund, ere I became a Singer and one able to company with my little people, I also ran the hills for a time in a different body. This is part of our learning. Orkamor knows this, so do others whom we visit now and then. At times we exchange parts of our learning. Now—I have told you something which you could use against the Thassa, tossing it as one might toss a firebrand into a standing yas crop to our ruin."

"And you—*you*—have been an animal!" There was first shock in his thoughts, and then, because he was a man of intelligence and of a mind more open than the planet-bound, he added, "But this is indeed a way to learn!" And I sensed that he lost then some of his uneasiness, so I thought I should have said the like to him earlier. Yet I also realized that I said it now only because there might be need for some hope should Orkamor's fears be true. Only—he must not look upon Maquad, nor know that story for the present.

We went into the inner hall of the temple and through that to the small garden where Orkamor rested his frail body, if not his compassionate mind. He sat there in a chair fashioned of hrata wood, deep-set in the earth so that the wood lived again and put forth small twiglets and branches, making a snug shield against the wind for one sitting there.

It was a place of deep peace, that garden, as was

needful for the use to which it was put. For here not only came Orkamor to be renewed in spirit, but also he brought those for whom the world had ended when someone they loved had arrived to abide with Umphra thereafter. There are places where the power we all recognize under different names manifests itself in a way to inspire awe and even terror. Very few are there where it lays a comforting hand upon the afflicted. This was such a place and all who entered there were the better for it.

Orkamor turned his head and looked at us. He smiled rather than spoke his welcome. We went forward to stand beside him.

"The day is new, for us to write upon as we will," he repeated a sentence from the creed of Umphra. "So fair a tablet should draw the best from us." Then he spoke to Krip Vorlund. "Brother, Yiktor gives you much to write upon these days."

"That is so," the off-worlder replied in thought.

Orkamor had the inner language. He could not have been who and what he was without it. Few of his race, though, have developed that gift.

"It is given to any man to learn all he can during his lifetime, no limit set upon that learning. Only to refuse knowledge is our choice, and he who does so cuts himself off from much. I have never spoken with an off-worlder before—"

"We are as other men," Krip Vorlund replied. "We are wise and stupid, good and evil, living by this code or disregarding that one. We bleed from wounds, laugh at jests, cry at deep hurts—do not all men whether they walk this world or that?"

"True. And this would be more true for those who, as yourself, see more than one world so they may make comparisons. Will you humor an old man, planet-bound, and tell him something of what lies beyond our skies and marches with the stars—"

Orkamor did not look at me, but I understood his dismissal. Why he would have the off-worlder to himself, I did not know, and it disturbed me somewhat. But that I put aside, since I could think no harm in Orkamor and perhaps it was only as he said, that curiosity moved him to do so. He was so much apart by reason of his calling that one forgets at times to remember he was also a man and had a man's interests.

I nerved myself then to do what I could not face the night before—seek out Maquad. Of that there is no need to speak. To drag the sorrows of the past out of memory and relive them is a weak and useless thing. But I marveled anew at what they did in this place for those without hope.

At nooning I came again into the courtyard where I had left the van. My little ones napped in the shade of a tree, but roused and came to me. Krip Vorlund was not with them. And I wondered, for I did not believe that Orkamor could talk away all morning, the press of his duties was too heavy.

Then I called to one of the priests who brought us food and water. But he had seen nothing of the barsk and told me Orkamor was in the meditation chamber where he might not be disturbed.

Now I was worried. While the priests of Umphra will raise no hand against any living creature, there

were others who might not think in their reaction to
the sudden appearance of an animal. I was returning
to the van when a secondary priest came in, his face
bearing a frown.

"Freesha, there is a message from the western
road, sent by a winged one. Those whom you seek
never passed the gate town."

I gave my thanks mechanically, only a small part
of my mind reacting to his words. The disappearance
of Krip Vorlund was my major concern.

"The barsk—" I began, though why this priest,
who had no contact with the supply duties of the
temple, would know, I did not guess.

"It was here, when I came seeking you before."
He looked around as if he might be able to conjure
that red-furred body out of the ground by eye-search
alone. "I remember I remarked to Brother Ofkad,
for never have I known a barsk to walk with man
before."

"How long ago was that, brother?"

"Two bell strokes before nooning. The gong
spoke even as I left to seek you elsewhere."

So long a time! I went to Simmle, spoke to her by
mind. She barked quickly, in some excitement, and
ran to the gate.

"It would seem, brother, that my barsk has gone
elsewhere. I must seek him."

I had warned Krip Vorlund before we entered the
Valley of the traps it might contain for those who did
not know its ways, or stay within the open ones.
Why had he left the temple, I could not guess. Surely
nothing that had passed between him and Orkamor

could have led to this utter folly. Simmle could follow any trail he had left with ease, but a barsk might cover much ground in the time lapse the priest had mentioned—always providing he had not fallen into any of the trapped ways.

Simmle and I had reached the outer gate of the temple when I heard a hail from behind and turned impatiently to see the young priest who had charge of the guesting court.

"Freesha, they say you seek the barsk."

"Yes."

"It cannot be far gone, for it was drinking from the bowl when the messenger came. It is odd—" He hesitated.

"Yes?" I was impatient to be gone.

"It was—it was almost as if the barsk were listening to what we said. It barked when I noticed it. And when I turned again it was gone."

Could the off-worlder have understood them? The temple priests among themselves spoke the high tongue—and with it mind-touch—until often their speech was sometimes but a word or two, the rest all thought.

"What did you say that the barsk appeared to listen to?"

He did not quite meet my eyes then. "He—Older Brother—asked where you were. I answered that you were in the inner apartments with the protected one. We—we spoke a little of that one. And then the Older Brother said that you awaited those who were bringing a stricken one, but they were not coming. After that he went hence and when I looked—the barsk was gone."

Had—could Krip Vorlund have been rash enough to go looking for his body? But why had he so rushed forth and not come to me?

I waved Simmle on—

"Find him, girl." I gave her the order which sent her racing ahead, and I followed, bewildered, shaken wondering what had changed in that short time when I had sought my own sorrow and forgotten about the purpose which had brought me here.

KRIP VORLUND

XI

I LAY ON THE EARTH and around me the smell of it, of the things that grew, roots set deep in its substance, and of the life that walked it, burrowed through it, was thick, teasing, testing. How far was I now from the Valley, how long the road I skulked along, I did not know as I lay and licked sore paws. I was now more Jorth than Krip Vorlund.

Man? Was there any longer a man who had once been Krip Vorlund? The priests of Umphra reported no party out of Oskold's territory with the husk of a man. Why, then, had I been brought to the Valley? What purpose had I been meant to serve for Maelen's desire, not mine? When I heard the priests talk among themselves suspicion had leaped into life, and I thought with new understanding of my interview with Orkamor in the garden of peace.

We talked of worlds beyond, but always he wanted to know of the men who sought out such worlds, of what made them become star rovers. And it seemed to me that he had been trying to learn what manner of man would become a barsk to save his life—as if, by such a chance, I had taken a step from which there might be no return, and if I would accept such a fate for all time.

When Maelen spoke of the exchange, there had been a kind of logic to it. She knew the dangers, ah, how well she knew them. For the priests I had overheard not only spoke of my missing body, but also discussed Maelen and what brought her to the Valley, not once but again and again. There had been another who had run in a beast's body, at her bidding perhaps. And there had been no return exchange. So the man's body husk now dwelt in the Valley, and of the beast they did not speak. Or was that unfortunate one caged among her little people?

That perfectly trained company—were they all, or most, once men and women, not animals? Was that how the Thassa recruited their beast shows? Perhaps the name they had given to their performers—"little people"—was entirely apt.

She had long wanted to add a barsk to the company, she admitted that. And I had walked into her trap with the naïveté of a trusting child. Or had she brought to bear on me some of her power when my mind had been bewildered? What mattered now was not what had happened and could not be changed, but what might still be done. My body—my man's body—where was it? If it still lived at all— And to find out I must search Oskold's land. What I would do if I found it, I had no idea. But for the present the burning need to find it possessed me utterly, past logical reasoning. Perhaps I was no longer quite sane—

Hunger and thirst were dim urges stirring now. I scented man, the odors of a farm holding. And, wincing as I rose on my sore pads, I slipped through the underbrush. How much of the beast served me, I did not know. Man's knowledge might be an awkward leash upon my hunting skill. In dim twilight, as I stole from shadow to shadow along a wall of loosely piled stone, I was drawn by the messages my nostrils caught and classified.

Meat—saliva dripped from my tongue, my belly growled its emptiness—the scent of meat.

I crouched between two bushes, peering underneath them to an open farmyard. A kas stood stamping heavy hoofs. There were also four of those domesticated animals—forsphi—whose long-fleeced coats provided the raw material for the weaving of a highly weather-resistant cloth. They appeared uneasy, turning their long necks, bending their heads at queer angles, to survey the wall near which I crouched. And one of them voiced deep, coughing grunts of alarm. Just as I scented them, so must they also have picked up my presence.

But what I sought was not one of those, half again as large as I. A fowl picked an erratic path much closer to my hiding place. It was a long-legged creature with a sharply pointed bill which it repeatedly stabbed into the ground. I tensed as it neared. Unlike the animals, it appeared not to have any sense of danger. I burst from my bush and charged it. The bird whirled with a speed which I had not thought possible, and I felt a sharp and piercing pain above one of my eyes. Only a quick flinch saved me from another attack and I fled, blood blinding me on the left, aware that only happy chance had saved my sight.

The clamor of the animals rose as I ran back along the wall and into such cover as I could find. I ran a long distance before my sore paws and laboring lungs forced me to a halt.

Barsks were supposedly wily hunters. But I was not a barsk, I was Krip Vorlund.

I had one advantage not shared by my man body, the night did not blind me. The dark might be my day, which it probably was for a barsk. And before morning I fed, ravenously, certainly not daintily, on a reptilian creature I pawed out from between two stones in a stream bed. Then I found a hollow between a fallen tree and a rock and slept, waking now and then to lick my paws and hope that they were not too raw to carry me onward.

It was better, I decided, to switch traveling by day when I might be sighted to night, which was the natural time for barsk prowling. So I dozed throughout the light hours and limped on when the moon was high.

The Three Rings about that lunar disk were very bright tonight. My barsk head went up and, before I could subdue the impulse, I bayed—my deep cry echoing oddly until it sounded, even to me, more than just that of a night runner saluting the sky rider. There was something in that splendid display which drew and held the eyes, and I could understand why those of Yiktor attributed psychic powers to the rare phenomenon.

Three-Ringed moon meant power—but there was only one power I wanted and that was to regain my own body. I returned to the stream and hunted again, with slightly better results, for this time I flushed a warmblooded animal I surprised drinking at a pool. As Jorth I feasted, thrusting man-memory away during that meal. Then I drank my fill and started across country in search of a road which might be my guide.

I came upon an east-west path running through the woods. For a wide space on either side of the thoroughfare underbrush and saplings had been cut back, leaving open space. I kept just within this cover going west.

Oskold's land did not appear to be thickly settled, at least not in this section. Before dawn I passed, giving it wide berth, another fort such as the one I had been imprisoned in. But this one had a settlement by it, though the houses, or rather huts, were very roughly built as though meant to be only temporary shelters.

It was an encampment, I thought, barracks for more men than the fort could house. Sentries walked beats on the eastern side, and there were several lines of riding kasi pegged out, not grazing free. I believed Oskold's forces were alerted, as if to repel some invasion. I passed too close to a kas, which snorted and then gave voice to a roar, making its comrades highly vocal in turn. Men shouted and lanterns flashed along the hut lines. I slipped away hurriedly.

If the outer limits of the domain were empty land, prairie uncut by the plow, the same was not true of the country into which the road now led me. And it had been wise to change from day travel to night. After leaving the camp, I skirted before dawn a village of some size, slinking through the fields which sustained it. Harvest had bared most of the land. But as I skulked by a farmhouse, I was startled by a sharp yapping and read in that the warning of a long-domesticated hound-hunter. Other animals took up the alarm until the village rang with their cries, and I saw once more lights on, heard a shout or two aimed at the wildly baying yard dwellers.

The reaction of the people of Yim-Sin and the words of Maelen had assured me that a barsk was a rare and dreaded creature. Suppose I was sighted, or some farmer turned loose hounds to hunt the strange disturber? To go on into thickly settled territory could be suicidal folly. I paced up and down within the thicket I had chosen for the day's layup. And I heard myself whining a little at my thoughts. But somewhere—somewhere in Oskold's land was the answer to the fate of my man body, and that I *must* know!

After my experience, I dared not hunt at another farmyard. But wild life was scarce and shy hereabouts, and my hunger drove me at last to a walled field. Tonight there was no bright display of three rings in the heavens, rather clouds massed there. And that veiling gave me extra courage to attempt once more an attack on domesticated prey.

The creatures in the field were fodo; I had already sampled what they had to offer in the dried meat Maelen carried. They were small enough, about the size of Tantacka. Perhaps long ago some common ancestor had been theirs, though generations of domestication and supervised breeding had made the fodo much heavier of body and shorter of leg, doubtless thicker of wits also. The only trouble was that they chose to huddle together for sleeping, and a charge at the whole herd might well spoil my hunt.

I prowled around the wall, testing the air carefully for the scent I had come to identify with the yappers of the farmyards. The wind swept toward me, carrying only the rich odor of the sleepers. Had I a partner I thought it would be easy. One of us downwind could have stampeded the fodo to the waiting jaws of the other.

In the end I decided that my fleetness was my best weapon and I ran downwind. I had very little time to wait. The snorting heap of sleepers pulled apart, rose grunting. I charged and seized upon a squealer, dragging it with me in spite of its struggles. Getting over the wall so burdened was difficult, but hunger is a mighty drive and finally I managed it, as well as the return journey to a mass of rocks and brush along the river which provided me with a fort, though I had no mind to be besieged there.

I ate enough to satisfy my hunger. Then I prudently waded downstream, thus hoping to destroy any trail which an outraged farmer might bring his hounds to sniff out. A bridge spanned the river, and under its arch I came ashore and licked water from my fur.

While still so busied I heard the pound of hoofs echoing hollowly. Crouching in the shadows I lay low. There were two sets of hoof beats—each heading from opposite directions, and the speed with which they came spoke of dire necessity. I thought that the riders would pass close to where I lay, and I listened for any greeting which might explain their haste.

The beat lessened; I believed that both riders must be reining in their mounts. I dared to hold my head higher, creep to the end of the bridge, hoping I might hear something of importance. I did not know any dialect save that of Yrjar—though the thoughts of the priests of Umphra had been as clear as words spoken in Basic. But I could hope for neither advantage now.

The riders had stopped. I could hear the heavy blowing of the kasi, and now the sound of men's voices. The words—no—those were only a meaningless series of sounds such as any human speech might be for a true barsk. Though—fiercely I stretched my esper to tap thought.

". . . sends for aid . . ."

Surprise, some anger. ". . . dares . . . after this . . . dares!"

Desperation, a burst of it so intense as to be almost a mind-blow. " . . . must . . . is hunted . . . the off-worlders . . . they have demanded full out-lawry.''

"No use. Our lord has returned their man . . . he has offered to pay blood guilt . . . that is all he can do.''

It would seem that the emotions of the two on the bridge were so high that their thoughts broke through to me more and more clearly, as a hearing of their words.

" . . . refuge . . . must have refuge . . .''

"Madness!'' The second messenger was emphatic. "Our lord is already gainsaid in council, those of Yimik and Yomoke turn on him. We have all the border to hold. If he brings in outlaws, then who will ride to defend him?''

"Let him decide—''

"Let him! You shall hear the same words. If the off-worlders have the power of Yu behind them, then outlawry can spread. They have the right to refuse bloodguilt price and ask for the other. What they have back now is no man—or do you name him so? You have seen him—''

There was no answer to that in words, only anger, fear. Then the cry of a man to urge his mount to the utmost. And one kas, that going west, beat out in a wild galloping. But the other rode, at not so harsh a pace, for the western border.

I dropped my head to my paws, hearing only the gurgle of the river. A man may lie in words, but his thoughts tell the truth. Now I had learned, so by chance, what I had come to seek—that my body was no longer in Oskold's land, but returned to my shipmates. For that the messengers had been concerned with my case I did not in the least doubt.

Yrjar was now my goal. The port—they would take my body to the *Lydis* where our medico would do what he could for that lifeless hulk. Suppose I did, by some miracle, reach the port and the ship, and even my body—what could I do? But Free Traders are open of mind. Maelen was not the only Thassa at the fair—there was the man Malec. Could I reach him, use him for explanation? Perhaps he might even make the exchange. So many doubts and fears between me and success, most of them formidable ones. But hope was all I had to cling to, lest I be swept away and drowned—man forever swallowed in beast.

Back then to the east, through the hills, down to the plains of Yrjar, where a barsk would be as conspicious as a scarlet cloak flapping in the breeze. Yet that I must do.

I drank of the water curling before me, my throat suddenly as dry as if I had not drunk for a day or more. And there was a trembling in my legs, a shiver along my spine. Still there was no retreat. Then I waded into the water and finally swam along the center current, heading yet farther to the sound before I came ashore on the eastern bank.

There was no longer need to follow the road and so meet any perils traveling thereon. The hills, dark and rolling across the sky, were guideposts enough. Beyond them lay the plains which cradled Yrjar, and the port. I sped through open fields, or trotted through forested places. I discovered that, though barsks were said to haunt the heights, yet their oddly small bodies and almost grotesquely long legs were meant for swift travel on the level. By sunrise I was well into the hills.

I passed at dawn that self-same fort where all my misfortunes had begun. Here, too, was extra garrison in evidence, men gathered in camp outside the walls. I made a wide circling to avoid their kasi lines.

As I ran I considered what I had learned from the messengers. He who had ridden westward, doubtless to Oskold's chief hold, had been bearing a cry for help—from Osokun and his men? It was said Oskold cherished his heir, but by the reaction of the second messenger some end had recently come to that. Oskold had offered blood-guilt price for my body—in other words he had attempted to settle by the one legal means on Yiktor the dispute between his son and the Free Traders, by offering Captain Foss the price of a crew member. Blood-guilt price could be offered for one killed inadvertently and without malice in time of peace. It was seldom accepted, almost never when the victim possessed close kin of the arms-bearing age, for blood feud was considered the more honorable solution. But if the victim left only females or boys too young to war within the required bonds of kinship, then the price could be accepted and the transaction recorded in the Temple at Yrjar.

Perhaps, because I was an off-worlder, as were the crew of the *Lydis*—who stood for my kin—the offer had been made with some hope of acceptance. But I wondered at Oskold's returning my body at all.

It would have been more logical for him to dispose quietly of that damaging piece of evidence against his son and then defy anyone to prove what had happened. Did their fear of the insane hold them so in thrall?

At any rate it was apparent that Captain Foss had demanded full punishment and Osokun had been outlawed. The disgrace had lapped over, so that old enemies of Oskold saw an opportunity to drag down father as well as son. And Oskold's land was close to a state of siege. I wondered whether Oskold would turn rebel against all law and custom by sending assistance to his son. If so, would Oskold's sword-sworn continue to support him? Loyalty between lord and man was a firm bond, withstanding death and torture, as many a ballad told in detail. But it worked two ways, a lord had to be as loyal to those who had given him leige-oaths. And such sheltering of his son for his own purpose might, I believed, count as open break-oath, endangering his men past reason.

Yrjar—I tried to picture the city in my mind. I found it hard to count the days since I had been kidnaped from the fair, and I could not even be sure that the fair was still in progress. What if—I put on a new burst of speed—what if the *Lydis* had lifted off-world? That thought was so appalling I could only push it from my mind lest I yield to the terror it evoked in me.

If the *Lydis* still stood on the port apron, would Malec still also be at the fair? If not—how— I licked my still tender paws and growled softly. Then I realized that the barsk might be gaining on the man. Was that what had really happened to him whom the priests of Umphra sheltered for Maelen? Had he gone in beast body so long that the animal had conquered, and had fled to the high hills with no longer any ties with man? I could have thrown back my head and howled, as I had bayed the moon with no human reason. But I stiffled that in my throat.

Griss Sharvan—he had been with me at the show—he had seen the return of the barsk, he had heard my story of what happened. And he might be open-minded if a barsk came to him now—be able to provide some contact. We all had esper powers, some more than others. Lidj—Lidj was the best aboard the *Lydis*—could I only get close enough. No, Krip Vorlund was far from beaten. In these hills I might move by day as well as by night—

I dug some small burrowing creatures out of the mold and ate, though they were only enough to stay the first edge of my hunger. And I climbed steadily up and up through the frosty air which bit at my laboring lungs. Patches of snow hurt my tender feet. I licked the snow and so gave my thirsty body a measure of moisture, though I thought often of the river where I had drunk so deeply and sweetly.

By midnight I found a pass which was no more than a knife edge of crevice, and was on the down slope to the plains. But fatigue drove me into hiding and the sleep I must have.

The sun was warm on my maned back when I awoke and looked about me through eyes slitted against the light, testing the breeze. Man scent, rank and strong used my nose.

There was the faint scrape of one hard surface against another, such as a boot sole might make slipping on rock. Whoever passed to my right and below was taking infinite precautions to go silently.

I wriggled forward, my head flattened against my forefeet as I tried to peer below. A man—no, men, for I saw another beyond the one so close to me— were creeping uphill. They had pulled over their scale shirts and surcoats roughly woven hooded cloaks, which were oddly patched with color. I believed that any eyes less keen than those of an animal would have found it near to impossible to sight them from a distance unless they were moving. A scouting party of Oskold's enemies?

It was of no consequence unless they found me, and now I began a retreat of my own, edging back into the brush before getting to my feet and moving undercover left and down from their advance. Twice I froze, keeping stone-still while more of the disguised party inched past. What their goal might be I could not guess, for I had seen no fort or post on this side of the hills. But their determination was plain to read.

Again I must turn south, for the creepers on the hill came from a larger party camped in the lower lands. All I had to guide me was the knowledge that Yrjar was somewhere to the west.

I lay up finally, waiting for night. And under a three-ringed moon I put on a burst of speed. So the hours of darkness passed while I alternately ran and walked, until my feet grew so painful that I had to rest. For a while I stood in a pool and there I also broke my fast, for a feathered creature, overlooking my presence because of my lack of movement, ventured too close. It was good eating, the best I had had since the fodo, and I cracked bones for the last taste of it.

Then I holed up in a thicket. But not long did I have to sleep. My head swung up and I listened, for this time sound, not scent, came first. Those were farm hounds and they hunted. Also whatever fled before them was coming in my direction.

As a man I had been hunted through these hills by Osokun's followers. Now as a beast was I also to know the chase. And there is a terror which comes from the sound of hounds on one's track. I held steady, listening, for I thought that I was not their quarry.

Then a slender-legged creature burst from the brush very close to me, passing in great leaping bounds. I recognized it for one of the wild ruminants of the plains, considered an excellent addition to the menu and usually hunted in numbers in the fall season so their flesh could be dried for winter storage.

This one had not been chased long and was running easily. But the pack was eager, too, and only a yip or two marked their coming, for they were running mute on a warm scent.

Again I moved south, angling away from the path the runner had taken. If I was lucky the hounds would be so intent upon their present game they would not pick up my scent. Or, if they did, was a barsk so formidable they would refuse to follow my trail?

The only trouble was that I neared open country. Not only were there no rocks or brush, no copses promising shelter from the sighting by a human hunter, but the fields had been harvested, leaving only stubble. And against that gray-yellow my own red coat must of necessity show plainly and in bright relief.

I caught the scent of water and remembered that a small stream ran from the pool where I had bathed my feet. Suppose I used that for my roadway, would it confuse my trail? What knowledge I had of such matters came only from tapes I had scanned for my amusement. And such hunting reminiscences, compiled from a man's point of view, might be very faulty indeed when applied to my present plight.

However, I could see no better answer, and waded into the stream to follow its course. But I had not gained much distance when a loud clamor from the place where I had lain sounded real menace. And I guessed the worst. The hounds had picked up my scent and, by some frown of fortune, had decided I was the better sport.

It was sheer panic which led to my downfall. I ceased to think. Like the plains animal that had fled, I ran, intent only upon leaving behind me that pack. And the rigors of my traveling had sapped my strength, so that though I strained to cover the ground, I knew that I could not draw far enough ahead. I leaped a wall, ran across a field and—

There was no longer ground under my pounding feet. I was in the air . . . falling . . . falling . . .

XII

SAND FLEW UP about me, my body jarred against the earth with a force which both drove the air from my burning lungs and dazed me. Then I heard, if dimly, the wild chorus of the hounds, and struggled to rise. My vision was blurred, but slowly it cleared enough to show me that I was imprisoned in a steep-walled pit. A man with fingers and toes to cling to the irregularities of those walls might have climbed out. For four paws with blunt nails it was an impossibility.

I threw back my head and howled. And that cry, rendered more resonant by the earthen funnel which held me, brought silence for a moment or two to the slavering pack now ringing the opening above. Excited by the chase though they were, none ventured to leap down and join me, but took out their hatred in their cries.

Then some of them were brushed roughly aside and I saw, from the angle at which I must hold my head, men looking down at me. The first shouted in open amazement and the others stared wide-eyed. One of them raised a crossbow and I wondered if I could possibly dodge any shot, penned as I was. But he who stood beside the archer struck down the weapon with an angry order.

For a time I lay panting while the hounds and one of the men kept watch; the others had gone. Then there was a thud, and a mass of cords landed on and about me. I jumped to my feet, which was just what they wanted. For the net was jerked entangled in its folds, being hoisted out of the pit.

The hounds leaped for me, to be beaten off by their masters as I was dumped, net and all, into a farm cart. So bound, I was transported to a farm and pitched into a dark shed.

About me the smell of animals, the acrid stench of man was thick. I panted, my lolling tongue and mouth ash-dry. Water—just a few drops to lick— But no one came near the shed as the hours wore away.

The shock of my landing in the pit remained in aches throughout my body, but the need for water became an all-demanding obsession. At last I tried feebly to use mind touch, of which I had been afraid, lest superstition lead to my instant death.

There were minds about me, yes. But though I tried with all my failing energy to implant in one of them my need for water, my harmlessness, there were none I could hold long enough to make my wants known.

I fell into an apathetic state, unable to keep fighting a lost battle. And so they may even have thought me dead when they did come at last, how much later I had no means of telling, save that it was dark outside when they pulled out the net and slung the package which held me into a cart once more. We passed a small pond and the smell of water roused me enough to whine, to raise my head. Then a blow sent me into unconsciousness.

Day now, bright sun hurt my eyes. And my ears were deafened by a clamor of shouts which I could not understand. The cart stopped and two men stood by its lowered tailboard, looking in at me.

"Water—" I tried to shape the word, but what came from my gaping jaws was a hoarse and despairing whine. One of the men leaned closer and when he spoke it was in the dialect of Yrjar which, very long ago, I too had spoken.

"Barsk—ten tokens—"

"Ten scale tokens?" exploded the other. "When, counterman, do you ever see a barsk here? And a live one—"

"Barely so," the first commented. "I will say perhaps he remains so until sundown. And that hide—it is cut—Even cured I could get nothing for it as fur."

"Twenty—"

"Ten."

Their voices became a drone, they wavered behind a misty curtain which now dropped before my eyes. I was very willing to drift into a beckoning dark which promised comfort and no more torment.

But I was roused to life again as the net was pulled from the cart and I was carried into a darker place, where the stink of ill-kept animals was ripe and heavy. Once before—my memory was like a spark to be extinguished forever—once before I had smelled just that stench. When? How?

Iron grip about my throat, hurting, choking— Feebly I tried to snap, to pull away. But instead that pressure impelled me into a small dark place, and then left me in cramped confines as a lid was slammed down. Two holes in the side gave small eyes of light, very little air. There was some straw, evil-smelling, for I was not the first captive to bide there. And the smell was not only of other bodies, but of minds also, filled with fear and hate, thick-ened by despair.

I tried to curl up my aching body, pillowed my head on my forefoot, seeking what small relief there could be in retreating from memory, from thought, from all around me. So I existed, or lingered; I did not live.

There was no water. Sometimes I thought or dreamed dimly of water, of how I had walked down those streams with the wavelets curling about my legs, sleeking my fur. And then it seemed that it had all been only a dream and there had never existed any world beyond this stifling box. There was no time, only an eternity of torture.

A snap overhead, the box top was raised to let in air and light. I think I tried to lift my head, but something heavy struck across my neck, pinning me to the noisome floor. And I could not see who stood surveying me.

"—near dead. You would offer *that* to my lord?"

"A barsk. When do you see a barsk alive here-abouts, Freesh?"

"Alive? Near dead, as I have said. And the hide—that is worth nothing either. You ask fifty tokens? You are fit for the Valley if you hold to that, fellow."

The pressure was gone from my neck, an instant later the lid slammed down to leave me once more in a prison. "Near dead—near dead—near dead—"

The words buzzed in my ears. "Barsk—near dead—"

A barsk was an animal. I was not an animal, I was a man—a man! They must know, must let me out. I was a man not an animal. That life spark which had flickered close to extinction in me a moment earlier flared up again. I tried to brace my weakened body against the walls of the box, to attempt to fight my way to freedom. It was no use. Muscles twitched, but there was no strength left in me.

"A man—a man!" I could produce no sound but a faint whine. But my thoughts shrieked to the world outside the box. "A man dies here—not an animal but a man!"

And with lightning swiftness a thought, clear and forceful, locked with mine. I clung to it as one loosed from a ship's hull in space flight during repairs would cling to his lifeline.

"Aid—for a man who dies—"

"Where?" came the demand so clearly that its very force brought answering energy to my mind.

"In a box—in a barsk body—a man not an animal—" I tried to hold that lifeline of thought which seemed to slip through the hold of my mind, as though the gloves of a ship-space line were greased and could not hold. "A man—not an animal!"

"Think, keep thinking!" An imperative order. "I must have a guide, so think!"

"Man—no animal—" But I could not hold, the line was slipping from me fast. Making a supreme

172

effort, I tried again. "Man—not a barsk—in a box—in— I not know where—but in a city."

Yrjar? Was that city Yrjar?

"In a box—as a barsk—a barsk— Not barsk—man!"

It seemed that I could not breathe, that the dark of space enfolded me too tightly, crushed me—

"Man—I am a man—" I clung to that, fighting hard. But the dark was here and in it I spun away to nothingness.

"Here!"

Through the dark again came that thrust of answer, swift and sharp to stir me. But I could not listen, there was nothing left but dark and an end of all struggle.

Light, far off, and voices which meant nothing. Then my head between two hands, raised. Dimly I could see a face.

"Listen," the order ringing in my brain. "You must help me in this much. I have said you are one of my little people, that you are a trained beast. Can you prove it?"

Prove it? I could prove nothing, not even that I was a man, not one who ran four-footed and killed with fangs in the dark.

Water poured across my swollen tongue, into my jaws, three times before I could swallow. Then again those hands cupping my head, the eyes meeting mine, reaching into me.

"Jorth—obey!"

That had once meant something, but I could not

remember. Someone had called me by that name and—

I bowed my head, tried to raise my forepaws. There were broad steps and a man in a black-and-yellow robe who had once watched me. So, I must bow, and do all we had planned together. We? Who?

"My animal—"

"There is no proof, Freesh."

"I return what you paid for him. Or do I call the street guard?"

Still those hands holding up my head. And once more water in my mouth, so I could swallow. With it came a measure of life. But the hands grasping me did not loosen.

"Be strong, we shall go soon."

Voices above my head washing back and forth. Then arms about me, carrying me out into greater light, where I whined and closed my eyes against the glare. He who bore me laid me down on a soft mat and I sprawled there, unable to help myself. Under me the surface shook, moved, I heard the creaking of wheels, their grating over stone pavement.

On went the wagon, and the odors of the town stuffed my nose. I did not try to look about me, to expand that much energy was beyond my strength. Rattle, grate, rattle—The cart came to a stop.

"—trained animal—"

Plop of a footboard being pulled down and put up again. The cart moved on. Fresher air, a breeze. Another stop, and someone dropped from the driver's seat to the bed of the wagon, knelt beside me. My head was raised and once more liquid poured between my jaws. But this was not only water, it carried a stinging addition. I opened my eyes.

"Maelen—" I thought that name. But this was not the Thassa woman who had plunged me into this desperate venture, but the man who had been with her at the fair. Memory returned like a faint picture much faded by exposure and the overlay of harsh events.

"I am Malec," came his answer. "Now rest, sleep, and have no fears. We have won a space of free time."

The meaning of his words did not wholly register with me as I did as he bade and slept—though this was not the stupor of approaching death.

There was a fire not too far from me when I awoke once more. And the leaping flames of that were very reassuring. Fire and man, his old comfort and weapon, so long linked in our minds with safety that our spirits lift ever when we look into it.

Beyond the fire was another light, and seeing that I growled—and was startled to hear that sound. For I had momentarily been Krip Vorlund when I roused, and it was a shock to find I still wore the guise of Jorth.

My growl I was answered from the shadows, where the full light of the fire, the beams of the moon globe did not reach. And my barsk nose, once more keenly in action, told me there were other life forms, many of them, around me in the half gloom.

A man came into the firelight, a kettle in one hand, a long-handled ladle in the other. I watched him pass along a line of bowls set out on the ground, into each measuring a portion of the kettle's contents. And so he came to me.

"Malec of the Thassa," I said mind-fashion.

"Krip Vorlund, from off-world."

"You know me?"

He smiled. "There is only one man who runs as a barsk."

"But—?"

"But you put on fur when I was not present? You have used Thassa power, my friend. Did you think that such would not be known?"

"*I* did not use it!" I countered.

"Not in that way of thinking," he agreed readily. "But it was used for your advantage."

"Was it?" I demanded.

"Was it not? Do you think you would have lived past your discovery by the sword-sworn of Oskold had Maelen not wrought for you as best she could— time allowing?"

"But the rest—"

He sat down upon his heels, so that now, I, up on my haunches, was a small bit taller. "You believe that she used you for her own purposes?"

I gave him the truth. "Yes."

"All races have that which they swear unbreakable oaths upon. So I can swear to you that what she did that night, she did wholly for you, the saving of your life."

"That night, perhaps, but thereafter? We went to the Valley—my body was not there, but she had another—"

He did not appear surprised. I do not believe I ever

saw one of the Thassa show that emotion as men of other races do. But there was a moment of silence between us, before he continued:

"What *do* you believe?"

"That there were dangers beyond what she told me. That she had her own reason for wishing me in the Valley and that was not to *my* good, but hers."

Slowly he shook his head. "Listen well, off-worlder, she did not send you into any danger she had not already tasted. And had you not gone your own road, you would not have been in such a plight as I found you. No Singer among the Thassa takes on the calling of power until he or she has worn, for a space, the guise of fur or feathers. Maelen had taken this way before your star ship even rocket-blasted the port apron of Yrjar."

"And that one in the Valley?"

"Did I ever say it is not a dangerous road to walk?" he demanded. "We do not slay the living things in the ranges, but that does not mean death holds aloof there. Maquad took upon him beast form, and a plains lord who went hunting without our leave shot a fatal bolt. It was one chance in ten thousand, for we did not know any walked our holy ground and we were not warned until too late. As for you, do you not think that Maelen will pay for her use of our power to aid a stranger? She believed truly what she told you, that Oskold's men would deliver your body to the temple and that all would be well. Had you remained there—"

"But my body is in Yrjar."

"Yes. And now we must make new plans, and I

will not deny to you that they must be made in haste. Your friends will not understand and in their ignorance may try cures which will instead kill.''

I shivered as along my spine sped a cold chill. ''Yrjar—we must go—''

''Not so. We have just come from Yrjar. I was able to bring you forth from the city only by saying that I would take you beyond any inhabited place. Maelen knows, or will know shortly, where you are. She will come hither, and then go to your captain, tell her story—we shall see if he is a man who will believe strange tales. Then we must plan to smuggle you into the port so Maelen can undo what has been done. And of this whole business''—he was frowning now—''I do not know what the Old Ones will think, for it has broken Standing Words, and put into the hands of those who do not share Thassa blood a secret weapon, should enemies desire such,''

''You mean that the plainsmen do not know you can so change bodies?''

''Yes. Think you—they are men who do not have knowledge of the spirit, only of body and mind. Tell the ignorant among them that there are those living on this world who can make a man into an animal, an animal into a man, and then—do you foresee what could happen?''

''Fear drives men to kill.''

''Just so. There would be such a hunt as would bathe the Quiet Places in blood. Already we know that this is spoken of us—by that off-worlder Gauk Slafid, who strove to use such knowledge as a bargaining level. Whether he gained this information from Osokun or others of Yiktor, we do not know. I hope he did not—at least not from Osokun, or Maelen's singing would not have saved you. The sword-sworns would have killed you that night, both barsk and man. Nor has any hint of it among the plainsmen since come to me. Now our Old Ones search for it by thought. We could be walking a thin edge of crumbling earth along the rim of a great gulf.''

"There is fighting, Oskold's neighbors turn against him. If one lord is embroiled with another, then do you not gain time?'' I told him of what the messengers had said and what I had seen in the hills.

"Yes, his neighbors see a chance to whittle away at Oskold, but think you how quickly he would seize upon such a story to launch them, away from his throat, at the Thassa! This could be a rallying cry to put the lord who gave it at the head of a united army. That is why I believe Gauk Slafid kept that knowledge to himself. For, if Osokun had known of it, that knowledge would have served him much better than any foreign weapon. He might have headed a 'holy war' against a common enemy uniting the land under him.''

"If you can change me back, I will be off-world and willing to swear no man shall ever hear of it from me.''

He surveyed me grimly. "The Old Ones would make sure no loose tongues would wag. I agree that the sooner we make the exchange and get you from Yiktor, the better. At present Osokun and his sword-sworns are outlawed. They can live only by raiding, and that with every man's hand against them. Sooner or later a combined force will track them down and finish them. I do not know if Oskold could be bought by any plea from his son to give even secret support. But, if he were so minded, he would have to do it *very* secretly, lest his own men declare him oath-broke and leave him. Outlawry is no light thing and those who aid any outlaw come themselves at once under the ban. It needs only three freeholders to swear to this to condemn a man. Oskold will have enough to occupy him with these invaders."

"And we wait now upon Maelen." I returned to what was to me the main matter. Quarrels of feudal lords had no part in my future, or so I believed.

"We wait upon Maelen. She goes them to your captain at Yrjar. As I said, much will depend upon how open a mind he has. Perhaps you can give her some message which will reveal the truth to him, some incident from your shared past which none on Yiktor can know. Then, if he accepts her story, we can plan further."

Free Traders were open-minded. They had seen to much on too many worlds to say that this or that might never happen. But this was so unique, could belief be stretched so far? Malec's suggestion was a good one. I set myself to thinking of some identifying story Maelen might use on my behalf.

When time becomes a factor in one's life, then it can wield a whip as sharp as those of the slave drivers of Corfu. Malec had his duties with the animals, but I had only those thoughts which worked sharp as thorns into my mind, keeping me pacing back and forth beside the fire. Whatever drink and food Malec had given me since my release must have carried a stimulant as well as nourishment, for I felt alive in every part of me—something I had not really done since I left the Valley on my futile quest.

He had done with his duties for the animals and came back to sit before the fire, turning down the moon globe. At last I sat beside him, wishing to be taken away from all the ifs and maybes which rode me.

"Why do the Thassa choose to run as animals?" I asked him abruptly.

He looked at me, his large eyes seeming even larger in his pale face. "Why do you choose to spin from world to world, calling none your home?" he counterquestioned.

"It is a way of life to which I have been born and bred. I know of none different."

"Now you do," he pointed out. "We are the Thassa, who have also been born and bred to a way of life. Once we were a different kind of people, akin to those now living in the plains. Then there came a moment of choice, we were shown another path to be explored. But all things cost and for taking this new road there was payment. It meant uprooting ourselves and turning from all which seemed safe and secure. No more would walls enclose us, we must gather close-knit to our kind. We set aside one life to gain another. Now, as these plainsmen see us, we are wanderers, people without roots. They cannot understand why we do not want what seems treasure and the future to them; they hold us apart. And because they have seen from time to time a little of what we gained by our choice, they hold us also in awe. We share all life as they do not— No, not all life—as yet we cannot share some things—the pushing growth of a tree, the putting forth of new leaves with the season, the coming of fruit. But we can take on a bird's wings and learn the sky after the manner of the feathered ones, or put on fur and become four-footed for a space. You know many worlds, star rover, but none do you begin to know as the Thassa know Yiktor and its life!''

Malec fell silent. His eyes turned from me, to rest upon the flames which he fed now and then from a pile of wood beside him. Now he no longer spoke with his thoughts, a wall stood between us. Though he did not wear the rapt look I had seen on Maelen's face, yet I believed he was close to that state of otherness which I had seen hold her that night in the van.

Night air fed many messages to my nose. After a time I went into the shadows about the camp, sniffing my way. Many of the little people slept in their cages, but others awoke and kept sentry. I do not think anything could have crept undetected upon that camp.

Maelen came before dawn. I smelled her scent before I heard the creaking of van wheels. There was a chittering behind me which was both greeting and signal. Malec struggled out of his blanket roll by the now dying fire and I joined him; we stood together as she came into the half light of the camp.

It was to me she looked. I do not know what I had expected, rebuke perhaps for my folly in leaving the Valley—though I refused to think it folly, judging by what I had known, or suspected, at the time. After all, how could the Thassa begin to understand what their accepted customs could mean to another?

But only weariness showed on her face—as one who had stood a long, unrelieved watch of duty. Malec held up his arms to aid her from her seat, and she came into them with a sigh. Before I had always seen her strong; now she was altered, though how I did not know.

"There are riders in the hills," she said.

"Oskold is beleagured," Malec returned. "But come—" He supported her to the fire, stirred its dying flames to feed it more wood. Then he put into her hand a horn he filled from a small flask. She sipped slowly, pausing between each mouthful. Then, cupping the horn against her breast, she spoke to me.

"Time passes, Krip Vorlund. With the dawn I am for Yrjar."

I think Malec would have protested, but she did not glance at him. Instead she stared now into the fire and drank all the horn held, sip by careful sip.

XIII

IT WAS A BRIGHT MORNING, such as brings the strong wine of wind to refresh nose and throat, a dazzling shaft of sun, the feeling in both man and animal that it is good to be alive. Before the sun had touched the ground where Malec had set our camp, Maelen mounted the riding kas her kinsmen readied for her, and started west. I longed to run beside her. The good sense which kept me behind was more prison than any cage bars that morning. We watched her out of sight, and Malec walked among the cages, opening each door so that the occupant could come or go at will.

Some still slept as balls of fur. Others blinked and roused, but only a few came out. Simmle shouldered past the door and bounced to me, uttering sharp yelps of welcome, her rough tongue ready in caress. But Malec dropped his hand upon her head and straightway she looked up to him, her tail drooping. She glanced from right to left, whined, and then trotted into the bush.

"What is it?" I asked of the Thass.

"Maelen said there are men in the hills. They may not all be intent on raiding Oskold. Somewhere the outlaws run."

"You think they might attack?"

"They need food, much else, if they are to survive. And there is only one way to get supplies, and that is to take them by force. We do not carry much to tempt them, but desperate men will fight for crumbs."

"The animals—"

"Some would be merely meat for the spit to such a party. Others would be killed, because men who are without hope kill for the sake of killing. If there comes trouble the little people can take to the land and be safe."

"And you?" He was making preparations as if he expected just such a raid soon. At his belt hung the long knife which was a part of normal apparel all over Yiktor. He had no sword, nor had I seen a crossbow in camp. Now he smiled.

"I, too, know the countryside as few of those who might so descend upon us. When our sentries give warning—then will the raiders find an empty camp."

Simmle was a sentry, I guessed.

"And you, if you will—" Malec continued.

Why not? As Simmle had done I went into the bushes, putting nose, eyes, and ears at his service. A few moments later I looked back at the vans. There were four of them—the lighter, smaller one which Maelen had taken, the three Malec must have brought from Yrjar. But who were the drivers for two of those? Save for the animals he was alone. Puzzled, I wondered about that—unless the kasi that had drawn them had followed behind the one he drove.

Though the cages had been set in a circle about the campfire, which still gave off a few lazy spirals of smoke, the rest of the gear had not been unpacked. I watched Malec go from wagon to wagon, busy himself in the interior of each for a space. Perhaps he was repacking contents for a longer pull.

As I had on my journey across Oskold's land, I skulked from bush to bush, going into higher land.

We were, I decided, in the fringe of the hill country. Although why Malec had brought us into what might well be dangerous territory, I could not guess. I kept on climbing until I found a ledge on which grew concealing brush.

Though the branches had lost most of their leaves, still I thought I was well masked by the growth; from this point I could see the camp, plus a good slice of the country about it. There was no road leading to here. But the tracks of the vans were still visible in crushed grass and earth and there was little chance of hiding that trail for the present.

Malec was invisible within one of the vans, nor, as far as I could see, had many of the animals issued from their cages. The scene was one of drowsy peace and quiet, lulling to watch. The wind had died down, little scent carried to me. I continued to test with my nose. Simmle must be prowling to the south; perhaps there were other guards, stationed to the west.

The sun climbed into a cloudless sky, bringing almost summer warmth as can happen in midautumn months. Malec emerged from a van, a yoke across his shoulders, buckets dangling from its ropes. He went down to the stream, which I could see only as a flicker of sun on water here and there.

Then—Simmle barked fiercely, once. I squeezed from under my brush shield. A puff of wind upslope had brought me warning. I leaped from the ledge into a lower thicket, wriggled through its spiky grasp. That one war cry from Simmle and then nothing— nothing but the scent and sounds which perhaps a human ear could not have caught, but which to barsk hearing were as loud as a fanfare of horns. I slipped through the cover, heading to camp, dropped to my stomach, and crept under the nearest van.

Malec wavered up the slope from the stream. Yoke and buckets were gone. He stumbled and slipped, one hand pressed to his breast, the other outflung, fingers moving vainly as if he tried to grasp some support which was not there.

He went to his knees before he reached the circle of the cages, and then sank slowly forward. From between his shoulders, dancing with his heavy gasps of breath, stood the shaft of a crossbow bolt. His hands pushed into the soil, and then his efforts ceased and he fell forward on his face, quiet and spent.

As if his struggle had been a signal, those in the cages burst forth and fled, voiceless and swift. They were gone, hidden perhaps to any man's eye, but not to my nose or ear.

I crept on, though such a mode of travel was hard for my barsk body. There was someone coming up the bank from the river, trying to move quietly, but with little success, from my point of view.

Continuing on under the shadow of the van, I began a circuit of the campfire. Malec had not moved, but his assailant was very cautious. Perhaps the other did not know that the Thassa had been alone save for the animals. I tried to reach Malec through mind-touch. He was still alive, but there was no consciousness to pick up my message.

I reached the end of the van. There were the cages, but I did not know if they were sufficiently high to hide me. Or dared I play a bewildered animal out in the open? As I hesitated, a tan streak ran to my left. Simmle! What was she doing?

She did not pause by Malec, but angled down in the direction of the one who scouted toward the camp. I got to my feet and flashed after her. I still had not seen her quarry when he screamed. A moment later I nearly fell over the furiously fighting tangle of man and venzese. He was crying out, trying to hold snapping jaws from his throat with both hands.

I jumped and tore, and Simmle got the grip she fought for. In those seconds I was more barsk than man, in me boiled a red rage I would not have believed I could house.

There was a shout, something whizzed so close to my shoulder that I felt the burn of its passing. Simmle still worried her victim and now I leaped a second time, striking against her, bearing her to the ground with my weight.

"Loose!" I beamed that thought order at her. "Loose—come!"

Again a bolt struck close. The smell of blood was fuel to my beast rage, but I fought against that emotion.

"Loose—come!" I had opened my jaws to seize upon eyes red and gleaming. She growled as one who warns another from legitimate prey.

"Come!" Again I launched myself against her and this time my plunge sent her sprawling away from the body. She growled, but got to her feet as a bolt struck where she had lain but a second before. She snapped viciously at where it stood quivering in the ground, and bounded with me up the slope.

They continued to shoot after us and I zigzagged, hoping Simmle would follow my example. We came into the camp only a few feet from Malec, who lay just as I had seen him fall. Simmle dipped her head to nose him and then sounded a shuddering howl.

"On!" I urged her. She swung around, showing her teeth as if to launch at me. Then some of the red light dimmed from her eyes and she ran with me, shoulder to shoulder, between the vans to the country beyond.

I had no idea where the other animals had vanished to, though I caught their mingled scent and thought they had taken this same route. I was not even sure how many there were, or of what different species.

"Up!" I ordered Simmle. She had swung around and paused, facing back toward the camp. Her usually sleek hair was rough along the spine, and her head was down between hunched shoulders, stained fangs exposed as her muzzle wrinkled in a snarl. She took a step or two down our back trail. Then she turned again and led me in a wild race in the brush.

We worked our way well up into the heights before we halted and lay panting, watching the camp. There were men there now, kicking at the cages where the doors swung open, thrusting swords into the interiors of the vans as if to hunt out anything which might be hiding there. From Maelen's they tumbled boxes, breaking open their fastenings to find supplies of the meat-and-grain cakes. All in sight seized upon these eagerly, wolfing them down with the greed of men who had missed many meals.

They had dragged Malec's body to one side,

bundling it out of the way under one of the vans. Two of the men walked along the line of the kasi where those animals snorted and pulled at their ropes, kicking out at any who approached too near.

The empty cages appeared to fascinate some of the men. They pushed them over as if unable to believe that they were bare of occupants, as if this rough handling would dislodge what must be within.

Into the disordered camp now rode a small party of three. One man supported another in the saddle of his mount, while the third came behind, as if to cover a rear attack. Now it was my turn to snarl. He who was being so tended I had last faced in the border fort. These were Osokun's outlaws who were making themselves free of the camp, and some time recently their leader had met with rough handling. His right arm was bound across his chest and his face was white and drawn. He was a sorry ghost of the cocky lordling who had tried to dictate terms to Free Traders.

The spoiling of the vans continued as the men sorted through the contents of boxes and baskets. Food appeared to be their first concern and they ate hugely, before putting all that was left into saddle bags. Some then went in a southwesterly direction and returned leading riding kasi. A few of the animals limped and all showed signs of hard and too long riding.

But the men were in no hurry to leave the camp. They lifted Osokun from his mount and put him on the divan they pulled from Malen's van. One of the men who had supported him heated water on the fire, busying himself with the tending of his leader's wound. It would seem, however, that Osokun was no longer in command, for the orders of another man set the plunderers to work righting some of the mess they had made. He bent on one knee by the van under which they had rolled Malec's body and made a slow, careful study of their victim. Then, by his orders, the others pulled forth the Thassa and carried him off into the brush.

Beside me I felt Simmle's tense muscles, I heard her almost soundless growl.

"Not yet," I thought to her, "not yet—"

Whether I could hold her, I did not know. But I was considering our plight. Maelen had gone to Yrjar and had said that time was short. She would speed in both going and returning. And from present signs the outlaws were not planning to leave the camp soon.

Instead they were fast restoring to the vans all they had dragged out of them, pitching in the plundered containers, but getting them out of sight. Another man was going around among the empty cages, not only righting them in their original positions, but even latching their doors. When they had done, the officer looked around and nodded. As far as I could see, they were setting up the camp to look undisturbed.

This could mean only one thing. They believed that in Malec they had not gotten all of the Thassa, and they were setting a trap for the others. Did they know of Maelen? Had they perhaps trailed her the day before, and waited now to seize her?

I tested the air. Many of those scents I knew. If the little people had fled, none had gone far. Already my nose located perhaps ten or twelve within a short distance of the place where Simmle and I crouched. I tried to open my mind to them and suffered a slight shock. Not only were the animals all there, but they were united in purpose as I could not think normal beasts of such diverse species could be. Flight was not in their minds, but battle was.

"No!" I struggled to deny that thought from mind to mind. But they withstood me. I was not Maelen or Malec, or any leader they acknowledged.

"Not now!" I tried to change, but I despaired of getting through to them. In the daylight, with the men below armed and alert, the furred army would have very little chance. "Maelen—"

In my mind I built up a picture of Maelen as I had seen her in her power, all ruby and silver, directing her little people on the stage. "Maelen!" I thought at them. "Remember Maelen!"

Simmle whined very, very softly—she remembered. But the others, could I reach them so? I almost shut out the world of sight, sound, smell, held only to the world of the mind, picturing Maelen, trying in turn to learn their response to that picture.

"Maelen!"

They were responding! I tamped down relief and excitement as I sensed that response, concentrated on what I must give them now.

"Maelen comes—"

Upsurge of excitement.

"Not yet—" I hastened to repair what might have been a fatal move. "But soon—soon—"

Some questioning now.

"Soon. Below—they wait for Maelen—" I was fumbling, trying hard, conscious that I might make a mistake which would send them in the very direction they must not go.

Anger now, rising hotly.

"We must find Maelen, before she comes!" I built up as best I could a mental picture of her as I had last seen her—but this time riding toward the camp, not away. "Find Maelen before she comes."

It was like a sea wave rippling downslope as that thought flooded from one small mind to the next. Then I knew they were moving out, not toward the camp and the enemy below, but to circle wide of that danger spot and head into the plains westward.

I lay where I was, continuing to watch the camp. Though I had no experience of warfare, I believed I was interpreting the enemy action aright. Osokun had been taken into Maelen's van, his nurse and guard stowing away there with him. The rest of the men hid in the vans or under them, save for one who was busy watering and feeding the kasi. One other, after conferring with the officer, disappeared westward, a scout I thought.

Now I spoke to Simmle. "Stay, watch."

Her lips wrinkled back from her fangs.

"Stay—watch—"

Her first objection faded, she growled.

"Not fight, watch—Maelen comes."

Her agreement was blurred, not the sharp return I would have received from Maelen, Malec, or a human. I could only hope that she would remain in the same humor while I was gone.

The scout was my present objective. I crept out of cover, needing to make a wide detour around the camp. Surely those in hiding there must have been puzzled as to what had happened to the vanished animals. They would be on the lookout for four-footed as well as two-footed travelers.

I had not seen any hounds with the outlaw band, and out in the open country I believed that none of us need fear any man unless we foolishly courted detection. So when there was a goodly slice of woodland between me and the camp, I dashed on at the pace which came natural to this long-legged body, and cut west. It was my intention to work back toward the hills, crisscrossing the way any scout must come, taking him unawares and far enough from the others to hide the deed.

Twice my path crossed that of others of Maelen's band and each time I asked concerning the scout, only to receive negative answers. But I lingered long enough to impress upon them the urgent need for secrecy until they could find their mistress.

It had been almost noon when Malec had been struck down. With the best of success, I did not believe we could expect Maelen to return before two days passed. And I hoped those setting the trap in camp would grow discouraged before the end of that time. The strategy I had used to take the animals out of danger would be successful, unless they lost patience and returned.

Taking out the scout might be profitable in two ways, I reflected, as I continued my personal search. If their man did not return, then they might either send someone to look for him—affording another prey—or else they would conclude they were in danger and retreat.

I came down to the river and there I saw the traces of how they had come upon us, for the signs of their riding were there. Drinking my fill, I pried one of the understone dwellers loose from his hole and snapped him up. There was no time for a true hunt, and food was fuel which the body must have.

Twilight closed in as I crossed and recrossed, running by scent as well as by eyes and ears. The passing of the enemy troop was easy to pick up though it was hours old. But why I found no trace of the scout began to worry me.

Then I remembered that one scent among all those others occurred again and again—that of a kas. I had dismissed it as a trace of the first party, yet sometimes it was so strong as to seem fresh, and a whiff of it brought me now to a closer investigation. A patch of soft soil gave me a mark needing explanation. It smelled strongly of kas, but the print left there was of no kas hoof, instead a shapeless splotch which bore no resemblance to any animal track I had seen.

I put my nose well down into the depression, drawing a deep breath into my lungs. Kas, so strong that it almost entirely hid all else. But under the kas was another scent, and beside that yet another. I crouched low and sniffed again. Hunter's wiles I did know as my man body would not have. There was kas, as strong as a stench, and under it some herb, and inside still—man. Suppose a man, seeking to elude those to whom scent was a powerful aid, would rub himself with an herb to deaden his natural odor, and then put on an outer covering steeped in kas? That could be the answer to my riddle and it was one I accepted. But to follow this kas—

Still doubting my ability to use barsk instincts, I went on. Perhaps the rest of our company had been befooled so. Back there Osokun, or the officer now in his place as leader, had a clever mind, and was using it to counter just what I had been doing.

Kas—I began to run the trail from that unclear footprint. It was strong, rankly so, but I had to puzzle out other odors from time to time, not daring to run on kas trace alone, for now and then it crossed early traces of the same beasts, perhaps the outlaw mounts.

The dusk gathered in. Still the kas trail pointed west, now in more open country where there was very little cover, and where any man, pausing to scout his back trail, could see a follower, I sat down upon my haunches, sending out a mental call—

My first answer came from the north. I recognized the hard-to-hold, in-and-out pattern of either Borda or Vors.

"One smells kas, is not. Where?" I attempted to send my message.

"No kas?" It was inquiry.

"Kas smell but not kas," I repeated.

"No—" That reply was emphatic.

Again I sent my call and had faint answer. "Kas but not kas?"

"Kas—yes—"

I turned south. Perhaps I was on a false trail, but I

must check it. But I was to discover that he whom I hunted was a master at this game. For I soon came upon the reek of kas strong and clear again. And my satisfaction at finding it was so great that I ran swiftly into the growing dark, trailing by nose, which was just what my quarry expected. I had drawn a deep breath before I realized my danger.

Smarting fire filled my nose, and the shock was so great I leaped straight up into the air, then pushed my nostrils into stubble and sand, pawing at my tormented flesh. The vile smell so clogged my whole head that my eyes teared.

I dragged myself across the ground, pushing my nose into the earth, scraping at it until my blunted nails tore the skin. I could smell nothing except the stink which now seemed a part of my own flesh. And that made me so sick that I rolled over and over, rubbing first one side of my head and then the other against the ground, until I was forced to raise myself and vomit.

There was a period until my wits began to work again. Either he who I tailed suspected he was being tracked, or else he had just used a general precaution. But he had flooded his path with some sickening liquid which had deadened my very important sense of smell. My eyes still watered and the tingling in my nose was a torment. But I had eyes and ears, and perhaps the aid of others.

Again I sent out a call. There were three answers from nearby.

"Kas—not kas—man—evil smell—"

Prompt agreement from all three, apparently the

smell had reached them. But from farther off, Borba:
"Man comes—"

Once more I rubbed my head against the earth. My eyes watered, but not so much I could not see. And this night was made for barsk activity, no shadow was as dense for me as it was for human eyes. I stood behind a rock, listening, watched, put aside the misery in my nose. Undoubtedly a real barsk or other animal would have been thrown off by that weapon. It was the misfortune of Osokun's scout that he did not now come to face a true barsk.

He moved slowly, and he was not a true man outline at all, rather a shapeless bulk, his kas-hide disguise hanging loosely about him, I readied myself—

Now and then he paused for long moments, probably trying to pick out some landmark.

Perhaps a barsk attacks with sound. I did not as I flashed forward, striking at that portion of the approaching rounded shape which I believed to be my best target. And cunning as he had proven himself to be, I took him by surprise.

XIV

I MADE THE KILL after the pattern Simmle had set me, then lay back panting on the ground beside the thing which had so recently breathed, walked, and been a man. Dimly I wondered that I did not feel the burden of my deed—it was as if in this I was far more barsk than man. That I had killed was a fact, but one which did not move me. We of the Traders use weapons in defense, but we do not carry war with us, preferring ever to find a way around a difficulty. I had seen men die before I planeted on Yiktor, but mainly from natural causes and accidents. And, when it had been otherwise, it had always happened in quarrels among aliens or strangers which were of no concern to the Traders, nor which involved any close to me.

But in this killing I was involved as perhaps those of my blood had not been involved for eons of time. Yet I did not care, save that I was in a manner satisfied with a job ably done. And there stirred in me a small fear that perhaps the longer I remained a beast, the stronger would the animal become, until there would run only Jorth on four feet, and he who walked on two would vanish.

This was no time to let fear stir me from what must be done, however, and I resolutely pushed aside that disturbing thought, to consider what action lay immediately before me. Should I leave this scout where he was, to be found by those who might come seeking him? Or would it be more baffling, and therefore upsetting to them, to have him vanish utterly?

"Dead—dead!" Out of the bushes came one of the long-nosed, big-eared animals I had last seen dancing to the drums on Maelen's stage at the fair, and mounted on its back was one of the ring-tailed riders. They both peered down at the scout and from them came a wave of satisfaction.

"Dead," I agreed and licked my paws, rubbing my nose still clogged by that choking stench.

The big-eared beast sniffed at the body and signaled repulsion before it retreated. I looked at the remains and decided to leave all as it was. The ground where the soil was softest, to leave a readable print. Both creatures looked at me in surprise, and their query was open to read.

"Leave signs—all against men," I tried. I could never be sure how well they understood. Perhaps it was only when my suggestions matched their own wishes that they would obey. But I was very doubtful concerning ideas.

They both stared down at the earth where I had made those signature prints. Then the smaller one jumped from the back of his fellow and planted both forepaws, the digits well spread, directly beside the marks I left. He stood up on hind legs to view the result, his head slightly on one side. The prints looked like those of small human hands.

The big-eared one shambled over and walked back and forth, his long-toed feet making a web pattern, before the smaller one remounted. I examined the ground. Now let those others find the scout. The record about him would give them a few thoughts. Three creatures of very different species looked to have shared the pulling down of the man. If the enemy could be led to believe that all the animals from the camp had turned against them, we could make them look twice at every lurking place behind bush or tree, have them hear attack in every leaf rustle. Of their own accord no such dissimilar company of beasts would combine against a common foe; it was not their nature. But the Thassa had powers which the plainsmen already held in awe.

The outlaws had been desperate enough to kill Malec. Perhaps now they would believe that not only natural but supernatural powers were allied against them. And for men already on the run, such knowledge would give a whip toward complete breakdown.

We left together, making for a space no effort to hide our going, but rather leaving plain tracks of three who traveled in company. After a time we began to conceal our trail, so that to any human tracker it would seem we had vanished into thin air.

Dawn found us in a dell where a spring bubbled. There were rocks among which we sheltered. My companions dozed, as did I, but we could wake in an instant to anything which was not ordinary. We were well to the east of the camp and, as nearly as I could tell, somewhere along the way Maelen must use on her return. But how soon we might expect her I did not know. My nose was still clogged, and with that foul odor ever about me, I could not test any breeze.

It was an odd day—the sun was cloud-veiled, but there was no hint of rain, rather a misty hiding of the horizon. There was the feeling that beyond the limit of one's sight was a significant and perhaps dangerous shifting, that one could not depend upon what was reported by one's eyes. And I wished at that moment that at least one of our company was equipped with wings, that we could have a spy whose vision of the country would be wider and better than our own.

But if there had ever been any birds or flying creatures among the Thassa little people, I had never seen them. So our sight was limited. What did happen during the day was an increasing contact with the rest of the scattered company. They linked minds at times so that fragmentary reports sped along a line wide enough, I hoped, to cover the whole front Maelen might cross in her return to the hills.

There were paired combinations such as the two who shared my refuge in the dell, the big eared animals and their riders. Apparently these partnerships did not exist only on the stage, but held continually. Borba and Vors, Tantacka, the ones who had drummed and some I could not identify, all reported. Simmle must have remained at the camp as I had asked, for I did not pick up any answer from her.

We did not venture further into the plains. It was better to reserve our strength by waiting for Maelen. I discovered during that day, as I tried to hold and read those minds, that the little people did not equate the Thassa with the plainsmen, whom they looked upon as natural enemies to be avoided and regarded with suspicion and wariness. The Thassa, however, were accepted wholeheartedly as kin and trustworthy companions. I remembered what Maelen and Malec had said—that the Thassa who would be Singers dwelt as animals for a space. What form had Maelen worn when she had so run the hills? Had she been one with Vors, or Simmle, or these with whom I now companied? Did one have a choice or was one assigned? Or was it chance, as it had been with me because the barsk ailed and was available?

Twice during the day I roved out into the open

country as stealthily as I could, seeking for any traveler. And on my second trip I sighted a mounted company heading toward the hills. But they were a troop riding under some lord's banner, armed men mustering perhaps—and they were some distance to the south. I knew they would sight none of us.

Impatience came with nightfall. We sought food, prowling up and down the line we had assigned ourselves. I found my luck was such as to keep my belly empty, for I could not scent any game. But water was not lacking and I learned that to go hungry does not cripple one.

There came the middle part of the night and with it a ripple of message. "One comes!"

Only one person, I thought, could awaken that response in those with whom I shared this vigil.

"Maelen!" I sent an imperative mind-call into the night.

"Coming." It was dull, a whisper, if such communication can be so judged.

"Maelen." In contrast my sending was a wordless shout. "Trouble—take care, wait—let us know where you are."

"Here—" Louder, a beacon to which we gathered from brush and grass.

She sat there in the moonlight on her hard-ridden kas. In contrast to the clouded day, the night was clear and the Three Rings burned in a glory of light. Her cloak was about her shoulders, the hood pulled over her head so that we could see no woman, only a dark figure on a stumbling mount. I ran into the open with my ground-covering leaps.

"Maelen—trouble!"

"What?" Again her send was a whisper, tired, as if strength had ebbed from her and she kept going by will alone. Now fear nipped at me, and I sped to her.

"Maelen, what is wrong? Have you been harmed?"

"No, but what has passed?" Her question was stronger, her body straightened.

"Osokun's men raided the camp."

"Malec? The little people?"

"Malec"—I hesitated and could find no way to tell it better—"is dead. The others are with me here. We have been waiting for you. They have tried to make the camp into a trap for us."

"So!" The weariness had gone out of her. She made of that word the whistle of a whip lash. "How many of them?"

"Perhaps twelve. Osokun is wounded, another has taken command."

For me anger had always been a hot and burning thing, but the wave of emotion which washed from her to touch me now was cold, very cold and deadly. Also it was very deep, and I flinched as I might have dodged a blow from her hand.

Moonlight became silver sparks as it struck the wand she held out. The light appeared to drip from that rod, until it held my eyes, made me dizzy. And she sang, first in a low murmur, but the words, the notes entered into one, became a tingling along the veins, nerves, muscles; and then louder and louder, to fill one's head, driving out all save a will and purpose that caught us up and welded us all into a single weapon which fitted her hand as perhaps no sword has ever suited the plainsman who bore it.

I saw that silver wand move and I marched in obedience to it, with all the others of that furred company, as Maelen and her sword-sworn took the field. Of that journey back to the hills I do not now remember anything; for, as those with me, I was filled with a purpose which crowded out all else, save the necessity for satisfying the hunger that Maelen's singing had set in me. And the answer to the hunger was blood.

There came a moment when we lay in hiding and looked down upon the camp. To our eyes this was deserted save by the kasi that stamped and nickered at their lines. But our other sense made it plain that those we hunted were still there.

Again Maelen sang, or else the echo of her earlier song moved in me. She got to her feet and started down the slope toward the vans. Back and forth before her she moved her wand. It had been burning silver in the moonlight. Now, though it was day, yet still it was bright, dripping fire from its tip.

I heard a shout from the camp. And then we were in upon them.

These were men used to dealing with animals they considered inferior beings, to be hunted, slain, tamed. But animals that had no fear of man, who combined for the slaying of men—these were so opposed to nature as our enemies had always known it that the very strangeness of our attack unnerved them in the beginning. Always Maelen sang. In us her song was a willing, a sending—what it might have been to the outlaws, I do not know. But I remember two men at least who dropped their weapon and rolled upon the ground, mouthing senseless cries, trying to cover their ears with empty hands. And such were easily dealt with. We were not all lucky, we could not be, but we did not know that until the singing ended and we stood in a camp we had taken at cost.

I was as one awakened from a vivid, frightening dream. I saw the dead, and one part of me knew what we had done. But another awakened from sleep and pushed aside such memories. Maelen stood there, not surveying the bodies, but rather staring straight ahead, as if she dared not look upon the havoc spread around her.

Her hands hung limply at her sides and in one of them was the wand. But it no longer shimmered with life, it was dull and dead, while her pale face was ashen gray, her eyes turned inward.

I heard a whimpering cry and toward her came Simmle, dragging herself along the ground, a great wound welling blood across her hindquarters. Then I heard other cries and whines as those who had battled, and were still living, tried to reach their mistress. But she did not look at them, only stared ahead.

"Maelen!"

Fear welled in my mind. Was it only a husk of womankind, or Thassa-kind, who stood there unheeding?

"Maelen!" I put into that mental cry all the strength I could summon.

Simmle whimpered. She had pulled herself to Maelen's feet, stretched out her head to rest it upon a dusty boot.

"Maelen!"

She stirred, almost reluctantly, as if she had no wish to return from that place of nothingness which had held her. Her fingers loosened and the wand fell from her grasp, rolled into the mud of blood and dust, a dead thing. Then her eyes came alive as she looked upon Simmle.

With a cry as desolate as any uttered by her animals, she knelt and laid her hand on the venzese's head. And I knew that she was safely back with us again. For a time then it was a matter of tending the wounded, seeing what could be done for what was left of the company. There were no outlaws left alive, but also too many of the little people were gone.

I dragged a bucket down to the river and filled it with water, brought it back once, twice, for Maelen's use while she wrought with her simples and herbs for the easing of the wounded. And on the third such trip my nose, recovering at last from the assault by stench, told me of danger—man scent, strong, recent, going off into the bushes. I put down the bucket and went to nose out that trail, though I had not gone far before the summons came via mind-touch for my return.

With a nagging suspicion that I had better follow that trail and soon, I returned. Someone had escaped the battle by the vans, and with a crossbow even one man could lie upslope and pick us off at his ease. Full of this I ran back to camp and Maelen, but before I could report my find she spoke:

"There is that I must tell you—"

"Maelen, there were—" I began to interrupt.

Almost imperiously she refused to listen, continued. "Krip Vorlund, I bring ill news from Yrjar."

For the first time in hours I returned to the plight of Krip Vorlund. And I was startled by the wrench needed to bring my thoughts back from Jorth's concerns to Krip's.

"The captain of the *Lydis* appealed to fair law when you were taken by Osokun's men. One of your shipmates was struck down and left for dead, but recovered to tell of what happened, identified the clan pattern he saw. Then it was a matter for the Overjustice, and a party went under claim-banner to Oskold's, where they found your body. They took it back to Yrjar, believing Osokun's treatment had broken your mind. The medico of the *Lydis* said that only off-world could they find the proper aid. Thus—" She paused, eyes meeting mine. Yet in hers there was nothing, for they looked beyond me, seeking something more than Krip Vorlund, or Jorth. "Thus," she began again, "the *Lydis* went from Yiktor with your body on board. This is all I could learn, for there are strange troubles abroad in the city."

Inside me somehow I knew she spoke the truth. For a long moment or so it had no meaning, nor did I listen to what else she was saying—it was as if she spoke some other language.

No body! The thought began to beat inside my head, growing louder and louder, until I could have screamed with the rhythm of the thumping. But as yet it was only a beating, not something I understood. Now she no longer looked into any far distance, but to me. And she tried, I believe, to reach through the beating to my mind. Only nothing she said meant anything. I was not Krip Vorlund, I would never be again—I was Jorth—

I heard sounds, I saw Maelen through a scarlet haze, her eyes wide, her lips moving. Her commands were far away, muffled by that beating. I was Jorth, I was death—I would hunt—

Then I was on the trail I had found in the bushes by the river. Hot and rich, the scent filled my nose. Kill—but to kill one must live a little longer. Be not too reckless, a barsk was cunning, a barsk was—

A beast with centuries of beast craft to call upon in mind. Let Jorth be entire. I withdrew, skulked apart as the remnants of what had once been a man, watching the going of the beast on the age-old business of the hunt. Three different scents I nosed out, one from the other. No kasi—these men fled afoot. And around one hung a sickliness which told of injury. Three, heading back into the hills.

They would be watching for a tracker, yes. This was a matter in which to use all skill. Nose here, nose there, watch ahead for aught which could be an ambush. Perhaps the cunning of man was still joined with that of the beast.

It would seem that they could not climb the steeper slopes. Perhaps the hurt one was too great a burden, for the trail followed the easiest footing. I found once where they had paused and there was a blood-stained rag I nosed disdainfully. But they kept doggedly on the march, heading toward the border of Oskold's land. Now I searched for other scents—those of the invaders I had seen in these hills. I was not of any mind to be robbed of my prey.

And ever there was a plucking at my mind from behind, though I held a barrier against that, refusing to open to call. I was Jorth and Jorth hunted, that was all that was real—just as perhaps Jorth would cease to be before another day. But if Jorth did so die, it would not be alone.

Up and up. I came to a place where two saplings had been hacked from their roots, and thereafter I followed only two sets of tracks, not three. Two carried the third, and their pace was much slower.

Now I left the trail, for we entered a gully between two sharply slanted rises, and I believed those I trailed would stay in the bottom of that cut. But I did not go at a blind gallop, rather did I slip from one cover to the next. Nor did I bury my nose on any close scent, remembering the trick the scout had played upon me.

Night came and still I caught no sight of them. I marveled a little at their ability to keep ahead, burdened as they were—unless they had left the camp before, not during, our attack, and so had more of a start than I had judged. The moon was with me, throwing into sharp relief the landscape, veiling part in shadows which cloaked my advance.

Then I saw them. The two on their feet leaned

against a large rock outcrop. Even as I sighted them, one slid down that support and sat, his head drooping on his chest, his hands falling limply between his outstretched legs. The other breathed in great gasps, but kept on his feet. While on a rude stretcher lay the third, and from him came small whistling moans.

Two were done, I decided, but that other who still stood—him I watched carefully. He moved at last, fell to his knees, and brought forth a small flask he held to the mouth of the man on the stretcher. But that one flung up his arm and struck outward, uttering a harsh, excited cry. The flask hit the boulder and burst, leaving a dark trickle on the rock. He who had held it gave a hoarse grunt, tried to reach the fragments, then raised his head and looked about wildly as if hunting something in the wilderness about them to relieve his misery.

All this time the man who sat had not moved. But now he shook his head slowly from side to side as if trying to clear it of some clouding mist. Then he pulled back to his feet, bracing himself against the rock. The moonlight fell now across his face, and I saw that he was the one who had guarded Osokun's rear when he and his companion had brought their wounded lord into the Thassa camp. I had not wondered about the identity of the three I had followed; somehow I had known from the first whom I would find here. Nor did it astonish me to see that I knew this one from an even earlier time, when he had done his lord's will in the narrow cell of the border fort.

Krip Vorlund—who was Krip Vorlund—what

call had he on Jorth the barsk for vengeance? It did not matter. These were my kill—

So much did I consider them my prey that I came into the open without any more use of cunning, and gave a war cry in the deep-chested growl of my kind. He that lay upon the stretcher would be helpless. The other two—let them fight for their lives. It was better that way.

I sprang for the man now standing. I do not think his fatigue-dulled mind and ears had really carried the message of my presence before my weight struck him full in the chest, crashed him to the ground, my fangs aiming true.

Easy—easy prey!

I snapped and tore, then was up, facing the other. He had steel, bright and clear in the moonlight, waiting in his hand as he half crouched between me and the stretcher. He shouted—battle cries? Calls for assistance? What did it matter—they were not for my ears and would matter to no one.

But the blade did, and we wove a pattern between us like the intricate design of some formal dance. I made him ever turn and twist and in the end that was my advantage, since his fatigue deadened his limbs with chain weights. At last my jaws closed upon the wrist of his sword hand. And that was the beginning of a swift end.

Panting from that dance of death, I turned upon the stretcher. He who had been carried on it was sitting up. Perhaps fear had overridden his weakness of body for those seconds, giving him a return of energy. I saw his hand move, a flash of light spun through the air, then came a blow between neck and shoulder as the knife bit hard and deep. But since he had not killed me outright, he had not saved himself.

Thus it was that I lay at last among my dead, and thought that here, too, died Jorth the barsk, who had once been partly a man. This was a good ending for one who had no hope of returning along the strange path leading to this time and place.

MAELEN

XV

SCALES OF MOLASTER. Days ago—nights and moons, days and suns, since I started on that strange path to adjust the scales of Molaster. But now they were as unbalanced as ever, and instead of doing good my efforts had wrought evil; I marveled dully that so much ill could be rooted in hope of good. I thought that Molaster was gone from my life, and that I was one who was lost and drifting on a tide I could not breast. Perhaps I had believed too much in myself and my own powers, and this was my punishment.

I stood in the camp among the dead, the enemy and my own little ones. And I looked about me, knowing that all this had sprung in part from my own acts, for which I must be the first to answer. Perhaps it is true, as some argue, that we are but the play pieces of great forces and are moved hither and thither for purpose not of our reckoning, certainly not of our desires. But, though such a belief is quieting to one's heart, putting aside guilt, yet it is not to be held by one who has known the discipline of a Singer. Thus did I refuse it now.

My spirit wept for my little people, and for Malec, though I knew that the White Road is not to be regretted for those we hold in close fellowship, It is sometimes far harder to remain in this life than to pass through the gate and into the way which leads elsewhere. We cannot allow ourselves to mourn for those who are gone; they have but discarded the old dress to put on a new.

So, too, for my little people. But those who still suffered, ah, for them did I also feel pain, fever, misery. And for another must I also bear the burden of life—he who had fled from the camp with such a threat riding him as to drive any man to death. Him I must find, if I could, for to him was I deeply in debt.

Also did I suspect that which was even worse, that my inner desires had willed just such an ending. And, if such powerful wishes be beamed, then they influence action to come. Although I had not sung this into being, could I be sure that I had not unconsciously twisted the future to serve my heart's longing? I knew that I had one escape to offer the man who had been Krip Vorlund from off-world, and, if he agreed, then—

I spoke to my little people soothingly, telling them what must be done. And I sang over my rod of office, though it was still day and not night, for I could not wait for dark. Then I set out food and drink for those who had been my companions for so long. Afterward I sat beside Simmle, telling her where I must go and why. The first streamers of sunset were in the sky when I went into the wilderness.

Had it not been for the power of my wand, I would not have kept to the trail. But when Krip Vorlund had entered into Jorth's body, the rod had wrought it, and it would seek him out for me as long as he walked the earth of Yiktor. I carried with me a shoulder sack of supplies, for I did not know how long I must journey, though a feeling in me said it could not be far.

Deliberately I refrained from trying to reach him by thought. Either he would shut his mind tight against me now, or else such a sending might distract him in a moment when he needed all his cunning for his own salvation. This much I knew—he had not run blindly away from the truth, but rather he had gone to seek battle. It might well be that he did not mean to survive such an encounter.

We have always known that when we take on the forms of the little people, we also take on a measure of their natures. And when a man was in the state of mind Krip Vorlund was, he would react to the most savage in his new form. Of all the animals the barsk was the most cunning, intelligent, and fierce, those three qualities having kept its species so long apart from all other life on Yiktor. Only because the beast had been so disordered by its treatment had I been able to work with it before the coming of Krip Vorlund to my upland camp.

Thus I could believe that the creature I now sought was for a time a savage hunter. And whomever it trailed must be some fugitive from Osokun's band. Osokun's body had not been found with the slain, perhaps he was the bait now. And with him, how many others? I had not known the number of raiders. While all we had surprised in camp were now dead, there could be more.

On toward the borders of Oskold's holding that trail led. Night came and with it the moon, which is ever favorable to the Thassa. Now I sang—not words to draw power from about me, but an inner questioning that kept the rod steadily pointing. And I did not tire, for through the rod flowed what fed by spirit.

When one sings one does not think, except for the purpose of shaping the notes. So I went with only one need in me—to find him who had been lost. For if Molaster favored me in even a very, very small way, there might yet come good from all this pain and ill.

The ground was rising, though all about me was in shadow. No longer was I fully of the world of which it was a stable part. Moon and shadow warred, first one and then the other seizing a strip of ground. I went swiftly, for the taking of one step and then the other does not matter to one who walks by song and rod.

Thus I came in the gray of dawn into a valley where death was a rank odor in the air, a feeling to daunt the spirit. I saw the bodies of three men. Two I had not looked upon before to my remembrance, but the third was Osokun. And as I approached where he lay on a rude stretcher as if he had been so borne to this place, I saw him whose need had drawn me here.

I thought-quested, believing that I might find the silence of body death. But, no! Flickering, yes, but still trapped was the spirit! By so little was I in time.

Thrusting my rod into the stained soil, I gave a flash of thanks to Molaster, and then set about looking for wounds on that red fur, so close to the color of the blood I feared to see.

There was only one which mattered. Driven deep was a short belt-sword which still stood in the wound. I began to work as I never had before. With my little ones the need had been rooted in love and pity, but now I must save a spirit, lest the last chance for either of us be lost. And I fought off death with my two hands, my knowledge, and the power of song.

We do not usually fight death to the last barricade. It is not meet among the Thassa to be so jealous of another's freedom as to deny him admittance to the White Road when he is already a step or two along it. To draw back the wayfarer is to blight his future. But this was a matter which was not for the Thassa to decide. And I have yet to find another race which shares our acceptance of the Great Law in the same way. To some species, I know, death was total extinction by their belief, and so they regarded it with horror which darkened most of their lives. I did not know how Krip Vorlund looked upon death. But I believed that he had a right to make his choice, was he to be numbered among those who saw death as an enemy rather than a gate. Thus I wrought as I would not have for one of my own.

The spirit was in him, but how long it would remain, or I could hold it, I dared not guess. In the hours of early morning I sang again, this time aloud, and drawing upon all the power I could summon. And under my hand that faintly beating heart grew, so I dared to believe, a thread more strong. Finally I picked up that limp body. It was lighter than I had feared, and I felt the bones under the skin, as if for a long time Jorth had been on short rations.

Back we went through the hills and all that way I sang, and held, and sang, fighting the battle to keep the one I held to the ways of earth. When we came to the camp, I found my little ones glad to see me, breaking in upon my concentration with their cries, their thoughts. I laid Jorth down beside Simmle. She still lived, which I had not thought possible. I tended her wound again, but looking upon it I knew that life such as would be left to her would not be enough.

Then I took her head between my two hands as we had often sat. And I asked her the Question. For a long moment we sat so, and then she gave me the Answer. Around us the rest of the company whimpered and cried a little. For the little ones are not Thassa, and it takes great courage for them to make such an Answer, their belief not being ours.

Now I made memories for Simmle, all the best ones, and let her wander in them, while all the pain of her body was gone. And she was happy and content. When she was most happy and content I gave release according to the Answer. But in me a sword was thrust, for memory is sour as well as sweet, and this one added more to my burden.

I wrapped the husk of Simmle, the part which was

no longer of any matter to us, certainly not to her who was free. And I put it among the rocks. Jorth slept deep in that place where, if there was to be any healing, it could begin. And of the others none were so hurt they would not mend.

Then I looked about the camp, knowing that I must be off to find what assistance I could, and that speedily. For where Osokun had come others might follow. Having broken my fast and that of my little people, I fell to the labor of preparing to move out.

One of the vans I must abandon and from that I brought what was most needed. Those who had despoiled our belongings had taken much, but I loaded in what was left of food and healing supplies. My little peoples' cages I set in two of the vans, making comfortable those riding in them. I put Jorth on an open pad of mats just behind the seat in the first of the vans. Then I ordered the kasi to move out, one van following the other, for those behind needed no driver; they would come in my wake.

The sun was paler, for the season was close to winter. To each part of the year its own magic. Some judge autumn a time for sorrow, for so much which is alive in the warmth seems then to die and vanish from the earth, and the coming of winter is dreaded. But each season has its own life and energies, and none can say that this or that one is not good because it fails in comparison in some parts with the others.

To the Thassa winter is a time of rest, of gathering in—both physically in clan groups and inwardly in spirit, a time of judgment and study. And this year I, Maelen, might face the justice of my race in a way not known for generations. But, though autumn faded, it was not yet gone from the land. And though the life spark in Jorth was faint, still it continued to abide.

Twice I saw mounted men ride in bands far off. But if my small train of wagons excited any comment among them, they did not seek me out. Perhaps it was better that we went our way openly by day, for the Thassa were always strange to the plainsmen and known to be wanderers. Whereas a journey by night would have aroused their supicion.

The kasi, having had a long rest in camp and being well fed and watered, were good for many hours of slow but steady moving, and I intended to press on past the usual limits of a day's journey. I would have to, for time was not my friend but a threatening enemy.

We paused from time to time that I might visit my little people and look to those who were hurt. What I missed most now was Simmle's presence beside me. She had been more to me than any of the others—because we were linked by that old exchange, having once been paired body to body, mind to mind. For that relationship there are no real words to explain. To me there would never be another like unto her. If I had been the one to go before, she would have felt the same emptiness.

I wondered, whenever I turned to look upon Jorth, whether, if his body would be his once again and the barsk spirit returned to its rightful envelope, this off-worlder would find himself united to other life forms in a fashion such as no one of his race or species ever had been before.

We moved on, back up along the Valley trail.

Now I thought of the Old Ones. What had come of the message Malec and I had sent from Yrjar? It had never been answered, he had told me that. There would come a time, which I could not and would not escape, when I must go before the assembly and speak of all I had done, give the reasons thereto. But I did not believe I had an excuse they would deem strong enough to stand against the weight of their anger.

I shut out such musings from my mind, for dark thinking attracts only ill fortune. Instead I built what I could for good by singing, choosing a growing song, as growing is close-kin to healing and what may root one is also part of the other. As the kasi pulled steadily toward Yim-Sin, I sang for both Jorth and my little people. In such singing all energy is bound into a single will-wish and all else slips away, as is needful.

On we rolled. Night came and I saw in the dark the glow of fire against the sky, marking some violence of man to man. Oskold's land lay behind the hills; we were now in the plains. Either he had carried war against the invaders, or the first quarrel had spread, involving many more. And I thought of the rumors I had heard in Yrjar that off-worlders meddled in the wrangling of lords, and that the *Lydis* had really gone off-world to escape some danger here.

In times of war among the plainsmen, the Thassa follow ever the old rule, drawing back into the high country and the safe places. So I thought other wagons would be moving through this night. But I did not try to use mind-touch to learn if that were so. I sang, nursing a small flicker of life, healing where healing was needful.

Perhaps because we moved under the Moon of Three Rings the singing held more power than ever before. I knew this was true as I turned on my seat and used the rod, drawing in the air above the skin-and-bones body of the barsk, sending strokes up and down without touching hide or hair, changing all power into one use. My wrist grew tired, my mouth dry, my throat sore.

I put aside the rod and leaned over. What had been a flicker of life now held steady. I was too tired to give thanks, save wordlessly, but now I knew that this lost one would live. And with returning life must surely come acceptance of what I had to offer.

We paused beside the turn into the main road to Yim-Sin. I loosed those of my little people who wished to be free and tended the rest. Borba came to me with a message that brought me into the road.

My nose could not pick up the story written there for most of my company. But there was no hiding from the eye that a large mounted party had passed this way. And, while I cannot use my nose to advantage, I can pick other subtleties from the air. Peril and anger had ridden this way and not long before us. To go on would be to face danger.

Yet I had no choice. What did these others hunt ahead? All men knew that this road led only to the Valley, and that was a place to be shunned, save for those whom fate had sent. I could not believe any raiders would voluntarily take this way.

There was only one reason, which hinted at such

recklessness and disregard for custom as to suggest madness among the men who chose it. The Valley had two entrances: one from the west, which was the road where we now stood, another from the east, where a trail came through Oskold's land. Had some one of his enemies, moved by insane hatred, decided to lead his men into the Valley and hence again down that other road, striking so into the heart of Oskold's territory?

For a leader so to outrage custom was almost unbelievable. Yet in time of war madness, much is done which afterward wondering men look back upon, unable to believe that such was so. Men driven by an unbridled desire to triumph over their enemies are released into a kind of callosity to do whatever they are moved by happenstance along the way.

I thought of the peace of Umphra and those who had guarded it for years upon untold years, and how they would not believe anyone would trouble them. They would be as insects under the sole of some unheeding giant's boot.

But what I suspected might not be so. And I had no other road. So I tended my company, and we rested until moonrise. This night I needed the moon, it was a draft to lift my spirit, to provide me with energy.

It came, unveiled by any clouds. But the moon was not too bright to hide the splotch of fire above. I looked at that, my lower lip caught between my teeth. For I believed it spurted forth at Yim-Sin. And such red flowering comes only from the plant of war. That which I feared must surely be!

I put the kasi back into harness and took to the

road. On its smooth surface we made better time. Time for what? To run into the red ruin of the sacking of Yim-Sin by crazed men? I had my own kind of weapons, but they were not for such battles.

To turn aside from this road would shortly be easy enough. There was a certain point ahead from which I could reach the high country and safety. If all Yiktor had gone mad—then it would be well for those still sane to gather together and keep in safety, letting the rest destroy themselves.

Behind me I heard what my ears had been waiting to report—a sound of feeble movement on the mats. I looked down. His eyes were open, but as yet no sign of intelligence sparked with them. A small new fear pricked me—had Jorth indeed won and the man been done to nothingness? This had sometimes occurred, though it was rare, when a man could not withstand the stress of beast nature.

I used mind-call. "Krip Vorlund!"

I made that as sharp as a summons to arms, with all the skill of such communication that I possessed.

Still those eyes were dull, naught dwelt within them. It was almost as if I now looked at the barsk I had taken from Othelm, an animal so deeply sunk in misery that it had withdrawn from life.

"Krip Vorlund!" Once more I forced that summons into his mind.

His head moved, as if he were trying to avoid some blow. Truly he had retreated, his mind now almost as far from me as his vital force had earlier been.

"Krip Vorlund!" I raised the rod, caught the

moonlight on its length, guided that down to strike upon the head of the barsk.

Out of him came a cry of pain and terror, a wailing such as I had never heard from any animal. And my little people answered him in their own ways. He was trying to pull himself up. But I put my hand on his shoulders, being careful not to touch near his wound, and with the weight of that kept him lying flat.

"You are Krip Vorlund." I made of each of those words a crossbow bolt, shooting them into his minds, setting them so firmly they could not be dislodged. "You are a man—a man!"

He was looking at me now, with a beast's eyes right enough, but there was a difference in them. He did not try to answer; left alone he would retreat again. I could not allow that, for I might not be able to draw him into life a second time.

"A man," I repeated. "And while a man lives, lives also the future. I swear to you—" I put the blazing rod between us and saw his gaze go from me to it and then back again, "I swear to you by the power which rests in this—and for me that is an oath binding past either life or death—that all is not yet lost!"

Was he alert enough to accept those words, understand them, and, understanding them, would he believe?

I could do no more in this time and place, the remainder rested solely with him. And what did I know of what moved this off-worlder and would set him on this road or that?

For a long, long moment I feared I had lost, that he understood but rejected belief.

"What remains—?"

His mind-speech was very faint; I could hardly catch it.

"Everything!" I hastened to hold, strengthen our contact.

"And what is everything?"

"For a space a new body—a man's body. So housed you can make your way unchallenged into Yrjar. Then you can either follow your ship into space or find a way to summon it back for you." Would he accept this?

"What body?"

This much encouraged me, his mind-touch was growing stronger. He was no longer rejecting contact with me as he had at first.

"One awaiting us—"

"Where?"

"In the hills." I hoped that I spoke the truth. I must believe that I spoke the truth or all was lost. He stared into my eyes.

"I think—you mean—this—" Again his contact weakened, but not this time by will; rather his body was failing him.

"I do. But you are sore hurt, you must sleep."

More than by my reassurance, I thought he was then ruled by weakness, the need for putting aside any decision or immediate action. He rested his head once more on the mat and closed his eyes as the van trundled on. He slept.

But for me there was no sleep. I could not take into

danger with me those other small lives far linked to mine. Once I had used them, or rather accepted their assistance. Those left must be made safe. I would not look upon another Simmle. When we reached the turn-off into high country, we would come to a parting of the ways. I could set a pattern in kasi minds which would keep them moving at their own speed for a day or two. Then—well—if no Thassa picked up the distress signal I would also loose, they could take to the wilds and a measure of safety. It was the best I could do for them now.

All followed as I had planned. I remained in the light van and sent the other two off by a pattern I impressed on the draft kasi. That would fade in a matter of hours, but the other small device I had triggered would keep them wandering in the general direction of the high country and would alert any Thassa to their aid. They were in their cages, but those were not latched and I left food and drink available.

I watched the vans out of sight and then I returned to my own seat. Jorth still lay in deep sleep. The two kasi pulling us were the best of our company, suited to hard going. I looked up at that fire glow. It was dimmer and there was light in the east. We would move on into the dawn of another day, into what peril, I did not try to guess.

XVI

LIKE ALL THE THASSA, I have ever loved the heights above the plains, where sometimes the breath clogs in the throat and there is such a dust of both country and man as to thicken the mind and slow thought. I do not know from whence my race came. The past stretches long and long, and is far lost in misty beginnings. Sometimes at in-gatherings we speak idly of this, speculating about this and that. It has been said among us that we are perhaps not even of Yiktor, but born of another world, in our time as new to this planet as the off-worlder riding with me. But if that is so, our coming is now so far behind us that not even any faint legend remains.

While we were still dwellers under roofs, our cities were of the mountains not of the plains, and that is why we made no difficulties over land when the plains dwellers came overseas to settle here. For they sought the lowlands as we the high places.

Now as the van climbed toward Yim-Sin, almost insensibly my heart grew a little lighter, as must any wanderer's coming into a land which welcomes him. Yet this time fear also rode with me. Had Simmle still shared my life, she could have scouted ahead, being my warning eyes and ears.

The sun climbed, but was much hidden by the peaks of the hills and we had neither its full light nor its warmth. I ate and drank as we went, but I no longer sang. For in me the power was much lowered by all the calls I had made upon it during these past few hours, and there might be need ahead for a weapon of some force. The signs of the troop which had preceded us could still be read.

Along the curves of the hills were the terraced vineyards, the leaves on the vines withered and purplish, proving the harvest well past its peak.

Down from the crest land came no good wind to rustle through them, rather one carrying the reek of burning. I no longer doubted what was to be found at Yim-Sin.

The smoke still coiled lazily from some heaps of ashes; and from places where the harvest had been stored came oily clouds. I wet a scarf and tied it about nose and throat, but my eyes smarted.

Umphra's temple alone stood unfired. But the great gate hung askew from its hinges and on it were marks of a battering ram. I stopped the van to listen. Very faintly from out of that inner court I heard a muffled plaint, not loud enough for true crying. About me I did not look too closely. Death had walked here and not as a friend. I climbed down from the van and went into that place beyond the broken gate.

It was plain what had happened. Yim-Sin had been taken by surprise, but a handful of her people had managed to reach here, hoping for a sanctuary not to be theirs. I searched for life, for the crying had stopped. And I found it in a child whom I took up in my arms, one who looked upon me vacantly and neither shrank from nor invited my hold.

Bestowing her in the van apart from Jorth, lest intelligence return to her and she be frightened by such a companion, I went again into Umphra's temple.

Senseless had been the slaying and destruction, as if those who had wrought it had been only shells of man with far worse than any human spirit within those shells. But that is how man can be when he thrusts aside all controls upon the kernels of cruelty and evil which dwell within him. I am a Singer, and to win my power I faced many dire trials and tests. I am of the Thassa, a people now pledged to a form of peace. What I saw that day in Yim-Sin was beyond all experience, and I came forth sick and shaking, unable to believe that this had been wrought by any who were still to be termed men.

If Yim-Sin had fared so, then what had happened in the Valley? But the Valley had safeguards, intended to protect, even from themselves, those who dwelt there. Would those safeguards have turned outward to save them from this?

I went back to the van and gave orders to the kasi. Then I took into my arms the girl-child I had found still alive, and to her I sang a small song to give her sleep for a time and open the deep place within her as refuge for her terrified spirit. When I laid her back within the van, Jorth raised his head and looked at us.

"What has happened?"

I gave him the truth of what I had found here and told him that death might now run before us.

"Why? Who?"

"Neither can I tell you. My only guess is that some enemy would come upon Oskold by way of the Valley."

"But I thought that the Valley, its roads, was sacred, untouchable."

"In war the gods are forgotten or outraged. It is often so."

"But would the plainsmen do such a thing just for

a chance at a sneak attack upon one lord?'' he persisted.

"I have thought that also, but I have no answer. There were fires out on the plains last night. I can only believe that this is not merely an invasion of Oskold's land but a conflict which has spread far more widely, perhaps already laps with fire and blood across the whole land. For what I have seen here there is not sane reason. Outlaws might act so, but there is no outlawed band large enough to take a town—and with Osokun and his men dead, who are the outlaws?''

"But we go on—to the Valley?''

"I have sworn to you an oath,'' I replied wearily. "What I can do to restore to you something of what has been taken, that I shall do. And the answer is in the Valley.''

"You propose to give me Maquad's body?''

I was not surprised at his words. He was not stupid, and the fitting of one thing to another to make the right sum was not difficult. "Yes, if you agree, Maquad's body. In that you can go to Yrjar, I with you. We can tell your tale, your ship may be signaled, they will return.''

"Many ifs in that,'' he commented. "Tell me, Maelen, why should you give me Maquad's body?''

"Because,'' I said dully, "it is the only one possible.''

"No other reason? Not that you wish Maquad to live again?''

"Maquad is gone. Only that which held him has life still—after a dim fashion.''

"Then you separate man from body, you Thassa." I did not know just what he was trying to say.

"You are Krip Vorlund," I returned. "Do you feel yourself less Krip Vorlund because you now dwell in another outer casing?"

He was silent, considering this. I hoped it was the right answer to direct his thinking. If he believed the body did not matter as much as that which was within it, then the exchange would not be so hard for him.

"Then to you, your people, it does not really matter what body you wear?"

"Of course it matters! I would be one lacking in wits to declare it otherwise. But we believe that the inner part is far greater than the outer, that it is our true identity; the other only clothing for the eyes and sense. Maquad's outer casing still lives, but that which was Maquad is gone from it and us. I can offer you his former dwelling place so that you can once more be a man—"

"A Thassa!" he corrected me.

"And is that not the same?"

"No!" his denial was sharp. "We are far different. As Jorth I have learned that a residue of the original inhabitant, as you would say, still dwells in this body and that it can influence me. Will it not be the same if I try another switch? Will I not be Krip-Maquad rather than Krip Vorlund?"

"Does barsk or man rule in Jorth?"

"Man, I hope—now—" But his answer was a little hesitant.

"Would not then Krip Vorlund be Krip Vorlund no matter what body he dwells in?"

"But you are not sure—"

"Is anyone," I burst out then, "to be sure of anything in any world under any sun?"

"Except death."

"Is death then a surety for you off-worlders? Do you believe that is just an end and not a beginning?"

"Who can tell?" he made answer. "Perhaps we can not demand any unqualified reply to any question we are moved to ask. So, you offer me a body more akin to my lost one. You say, take and go to Yrjar, tell your story, and ask for the return of that which is yours. Yet it would seem that we must deal not only with our own affairs, but with a war lying between us and Yrjar."

"Think, Krip Vorlund, have I ever promised you that this would be an easy thing?"

"No," he agreed. "Nor can you either promise me a body—if those we trail now have used the Valley as they used Yim-Sin."

"The Valley has safeguards the village did not. It is able to protect those who dwell there, and it may be there is a good defense against these raiders as well. I have offered you the best I can, Krip Vorlund. No one, man or Thassa, can do more than that."

"Agreed. What will you do with this child?"

"If the Valley is still intact, Umphra will care for her. If not, she goes with us."

For the first time, he appeared to note the loss of the rest of our company, for he asked:

"Where are the animals?"

"I have sent them to where I hope my people will

find them. If not, they will be free to roam as they choose.''

For a while he was silent, and then he said, ''Both our lives have been changed by that walk we took together in the fair of Yrjar. I would not believe this story had I not lived it.''

''Stuff for the weaving of a legend,'' I agreed. ''I have heard it said that if you dig far enough into any old tale you will unwrap at least one small kernel of one-time fact.''

''Maelen, what was Maquad to you?''

I was off-guard and perhaps he had sensed that. The sudden shot brought the truth from me.

''He was the life companion of my sister by birth, Merlay. When—when he went from us, I thought she might follow. She still turns her face from the fullness of life.''

''Tell me, would that alliance be again in effect did Maquad return?'' His second demand was as sharp as the first.

''No. You would wear Maquad's body, but you are not Maquad. Looking upon you, however, she might be moved to accept the truth and awake once more from dark to light.'' There it was, my poor frayed wish spoken into words at last.

''But would your people know I was not as I seemed?'' He appeared not to have heard the ending of my speech.

I smiled wryly. ''Do not think you can hide your true identity from any Thassa, Krip Vorlund. They would know you at meeting. And, I must tell you this also, they will not approve of what we would do. I defy all our Standing Words when I give to you Maquad's dwelling, even for a short space of time. They cannot prevent that act, but it is one I must answer for in time to come."

"Then why—?"

"Why must I do it? Need you ask that, off-worlder? This tangle is of my snarling, mine must be the unraveling. I am pledged by the strongest oath of my people to see that you have all aid within my power. I cannot tell why this has been so set upon me. But one bears the burdens sent by Molaster, one does not question them."

He asked me no more, and I was glad that he meditated upon his own thoughts. For I was busy in my own mind. I had told him the exact truth. He would wear Maquad's body and he would not be Maquad. But just as the beast influences a little the human in-dweller, so would the shell of Maquad influence him. And this off-worlder was sensitive with esper power.

Maquad had been a singer of the second degree. He had been searching for knowledge to lead him higher when he was slain in four-footed guise. The animal of his exchange had been young, not used before, and so it lapsed after a period of violence into a cataleptic state which no mind-send could reach. But the beast portion had not, could not, reach all of the human brain, just as the human could not entirely possess the animal. There was a residue left in Maquad, if not the same Maquad of his memories, of more—Even the Old Ones do not know the full extent of changes so wrought. In all our history there was never a case of a human's return to a human or Thassa body not his own. Suppose, just suppose, that in Maquad's body that residue would awake and influence— I could not be sure, but even a part-Maquad might brighten Merlay's days for a space, draw her back to us again!

I stared out past the kasi and the road, and saw neither animals nor way but only her face and the change which might come to it were Maquad—or part-Maquad—to walk with her for a time! Although if what I longed for did not come, still I would abide by my oath—we would ride to Yrjar and try to change what might be unchangeable.

Also I thought of the Valley and what might be happening there this day. By all signs those who had finished Yim-Sin must have reached there by now, and the time space between us lengthened as we climbed so slowly. We passed the sections where sentries had once stood to ask the business of wayfarers. There were no sentries and I did not pause to seek them. I was not minded to hurry our ascent, to arrive while a battle might still be in progress. The Valley safeguards would make no distinction between friend or foe. And who knew—perhaps some measure of sanity would return to the raiders aloft.

The child slept and perhaps Krip Vorlund did also, for he lay quiet, his head pillowed on a forepaw. Nor did he speak to me again. We made a nooning in the wilderness where only the road broke the land. There water bubbled in a mountain stream and I loosed the kasi to graze and rest.

"No sign yet?" The off-worlder asked when I brought him a bowl of water.

"None save they came this way. But who they are, or why they do this—" I shook my head.

"Your powers," he commented, "appear to have their limits."

"As all do. You have mind-send. But do you also teleport or the like?"

"No. There are those who can, but I have yet to meet one. Only I had thought that the Thassa—"

"Could perform stranger acts than that? Sometimes, but the site *and* the time must fit the pattern. Given both I might beam-read and get a half view of the future, or rather *a* future."

"Why *a* future? Do futures change?"

"They do, because they depend upon decisions, and does a man remain always subject to the same thoughts, hour after hour, day after day? What seems right and meaningful at this moment may not be so later. Therefore the future in the broad sense, yes, that can be read. But our relation to the future changes through our need to face this crisis or that. I could tell you the fate of a nation, but not of the individual men of that nation."

"But you might tell the fate of the Valley?"

"Perhaps, given the right time, which I am not. For that is beyond my grasping."

"And soon we may learn for ourselves," he said. "When I first met you in that dell—how long ago was it? I have since lost all numbering of days."

I shook my head. "Days bearing numbers are not the concern of the Thassa. Long ago we ceased to deal with such. We remember what has chanced, but not this day or that."

Had he been man at that moment, I think he might have laughed.

"You are so right, Freesha! Enough has happened to me on Yiktor that days have certainly ceased to count in number. But when I came to your camp fresh from Osokun's fort, I thought I was caught up in some vivid and unpleasant dream. And to that belief I am inclined to return now and then. It would explain what has happened so much more easily than to think that waking I have lived—am living—this."

"I have heard that off-world there are methods of inducing such dreams. Perhaps you have tried such and so are ready for such a belief. But if you have been dreaming, Krip Vorlund, I am awake! Unless I am a part of your dream—"

He ate from my fingers the meat cake I crumbled, then drank from his water bowl. The child stirred and moaned.

"You put her to sleep." That was more statement than question.

"Thus she could not remember, or fear."

I took her up in my arms now and put to her lips a small cup wherein I had mixed water and the juice of healing herbs. In her sleep she drank, and then her head turned on my shoulder and she passed into deeper slumber.

"Maelen, are you wed? Do you have a child?"

I thought suddenly, in all this strange adventure we were sharing neither of us had asked such a question of the other, nor had we cared what had passed before.

"No. I am a Singer. While I sing, I have no life companion. What of you, Krip Vorlund? I had heard that the Traders have families. Is it with you as it is with the Singers, that you can be but one thing at a time?"

"In a manner." He told me of the life of his people, wedded to many stars and not one alone. They had life companions, but only when they had reached a certain rank within their companies. Some times a planet woman might accept Trader life for the sake of a man; but that a Trader abandon his ship for any world because of a woman was unthinkable.

"You are like unto the Thassa," I said. "For you, to be firmly rooted in one place is to die. We sweep across the earth of Yiktor and her seas at our will. We have certain places such as your space cities where we gather when there is need. But for the rest—"

"Gypsies."

"What?" I asked.

"A very ancient word. It means a people who live ever traveling. I think there was a nation of such once, very long ago, and worlds away."

"So the Thassa have their like across the void. I spoke once of a ship and my little people, and the visiting of other worlds."

"Such might still be done. But it would cost more tokens than lie even within the temple treasury of Yrjar. And such a ship must be built on another world after much study and experimentation. A dream indeed, Maelen, for no one would have such treasure as to bring it to life."

"What is treasure, Krip Vorlund? Does it not take different forms from world to world?"

"It is what is rare and valuable on each particular planet. Rarity plus beauty in some cases, rarity plus usefulness in others. On Zacon it is knowledge, for the Zacathans look upon learning as their treasure. Bring to them an unknown artifact, a legend, something which hints at a new sentence in the history of the galaxy, and you have brought them treasure.

"On Sargol it is a small green herb, once common on forgotten Terra, utterly irresistible to the Salarki, who would willingly exchange gems for it. And those same stones on another planet—one no longer than the nail of your smallest finger, Maelen—will allow a man to live as a lord of Yiktor for five years or more. On Hasku it is feathers, sprokjan feathers. I can recite you the list of treasures for a quarter of the galaxy, as they pass through our warehouses."

"So, to each world a treasure, and it varies so that what seems a fortune on one planet will on another be worth nothing—or perhaps more?"

He laughed inside his mind and even the barsk jaws fell apart in a faint likeness to a smile.

"Usually less rather than more. Gems—those are best, for gems and things of beauty speak to more than one people and species as worth taking and keeping safe."

"This world wherein such a ship as would carry my little people might be built, what manner of treasure do they there prize?"

"All that is high wealth. They are an inner planet and the men there are satiated with the best of a hundred worlds. What they have to sell, their ships, draw all the treasures they will accept. It would have to be something very rare, perhaps never seen before, or so large an amount of trade credits as would wipe out the contents of half our warehouses.''

I laid down the sleeping child, making her comfortable, but setting a barrier between her and the barsk again, so that if she woke she would not see that animal. Then I brought the kasi back to their duty. Once more we traveled the road. But I thought now and then of the nature of treasure and how different worlds rated it. I knew what the off-worlders took off Yiktor and I guessed such cargo passed as ordinary things. We had gems, but they were not such rare objects that off-world traders struggled to buy them. I decided that Yiktor might be termed, in the eyes of such experts, a relatively poor planet.

The Thassa did not, as the plainsman, try to gather portable wealth. When we had more of any one thing than we needed, we left the surplus at one of the ingatherings for those who lacked. Our beast shows brought us many tokens, but we did not build up reserves from them. For we considered them a form of training for both animal and Singer. They also gave us more reason for a roving life.

But to lay up any treasure and guard it—that is foreign to us. And if we had done it in the past, before we left our cities, we had forgotten it.

As we began once more our slow journey to the Valley, I asked of Krip Vorlund, ''What is your greatest treasure? Gems? Or some other rare thing?''

''Do you mean mine personally, or what is so regarded by my people?''

"Both."

"Then I shall answer you with one word, for with both me and my people it is the same—a ship!"

"And you gather naught else besides?"

"What we gather, and it is as much as we can of the treasures others want, it is only that we may finally spend all we have so garnered for a ship of our own."

"And how many of you ever achieve such?"

"Perhaps as many as find lordships on Yiktor. The struggle is as hard, though in another way."

"You—do you believe you will ever have this treasure?"

"No one willingly loses any dream, even when the point of being able to realize it is past. A man, I think, continues to hope for good fortune until he dies."

We camped that night, but not for the whole space of darkness, only for a few hours. I watched the moon rise, but I made no move to draw its power—not then. One cannot store it too long, and to tap it and be forced to loose it before using it to any advantage is a stupid waste. So I did not raise my rod, nor did I sing outwardly or inwardly. All that I did was to aid the kasi with thought power when and where I could.

The moon hung low when we came to the lip of the descent into the Valley. And, as was always true at nighttime, the mist covered thickly, hiding whatever might lie below. From where I sat I could see no change, no sign that any danger had passed this way. But my sight was very limited.

I heard the barsk stir, looked back to see he struggled to get to his feet. I restrained him with an outflung hand.

"We are above the Valley. Lie you still, rest while you may."

"You are going down?"

"I shall take precautions." I brought out my rod. The moon was not at its height, but it was there. I began a deep song, an inward chant, and the kasi started down into the Valley.

KRIP VORLUND

XVII

WHEN I FIRST AWOKE and knew that I was still alive, tended by Maelen and once more in the Thassa van, it seemed that the dream in which I had been caught had come full circle. There was an acceptance in me, the kind with which one faces incongruities met in a nightmare, wherein nothing surprises. But I came to learn during the following hours that this Maelen was one I had not met before. I now saw Maelen not unsure, but rather as one to whom duty had become the lead star of life. And, in spite of my own need to know what must be faced, I could never press past certain boundaries she held.

As we descended into the mist-cloaked Valley, she kept the van to the exact center of the road. I read in her mind that those precautions or defenses which she had spoken of could well be our undoing even though we came in peace. That they had been the bane of those we trailed was a hope we shared.

Another worry nagged at me. Though my mind was alert, yet the body housing it was weak and would not obey my commands. Were we to be attacked I could offer nothing, not even in my own defense. I could lift my head, stretch my legs as I lay upon the mat. But if I drew a deep breath pain followed and there was a languor, which came and went, to disturb me. Maelen had healing powers, that I knew, but would they succeed with the wound in my breast—? There was good reason to believe that Osokun's blade *had* bitten too deep, and that survival in my present body did not mean recovery.

I had gone to seek death when I had trailed Osokun and his sword-sworn, the shock of the news Maelen brought from Yrjar sending me into that temporary madness. But there is planted, at least in my own species, a stubborn resistance to the end of existence. And now a small measure of hope bulwarked what spirit I had. The alternative Maelen suggested had possibilities. Equipped with a Thassa body, I could indeed return to Yrjar. The Traders shared a consular representative on the planet; I had met him when the *Lydis* landed. I could go to Prydo Alcey, state my case, let him send a message to Captain Foss. It ought to be easy to frame some message such as only Krip Vorlund could send to certify my identity. Then, with my own body returned, another switch and I would be truly myself.

Of course there were many pitfalls between this

present moment and that to-be-wished-for result. And several might lie directly before us. I tried to move, to lift my heavy head and loose-muscled body so that I might see over the driver's seat. But I could accomplish nothing and lay panting and weak, alarmed at my state.

It was only when I lay so that I became aware that Maelen was engaged in more than merely directing the kasi down the road. There was an aura about her which tugged at mind—send powers. I was lying now so that I could watch her profile, her half face stern and set. Her hair was not piled in elaborate rolls as it had been at our first meeting, but bound about her head smoothly as to form a silver helmet. And the arabesque of ruby and silver which had then been on her forehead was gone. Now her eyes were half closed, the lids well down as if her gaze turned inward, or on other things than the sights of this world.

But there was such a brightness on her face as to dazzle me a little. Was it the moon against her very fair skin, or did some of it come from within, the reflection of power stored there? Always before I had seen the human in the Thassa; now she was more alien than any of the animals with whom I had shared life and battle these past few days.

"Taking precautions," she had called this. "Arming" was the name I would set upon it. I dropped my heavy head. I could no longer see her; yet the consciousness of her, how she sat, what she did, was so with me that it was as if I continued to watch her.

There grew up about us a new sensation as the van

rumbled on—a kind of warning. It was as if some scout on a distant hill waved away our advance. As we did not heed that warning the uneasiness grew sharper, feeding into the mind a shadow of foreboding which became steadily blacker. Whether this was one of the defenses of the Valley, I could not tell. But apparently it did not affect Maelen, or swerve her from our advance.

I heard the child stir uneasily beyond the blanket, making small sounds of distress. But whether she slept and dreamed ill dreams, or waked to find them reality, I did not know. For I was ridden now by my own distresses. Lassitude in me was growing. At moments it was clear where I was and what was about me, at other times I swung out into a void of nothingness where the resulting giddiness frightened what sense I had left. And I could not tell whether the mists which fuzzed my sight when I tried to fasten on some part of the van were of the real world or born of my increasing weakness.

The journey was endless. Time vanished, or rather the measurement of it did. I lay in the van and heard the whimpering of the child— I was gone—as if — rested on a shuttle racing back and forth weaving a future which eluded me.

Around, the air throbbed and beat—in time to the swing of the shuttle which bore me? No, this was a pulsation which broke that rhythm, anchored me in the van. Then I heard a sound which was part of that beat, a chant, I thought. It did not come from Maelen, but from the Valley, and it grew louder with every forward step of the kasi.

Oddly enough that beat of sound, of power,

strengthened me as if it poured back into my slack body the essence which had ebbed since Osokun's knife had sought my life. I lay, feeling that wash into me. Some ebbed again, yes, but each receding wave left a residue behind to hearten me. I was no longer only holding on grimly to what life I had, I was once more able to think beyond my body and my own concerns.

Once more I struggled up and looked at Maelen. Her head was thrown back now, her hands raised before her. Between her two palms, pressed together, was her wand. It seemed to spin, throwing off sparks of silver which struck her head and breast and then vanished. And she was singing—not like the chant which still filled the air, but very high and sweet, notes which pulled at me.

Somehow I braced my forepaws hard against the floor of the van, and managed to raise myself. Now my eyes were level with the seat on which she sat. I glimpsed the world below; it was still night, or very early morning. The moon was no longer bright, but ahead, down, there were other lights to be seen.

That was not the yellow-red of fires, nor the blue shade of the lamps I had seen in Yrjar. Rather these were moon globes as Maelen carried, only they were not fixed but moved about as might lanterns.

And it was from that place of lights that the chanting arose, stronger and deeper. I dragged myself farther up until, it spite of the pain it cost me, I could place one foreleg across the seat, resting my head upon it. Maelen did not notice me, she was still wrapped in her singing.

Two men carrying moon globes came to meet us. I

saw the white-and-yellow-patterned black robes of priests. But they did not greet Maelen or try to halt us, only stood aside one to right, one to left, and were silent as we passed between. Their faces remained impassive and they continued to chant words I did not understand.

We passed more of the priests of Umphra engaged in tasks along the road. I sniffed the stench of burning, and beneath that barsk nostrils picked up also the reek of blood. No, the Valley had not escaped the doom which had come to Yim-Sin. Yet I believed the doom had not been as complete here as it had been in the village.

The kasi turned without any outward sign of control from Maelen and we went through the gates. The portal which had hung there was splintered and scored, and in it bristled bolts from crossbows. The mist was now the smoke of destruction. We entered the first temple courtyard.

For the first time Maelen moved, raised the wand until its brilliant shaft pressed against her forehead. The light which had spun from it was gone and, as she dropped her hands once again, it was a simple rod. Her eyes opened.

A priest came to us. There was a bandage about his head, and he carried his right arm in a sling.

"Orkamor?" Maelen asked him.

"He sees to his people, Freesha."

She nodded gravely. "Evil has been wrought here. How great that evil, brother?"

"Much that was long and long in building has been broken." His voice was somber, his face drawn, with the deep-set eyes of a man who has been forced to witness the destruction of what had been very much a part of him. "But the foundations have not been destroyed."

"And who did this? They did worse in Yim-Sin."

"That they told us. As to who they were—men who have fallen under a darkness grown from seed brought from elsewhere. They have not, however, prospered in their wickedness."

"They are destroyed?"

"They destroyed themselves. For they did not heed the safeguards. Only, behind them they have left ruin."

"Those—those whom Umphra holds under his cloak—" she began, almost timidly. "How fare those, elder brother?"

"Him you hold in your heart-hand, Freesha, survives. Others—some Umphra has at last loosed upon the White Road."

She sighed. Her wand lay across her knees, her hands rubbed her forehead.

So Maquad was still alive; I clung to that much. My lassitude was creeping back. I could not find it in me to care greatly that her plan had not been swallowed after all. The pain in my breast gave me a sharp twinge, and I slipped from my half sprawl across the seat to huddle on the mat once again. It was as if my last small reserve of strength left me.

Light—shining into my face so that it smarted through the small slits between my nearly closed eyelids. . . . I tried to turn my head away from that light, but I was held to it and I breathed in vapor which was sharply aromatic, clearing my head. I opened my eyes and found that I now lay in a room and Maelen bent over me, a bowl in her hand holding a golden liquid. From this rose the fumes which had summoned me back.

With her was another, and that old, benign face I knew. Once, a very long time ago, we had sat in a quiet garden and talked of life beyond the star which was Yiktor's sun, of how men carried out their destinies in many strange places. This was Orkamor, servant of Umphra. I tried to say his name.

"Younger brother"—his words formed in my mind—"is this your wish, truly your wish, to put off the body you now wear for another?"

Words—words—but, yes, that was my wish, of course it was! I was a man—a man! I claimed a man's body. And that rose in me as no mere desire, but as a demand which was centered with all the strength I could now summon.

"Be it as you will, then, sister, brother—"

Orkamor receded from my vision as if he floated away. Once more Maelen leaned above me, holding the bowl that its reviving fumes might clear my brain.

"Say this, Krip Vorlund, word for word: 'I wish this by the power, to put aside fur and fang, to walk again as a man!'"

"I wish—this—by—by—the power, to put aside—fur and fang—to walk—to walk again as—a man!" Triumphantly I finished that plea, wishing I could shout it aloud from some mountain top for all the world to hear.

"Drink!"

She held yet closer the bowl of aromatic liquid. I lapped at its contents eagerly. It was as cool water from a mountain stream. I had not realized how I thirsted until I swallowed. It was good—good— I drank until the bowl was emptied, until my tongue found no lingering drop.

"Now—" She put aside the bowl to bring forward one of the moon globes. And though the room had seemed light to me, yet did that lamp make it brighter.

"Look into this," she bade me. "Loose, look and loose—"

Loose? Loose what? But I set my eyes upon the globe. It was a world of silver such as one might see rise up on the visa-screen of the *Lydis* as she made planet fall in a new system—a silver world reaching out—drawing one . . .

Who wanders on silver worlds, and what do they see there? Out of some depth that thought came to me. But this was waking not dreaming. Yet still I would not open my eyes to see, for there was a difference now and some wary part of me wished to explore that difference slowly.

I drew in a deep breath, waiting for my nose, for the barsk senses to tell me all they could. But it was as if those senses had been deadened, shriveled. There were scents, yes, the perfume of some growing thing, and others, but all weak compared to those I had known.

As yet I had not tried to move. But when I had breathed so deeply, that pain which had become so much a part of me—it was gone! Now I opened my eyes. But—distortion! Colors were less sharp in some ways, stridently screaming in others. I blinked, trying to make my surroundings return to normal. But they did not. It required effort to focus, to make my eyes once more my obedient servants. Once—once before this had happened— Memory stirred in me.

I stared ahead. There was a wide surface, a wall, and in it a window. Beyond that branches waved in the pull of the wind. My mind readily supplied names for all of these, recognized what my eyes reported, even though they saw everything differently. I opened my mouth, tried to lick sharp fangs with my tongue. But the tongue which moved there was not long, it swept across teeth—these were not the tearing implements of a barsk.

My—my paws? I ordered a foreleg into my range of vision, somehow not daring yet to raise my head. There was an arm moving slowly upward for me to see—a hand—fingers which curled when I ordered—

Arm—hand—? I was not a barsk—I was—a man!

Abruptly I sat up and the room, still somewhat distorted in my sight, swung giddily. And I was alone within it. But I raised human hands, two of them, to stare upon and I looked down at a human body! The flesh was pale, so pale it made me a little uncomfortable to look upon it. That was not right—I should be brown, very brown. I huddled on the edge of the bed where I had lain, looked searchingly at the length of my new body, at its pallor, the thinness which was close to emaciation.

Then I dared to raise my hands, to explore by touch my face. It was human right enough, though by touch alone I could not estimate its difference from the Krip Vorlund who had been kidnaped from the Yrjar fair. I wanted a mirror. I must *see*!

Stumbling a little, for it was a strain to walk erect once more after running for so long on all fours, I got to my feet. I inched one of those bare feet forward in a step, my hands out to balance me as I teetered from one foot to the other. But as I reached the window and then turned, my confidence in such a method of progression returned. It was as if I revived an old skill forgotten for a space. I looked about for the furred body which was Jorth, but it was gone—nor did I ever see it again.

The room was very small, the bed occupying much of its area. There was a door in the opposite wall and a coffer which also served as a table, judging by the cup and flagon set out upon its lid. From the window the wind swept in cool enough to send me shivering, and I tottered back to the bed to pull its upper covering off to wrap about me. I still longed to see my face. Judging by my body I was Thassa—Maquad—

But to my surprise I found in me some regrets for those senses which had served Jorth so well, but which were barsk. It would appear that the Thassa had limitations which matched those of my original self.

With the bedcover as a cloak about me I went to the coffer, thirst moving me to investigate the cup there. It was empty, but the flagon which shared its tray was not and I poured slowly the golden liquid.

That was cool, satisfying, and in my body spread a new sense of well-being, of unity with this new habitation. I heard a low cough and looked up at the priest with the bandaged head, whom I had last seen as he greeted Maelen. He inclined his head and crossed over to lay his burden on the bed, clothing, gray with touches of red, such as the Thassa favored.

"The Eldest Brother would speak with you, brother, when you are ready."

I gave him thanks and began to dress, far more sure about my movements now. When I had finished I guessed that I must look like Malec.

Malec! Another thrust of memory, and with it anger. Malec had brought me out of the hell of that barsk in Yrjar—and what had been his end? I had known so little of him, and I owed him so much.

Although my new sword, and certainly no wand such as Maelen carried. Yet in me was the desire for a weapon to fit my hand when I thought of the killing of Malec.

There was no mirror, I could not see the whole of the guise in which I now walked. But when I went out of that room, I found one of the boy priests waiting for me. He limped as he led the way, and in his face was the same emptiness of shock and fatigue as had marked his superiors. Also, in this place was still the smell of fire, though not as strong as Jorth had scented it.

We came into that same small garden where Orkamor had received me once before. And again he sat in the tall chair of sprouting wood, though the leaves on its now were sere and withered. There was a stool there, too, and on it Maelen, her shoulders drooping, her eyes sunken and dull, marking one who has expended a great effort to her own ill advantage. In me was the impulse to go to her, take those listless, limply lying hands in mine, and rouse her. Strange had she seemed to me in Yrjar when I had seen her confident, and strange had she been during all our journeyings; but now no longer. She seemed only as one who had claims upon me and who was worn and tired. But she neither looked up nor welcomed me.

Orkamor's eyes met mine, reaching in and in as if he meant to search out every thought, no matter how deeply buried it lay in my brain. And that searching was as keen as if he sought for a flaw he knew lay there. Then he smiled and raised his hand, and I saw there was a great, angry-looking bruise across its back, and one of his fingers was splintered and stiffly bound. But the gesture he made was of welcome, and, more than welcome, of happy surprise.

"It is done, and done well."

He did not speak aloud, and his words must have rung in Maelen's brain also, for she stirred, her head coming up a little, turning slowly, her eyes to rest upon me at last. I saw surprise and a kind of wonder in them, which astonished me in turn. For if she had wrought this change for me, why should the results amaze her?

She spoke to Orkamor. "Is this well done, Eldest Brother?"

"If you mean, sister, have you accomplished as you wished—yes, it is well done. If you mean will it lead to more complications, then I cannot answer you yes or no."

"The answer"—if thought could be a whisper, then was hers now—"is mine now. Well, what is done is done, and what must *be* done— With your permission, Eldest Brother, we will ride forth to see the end of all this."

Still she had not spoken to me, and now it was as if she did not want to look at me again. For after that first measuring stare, she turned her head away. I was curiously chilled, as if I had put out a hand in greeting, only to have it refused, myself ignored. And yet I could not make any move to draw her attention again.

We went inside to find food and drink. Maelen ate as one who must fuel an engine for running. And I did the same, discovering my body welcomed what I gave it. But still she was behind a wall I could neither breech nor climb.

I judged it midday when we came out into the courtyard of the temple. There was no sign of the van, but two riding kasi awaited us, journey cloaks across their saddle pads, bundles of provisions hanging ready. I would have aided Maelen to mount, but she was too quick for me, and I went to my own kas. Could it be she shrank from any contact in aversion?

We went through the devastation in the Valley. There were fire-blackened ruins, other signs of the fury which had hit to cripple, but not totally to destroy. Maelen pushed ahead along the road to Yim-Sin. It was plain she was in desperate haste to fulfill the rest of her plan, to return us both to Yrjar and resolve, as far as she could, the tangle fate had snarled about us.

Nor would she look at me during that upward climb, even touch thought with me. Was it so revolting to her that I now wore the body of one who had been closekin and who might be now deemed doubly dead? I chafed at that. Nothing of what had happened to me had I asked for.

But I had, memory responded. Twice I had asked through some Thassa ritual for these changes. And twice perhaps they had saved me from death. For the first time I wondered who would inhabit the body I now wore when and if I finally regained my own. Would Maquad indeed die then, totally and finally?

Since the pace Maelen set took us much farther than the former speed of the van, we were well out of the Valley before sunset. By sunrise we might again see the ruins of Yim-Sin. Then across the plains to Yrjär—But what was happening on those plains? And because I must look a little into the future, I forced myself on my companion.

"What could the servant of Umphra tell you about what might be happening on the plains?"

"Those who came from the west," she answered, "were strangers. It seems there is a new enemy abroad in Yiktor, more ruthless than any plains lord has ever dared to be. And that force comes from off-world."

"But the Traders—" I was too astonished to grasp it quickly.

"These are not Traders like unto the men of the *Lydis*. These newcomers fight to carve themselves a rooting in our soil, gather to themselves power, build their own kingdom. Some of the lords they have already overwhelmed, having worked secretly for a time to sow dissension among their people; others they have gathered to them with promises of much treasure to be later shared. They have set one against another, stirring ever the caldron of war with that spoon which will make it boil the most furiously. I do not know what we shall find now in Yrjar. I do not even know if we can reach the city. We can only try.''

What she said was not too enlightening, and not at all promising. It sounded as if this had been longer building than we had suspected— To plunge into a land where every man's hand was raised against his neighbor was daunting. But the port was at the outskirts of Yrjar, and there lay my only chance of reaching the *Lydis*.

Yrjar lay some distance away, and as I chewed upon what Maelen had said, the journey appeared to double. Were we wise to take the road at all now?

That thought was already shaping in my mind when the summons came. It was sharp and strong, as ringing as any horn call. But ti did not reach me through my ears.

There was an after moment of silence, then once more the pealing, demanding order we could not disobey. I heard a small cry from Maelen, of protest—

Then, before we willed it, we had turned our mounts to the right, out of the road into the wilderness of the northern ridges, answering a call which body and mind must obey—the horn-in of the Thassa, which sounded only in times of great import.

XVIII

WHAT I HAD SEEN of Yiktor had been much like any other world of its type—plains backed by hills, covered with vegetation varying in shade. But Yrjar, the fort of Osokun, Yim-Sin, the temples of Umphra, had their counterparts on many planets and were also familiar to me in part. Where we rode now was very different.

The horning set such bonds upon us that we could not have disobeyed its order. And we rode on and on, ever north, always into higher country. The rises here were not softened by any growth of trees, or even slightly veiled by brush and shrubs. Only small patches of grass, now killed by the first breath of winter, broke the general desolation of the stone.

For this was truly a desolate country. I have visited planets burned off in some nuclear war of such antiquity that it antedated the coming of my own species into space. That is ruin to daunt the heart of any who look upon it. But this was even more alien than that. It was a vast loneliness which rejected life as our kind knows, a stark stripping to the bones of Yiktor itself.

Yet there was life here. For when we rode deeper and deeper into this wilderness of naked stone and sand, we saw traces of those who had gone before us, tracks left by vans, hoofprints of riding kasi.

It was as if we lay under some spell, for we did not speak to each other, neither did I have any desire to turn back to the plains and what had once seemed my pressing business there. Night came. From time to time we dismounted, rested our kasi, ate of the supplies in the bags, walked up and down to ease our own bodies, only to remount and take up the trail once again.

At dawn our road wound between two towering cliffs. I thought that at some immeasurably early time in Yiktor's history this must have been the bed of a great river. There were sand and gravel and rumbles of bounders which looked water worn, but no living thing, not even so much as a single tuft of withered grass. And that river bed brought us into a huge bowl, also ringed by heights. If we had come up the river, now we entered a lake bed.

Here for the first time had man, or some intelligence, broken the austerity of the wilderness. Cut back into the cliffs about the lake bed were a series of wide openings, each bordered with carving which had once been chiseled deep, but now worn away to faint, unreadable tracings.

These cliff dwellings had inhabitants, for there were vans drawn up before them, the smoke of fires drifted into the morning air. Animals wandered about. But men, or Thassa, were missing. Maelen took the lead, for once we entered the basin the compulsion which had kept me every by her side lifted. She guided her mount to a picket line, slid from its back, and straightaway loosened her saddle pad, freeing it. The kas shook its head and then lay down and rolled in the sand, snorting vigorously. And mine, as I stripped it, did likewise.

"Come." For the first time in hours she spoke to me.

I dropped my saddle pad beside hers and we went across the valley, heading for the midpoint of the opposite wall. There was a rock doorway easily twice the size of the others flanking it. I marveled at the vast labor its carving had demanded, but I could not detect any meaning in the patterns which were outlined, for they were far too badly eroded.

Where were the Thassa? All I could see were animals and vans. But as we approached the cliff door I had my answer. From it came a sound which was more than mere chanting. It partook also of the movement of the air in a way I do not have any words in off-world vocabulary to describe. I fell into the rhythm of it unknowingly and then realized what I did. Beside me I heard Maelen's voice raised in song.

We passed from the light of the valley under that heavy portal into a hall. It was not dark, globes hung high over our heads and we walked through moonlight, although a few feet outside the sun struck hot across the rock.

And the Thassa were there in numbers I could not count. Before us there was a pathway open to the very center of the place, and down that Maelen went; I, less surely, a step or two behind her. Always that singing rang in our ears, beat in our blood, was a part of us.

So we came to a space where there was an oval

dais or platform raised a few steps above the surface
of the floor. And on that stood four of the Thassa;
two were men, two women. Although they were
firm of flesh, bright of eye, yet about them was such
an aura of age, authority, and wisdom as to set them
apart, even as their present positions set them bodily
above the rest. Each carried a wand. But these were
not the relatively short rods such as Maelen bore;
rather did they top their holders' heads when one end
was planted firmly on the floor. And the light which
shone from these shafts rivaled and paled the moon
globes.

Maelen did not mount the two steps to join them,
but stood in the open just below. And when I hesit-
antly came up beside her, I saw that her face was
closed and bleak; yet still she sang.

They all sang until it seemed to me that we did not
truly stand on firm rock, but rather that we wavered
back and forth in the currents of an ocean of sound. I
felt that I did not look upon Thassa but upon other
people—or spirits. My vision of them was never
complete; rather were they shadows of what might
be the truth.

How long did we stand so? To this day I do not
know, any more than I can dimly guess the meaning
of what was happening. I think that by their united
will as a people they built up certain forces, and from
those they drew what they needed for their purposes.
This is a very fumbling explanation of what I involuntarily joined during that day.

The song was dying, fading away, in a series of
slow, sobbing notes. Now it carried with it a vast

burden of sorrow, as if all the private griefs of an old, old people had been distilled through centuries, and each small ultimate drop of despair preserved for future tasting.

It was not for other ears, that end-song of the Thassa. I might wear Maquad's body, and in some small ways respond to Thassa ways, but I was not Maquad and now I put my hands to my ears to shut out the song I could no longer bear. I felt tears on my cheeks, sobs burst from my chest, although those about me gave no outward sign of the unbearable grief they shared.

One of the four on the dais moved. A wand swung out and pointed to me. And then I no longer heard! I was free of the cloud I could not bear. So it was until the song was done.

Then the second of those commanding that assembly moved. This time the wand pointed to Maelen. From her fingers her own symbol of authority freed itself, to fly to the greater rod as iron might be drawn to a magnet. She gave a little gasp and put out her hand as if, too late, she would have caught her errant wand. Then both hands fell to her sides and she stood motionless.

"What is your tale in this time and place, Singer?"

The question, which resounded in my head as well as in hers, was not voiced aloud, but was none the less plain.

"It is thus—" She began our story, telling it simply and clearly. None of them interrupted her while she spoke, nor commented on any part of our incredible experiences. When she had done, she on on the dais whose wand had entrapped Maelen's spoke:

"This, too, was in your mind, Singer; that there was one of your blood-clan who knew heart hunger, and that if the semblance of the one for whom she hungered be returned, perhaps good might come of it."

"Is this not so?" the man to the right of the speaker asked.

"In the beginning, I do not think so. Later—" Maelen's hand rose and fell in a small gesture which I read as resignation.

"Let that other who is so concerned stand forward," summoned the woman.

There was a stir and from the right came a Thassa woman. Although I could not read age among them, I believed that she was perhaps even younger than Maelen. She held out her hand to Maelen, and their fingers interlocked in both greeting and deep affection.

"Merlay, look upon this man. Is he the one whom you have mourned?"

She turned slightly to look at me. For a moment there was a kind of awakening in her face, a light in her eyes, as one might look when fronting a miracle. Then that light was gone, her face veiled and still.

"This is not he," she murmured.

"Nor could ever be!" the other woman on the dais said sharply. "As well you know, Singer!" And her sharpness was keener yet as she spoke to Maelen. "Standing Words are not to be altered, Singer, for

266

any personal reason. You have sworn oaths, do you now admit yourself foresworn.''

The other man on the dais, moved now, raising his wand and swinging its tip lightly through the air between the three and Maelen.

''Standing Words,'' he repeated. ''Yes, we lean upon Standing Words as our anchors and supports. Yet it seems to me that this sorry coil was begun through Standing Words. Maelen''—he was the first to speak her name and I thought there was some compassion in his tone—''first saved this man because of a debt. Nor is she responsible thereafter for much which happened. Therefore we lay upon her that she do as she has thought to do, return with him to Yrjar and there undo what has been wrought through her powers.''

''Which she cannot do,'' said the sharp-voiced woman, and I read satisfaction in her speech. ''For have we not had news of what will happen to Maelen the Singer if she is seen there?''

Maelen raised her head to look at the other in open surprise.

''What mean you, Old One? What danger lies in Yrjar?''

''The off-worlders who have raised fire, shed blood, and loosed the barsks of war have said that Maelen enchanted Osokun and drove him mad, and that they will have her dead—many believing them.''

''Off-worlders? What off-worlders—and why?'' For the first time I broke into what had seemed none of my affair, only between Maelen and the rulers of her people. But off-worlders—what *was* behind all this?

"Not of your breed, my son," the man who had spoken for Maelen replied. "But rather that one who sought out Maelen before the beginning of all this and wished her to be his tool, and those for whom he carried a sword in this matter. It would seem that you and yours have some powerful enemy off-world, who have now brought the quarrel to Yiktor."

"But—if you mean the Combine men—" I was startled. "I have no personal enemy among them. Long ago their kind and mind warred, that is true. But of late years our differences have been settled. This is madness."

One of the women on the dais smiled sadly. "All war and slaying is madness whether it be between man and man, or man and animal. But for whatever reason these bring their fight to the plains, it is true they have set a price on Maelen. Perhaps they fear she knows too much of them. To venture into Yrjar—"

"As Maelen," spoke the girl who stood hand in hand with my companion, "perhaps not. As Merlay—?"

The eldest man considered. Then he shook his head, almost regretfully. "There is the matter of time. Already the Third Ring begins to fade from the night sky. And only under it may an exchange of Thassa with Thassa hold true. You would not survive more than four days."

"It need not be so," continued Merlay, "if the exchange is not made here, but in the hills which border the plains. Then to Yrjar—four days will suffice.''

Maelen shook her head. "Better I go in my own body than risk yours, sister. I pay my own debts.''

"Have I said that you do not?'' countered Merlay. "I only ask that you follow wisdom and not folly. You have said, Mylrin,'' she appealed to the leader, "that Maelen has a right to bring this venture to the proper ending. There are those in Yrjar who knew that Maquad and I were life companions. If we go together, will we be suspect? This is the best way.''

At length it was decided that she had the best plan. I was not consulted. In fact, at that moment, I was thinking too much about the off-worlders. According to Maelen, Salfid had been mixed up in Osokun's intrigues from the first. He had threatened to tell of the Thassa body-changing to force Maelen and Malec to his aid. But as far as I knew he was no more than a very junior officer on a Combine ship. Why would any Combine wish to war here on Yiktor? They had done the like on other primitive worlds in the past, we knew gory stories of that—so that they might fish in troubled waters when both sides were exhausted. But Yiktor, as far as I knew, had no resources so rich as to tempt them to risk attention from the Patrol.

I was puzzling over this when we started back on the trail. Maelen and I, Merlay, and two of the Thassa men were mounted on the pick of the riding kasi. We covered the distance at the best pace the animals could keep. But it took four days of hard riding to reach a nook in the lower plains for the camp we wished.

That night we slept and through the next day we rested also, for that which must be done between Merlay and Maelen required bodies not strained to the edge of endurance. In the meantime I tried to discover what I oculd about the off-worlders. When they knew my concern the others discussed it with me, but among us we could light on no reason why Yiktor was a target for such interference.

"Treasure," Maelen said. "You spoke of treasures which are many and diverse. You said what is worth perhaps a man's life or a country's freedom on one world may be nought, less than a child's toy on another. I do not see what treasure we have here which could bring upon us disaster from the stars."

"Nor do I," I agreed. "You have told me there was nothing new and startling displayed at the fair. And all wares there were already known to the Free Traders. We could make a profit on a cargo from Yiktor—or we would not come—but only a reasonable one, not one to attract a Combine into one of the old-time raids."

"Mathan," one of the Thassa guards said to his fellow, "when we ride hence again, it might be well that we do not say, 'This is not our life, let the plainsmen do as they will about it.' For it might be that our whole world will be involved and it *will* be our concern."

"There is the off-world consul in Yrjar." I clung to my last hope of learning the why and wherefore of all that had happened since the *Lydis* had planeted here. "He must have the answer, or a part of it!"

On the second night the Thassa wrought their magic. This time I was no part of it, but was sent to await the one who would come out of the small tent they had set up to veil their actions. And when she did, booted and cloaked, ready to ride, we were off for the plains together, while the others remained.

The signs of war were here, though we took as covered a route as we could. I began to wonder if we could get through to Yrjar. We might well arrive to find the city under siege. She who wore Merlay's body, but was Maelen, did not agree with my pessimism. Yrjar had always been a kind of neutral meeting place, even when the fair was not in progress. And if the uprising was indeed inspired by off-worlders, they would make sure first of keeping the spaceport free. Warfare on Yiktor had always been more a matter of raids, hit-and-run attacks, rather than lengthy sieges to reduce well-fortified places. There was small profit in that, and loosely organized fighting units quickly lost patience.

Luckily we would not have to go into the walled portion of the city in order to reach our goal. For the building which housed the consul was on the edge of the port field. So we swung south to avoid the main roads into Yrjar and came in on the field. There was only one ship there—an official courier, and I noted that it was set down unusually close to the consular buildings. For the rest the port was deserted. We came in warily, tired from two long days of riding since we had left the camp in the foothills. Our kasi were close to done and we would have to have new mounts if we rode forth again—or rather Maelen, in her guise as Merlay, would. For if all went well, my only exit from Yrjar would be by ship.

We reached the edge of the field without any challenge and I did not like the silence, the feeling of being the only living things abroad in a forsaken world. With caution we worked our way to the gate of the consular compound and then were challenged, not by any guard, but by a force beam. The whole building must be englobed!

I slapped my palm against the voice box on the outer post, though a Thassa palm against that would mean nothing to the lock, and then I stated to the speaker that I had urgent business with Prydo Alcey. For a long moment, a very long one, I thought I might either be talking to an empty office, or else I was such a suspicious figure that I could expect at any moment to be crisped by a beamer. But then the plate lit up and I saw the face of the consul, knew that he must view me in return.

When I stated my business I used the Trader tongue, and now he looked out of the plate in amazement. He turned his head and spoke to someone over his shoulder, then he looked back to me.

"Your business?" He used the speech of Yrjar. But I answered in Trader tongue.

"Urgent, and with you, Gentle Homo!"

I thought he was going to deny me, for the plate went dark and he made me no answer at all. But a few seconds later the door of the inner court opened and he stood there, backed by two guardsmen. With the force shield in place, however, they were certainly safe enough from any weapon known to Yiktor.

"You are—?"

I decided to answer with the truth and hoped the apparent lie would spark his curiosity enough to let me tell the whole of it.

"Krip Vorlund, assistant cargomaster, Free Trader *Lydis*."

He stared and then gestured. One of the guards slapped the wall, and the sheen of the force shield was gone—for a moment. But both guards now held beamers on us as they motioned us in. We rode our stumbling kasi into the courtyard and I heard a swish as the screen went up behind us.

"Now," Alcey said quietly, "suppose this time you begin with the truth."

All men who travel the star lanes must develop the ability to accept weird things beyond the normal edge of belief. But I think that the consul of Yrjar found my story more bizarre than any he had heard before, except that, Thassa though I looked, I was able to supply so many off-world details that he had to admit only one who had served on a Trader could have given them. And when I had done he looked from me to Maelen and then back again.

"I saw Krip Vorlund when he was brought in—what was left of him. Now you arrive and tell me this. What do you want?"

"Get in touch with the *Lydis*, let me send a message. I can provide details which will prove the truth."

He smiled then, and it was the type of smile to dry up any flow of speech.

"You have my permission to signal off-world anything you wish, Vorlund, if you can."

"If I can?"

"I am, as you might have guessed from your welcome, no longer a free agent on Yiktor. There is a blanket satellite operating on short orbit up there—" He pointed to the ceiling over our heads.

"Blanket satellite! But—"

"Yes, but—and but—and but! A hundred planet years ago this might have been a reasonably normal situation. Now—it comes as somewhat of a shock, does it not? The Korburg Combine, or at least some agents stating they represent that Combine, have landed and believe they have the situation well in hand. I tried to get off a courier last night and was warned there was a stop-circuit set up. Because I have seen other evidences of their ruthlessness in operation here, I did not take the chance."

"But what do they want?" I demanded. As he had said, a hundred years ago such piracy would have been usual, but now! The appetites of the big Combines and Companies had long been curbed by the Patrol; there were drastic answers to such action.

"Something," Alcey returned. "Just what has not been made entirely clear. So your problem"—he shook his head—"now becomes a relatively minor one, except of course for you. There is this—" he hesitated. "I may not be doing right to tell you this, but you should be prepared. I saw your body when it was returned here. Your medico, he was not sure you could make it, but the *Lydis* had been warned out privately by one of their local merchant contacts.

They agreed to carry a message from me to the nearest Patrol post. We had only hints and rumors then, but enough to know they must lift ahead of time. And you—or your body—could well not have survived that lift. The medico protested it on your behalf."

I glanced down from meeting his eyes to the hands resting before me on the table top. Long thin fingers, ivory skin, strange hands—but they did my will, moved at my command. What if—if he was right in his foreboding that the Krip Vorlund taken away in the *Lydis* was dead, now perhaps spaced in a coffin suit after the manner of my people, so to lie among the stars for all eternity?

Beside me Maelen stirred. "I must be going," she said, and her voice was faint, very weary. So she recalled my thoughts—the change between her and her sister could not last much longer. With every passing moment their danger grew.

"But you do not know what Korburg wants here?"

"This much. There have been recent changes in the Council, especially as it touches the government of some inner planets. This world might provide a refuge or way station—temporary, of course, but perhaps necessary for some Veep when a coup on his home world has failed, a place from which he could come back with an army trained here."

It sounded unlikely, but his preparation for guessing right was better than mine. It remained clear that there was no hope at present of reaching the *Lydis*. If Captain Foss had made it to the nearest Patrol post—

Then it would only be a matter of time before they would visit Yiktor. On the other hand Maelen had very little time left. And we would be safer to return to her people to wait out the struggle. I asked for a recorder, and with both of them listening taped a message which I thought would identify me to all on board the *Lydis*. Then I told Alcey what I would do and he agreed.

The consul furnished us with fresh mounts, though they were not as wiry and mountain-trained as the two who had carried us to Yrjar. At nightfall we rode from the port. This time we were not so lucky in escaping notice, for we were trailed and only Maelen's power acting on the mounts of the pursuers let us pull ahead. The singing left her further drained and she urged us to greater speed, lest she fail before we found the camp.

Toward the end of that nightmare journey I carried her before me in my arms, since she could no longer sit on her animal. We put on a last burst to come to the secluded ravine between two steep hills where we had left the others. The tent was there, rent and crumpled on the ground. And half entangled in the folds lay one of the Thassa.

"Monstans!" Maelen broke from my hold and stumbled toward him, falling to the ground by his side, yet struggling up to look into his still, white face. She caught his head between her hands, bent to set her lips to his, sharing her breath with him.

I saw the tremor of his eyelids. The whole front of his tunic was stained scarlet, but somehow he had held on to the last dregs of his life force until our coming.

"Merlay"—it was a whisper in our minds, not any words shaped by those pallid lips—"they have taken her—think she—is—you—"

"Where?" Our demand was as if in one voice.

"East—" So much had he done in our service, but no more. The life he had held to swept out of him in one small sigh.

Maelen looked to me. "They seek my life. If they believe that they now have me—"

"We can follow." I had to promise that. And, for good or ill, I knew I would keep my word.

XIX

I SAW THEREAFTER how determination of will can carry one beyond the limits of body strength. For she whom I had brought before me drew upon such will to send her on from the destroyed camp.

"Mathan?" I searched about for some trace of the other Thassa before I left the body I had wrapped in the tattered tent. Maelen sat on her saddle pad, both hands pressed to her face. Now she spoke, her voice muffled by her fingers.

"He has gone ahead."

"A prisoner also?"

"My power fades so fast. I cannot say." She dropped her hands to look upon me. Her eyes were dull. It was as if even as I watched, life ebbed from her. "Tie me," she begged. "I do not know how much longer I can ride."

I did as she wished before we left the ravine, following a trail the raiders had made no effort to conceal. There were many kasi tracks and, while I could not be sure, I thought that more than a dozen riders had passed this way.

The way we took was not a road, yet it had been used before, and it pointed through the hills ever westward toward Oskold's hold. Maelen made no effort to guide her mount, which nevertheless followed closely the one I rode. She once more shaded her face with her hands, and I thought that now she shut out the world both physically and mentally, so she could either reach or hold some tie which would pull us to what we now sought.

Night became day and we found a camp where there were embers of a fire still warm to the touch. Maelen's head now hung forward heavily on her breast, her arms limp at her sides. She roused only to much urging from me. But I got water between her lips, saw her swallow as if that act were both painful and difficult. More than a little liquid she refused.

It was strange to see one I had come to accept as having more than human powers become so dependent. But her half-open eyes focused on me after I had made her drink, and there was knowledge and recognition in them.

"Merlay still lives—they take her to some overlord—" Her voice was the merest threat of whisper.

"And Mathan?" I held to the hope that the other Thassa had escaped death or injury, that he might eventually join us in whatever frail attempt we must make to free Maelen's body from the raiders.

"He is—gone—"

"Dead!"

"Not—so. He has gone to call—" Her head fell forward again and her too slender body swayed in the bonds which held her on the kas. I could not rouse her again. Thus I stood in the deserted camp of the enemy and wondered what was to be done. Manifestly Maelen could not continue, and to go on alone was rank folly. Yet neither could I abandon the trail.

"Ahhhhhh—" Half sigh, half crooning cry from Maelen. I hurried to her again. But, though that sound continued from between her lips, still she did not come out of the stupor.

There was a rustling in the bushes. I whirled, the Thassa sword-knife fitting in my hand awkwardly, since it was a weapon new to me. From the branches, downdrooping and still hung with leaves, came an animal—an animal? No—more than one, and not from just one side. Nor was the beast that had first pushed a fangfringed muzzle through the vegetation a pattern for the rest. No, here were the Borba and Vors, and their like Tantacka, here was the like of—Simmle— More and more of them!

And the beast who led that silent, purposeful advance was one new to me, long and lithe of body, feline in its movements, with a prick-earred head, and—and eyes with the spark of human intelligence in them!

"What? Who?" I tried to beam an inquiry at their leader.

"Mathan!" The identification was sure.

Those others, were they also Thassa? Or some of those whom Maelen had sent into the wilderness? Or companions of other beast masters and mistresses?

"Part and part," Mathan gave me answer.

He loped soft-footed to Malene's kas, stood upon his hind legs to look upon her.

"Ahhhh—" Again that cry from her. But she did not open her eyes or look at him and that company. For a company—no a regiment!—it was.

More and more rustling in the brush, heads out into the open, animal eyes regarded me narrowly.

"She cannot ride any farther," I told Mathan.

Furred head turned, round eyes met mine. "She must!" With his teeth he caught one of the ties which kept her on the on the pad, gave it a sharp tug. "This will hold. She *must* come!"

If he had passed some command to that army, I did not hear it. Now they flowed past Maelen and went westward and were swallowed up in the cover. Of their number I could not be sure, save there were more of them than I had ever seen gathered together before. But the feline Mathan paced just before us as we rode on. I tried to stay beside Maelen to steady her. She slumped forward now, lying against the kas's neck, wholly oblivious of us and the road.

There was a coming and going of animals, occasionally some would return and look at Mathan. I was sure that messages passed between them, but I could not pick up any information. We had progressed well into the hills, taking a way which did not lead to any gap but up steep ascents, where I dismounted and walked beside Maelen. There was no sign of any trail here, and several times we inched along a knife-edge advance. I dared not raise my eyes from the footing, lest I turn giddy.

At last we came out on a level space. Snow lay here, and fine flakes of it stung my nostrils, were glitter points in the air. If the plains had not yet quite felt the last of autumn, here winter already licked at the land. I fastened the cloak tighter around Maelen; she stirred beneath my hand. I felt a shudder run through her thin frame, heard her gasp and then cry out. She struggled against my hold, sitting up as she had not for hours, to look at me, at the rocks and snow, with eyes which were first wild and unseeing, then had recognition in them.

"Maelen!" The voice she used was shrill, carrying enough to bring an echo. There was a deep growl from the beast with Mathan's eyes. And too late she put her hands to her lips as if to stifle that cry.

She who had been so drained and helpless was now erect, as if strength flowed into her in great waves. There was even a delicate flush on her cheeks, more color than I had ever seen on Maelen.

Maelen? It was clear to me now—this was not Maelen. Merlay had returned to her own body. But before I could say that, or ask the reason, she nodded to me.

"Merlay." She gave me the answer I had guessed. Maelen's time had run out, the exchange had been made without any ceremony or outward sign.

"And Maelen?" My words, Mathan's thought sped together.

"With them." She shivered and I knew it was not from cold, though the wind was a breath of frost.

She looked about, from peak to peak, as if searching for some landmark. Then she pointed to one to the right, yet well ahead.

"They camp on the far slope there."

"For how long?" Mathan demanded.

"I do not know. They wait for someone, or some message. They hold Maelen by the orders of a leader I never saw. But I do not think we have much time."

Again a growl from Mathan's throat. He was gone in a flash of gray-tawny fur, and I knew that all those others he commanded in his strange regiment were running with him. Merlay looked to me.

"I am no Singer. I have no power to aid us now, save that I may be your guide."

She urged the kasi on in Mathan's wake, and I after her. For these few moments I wished I had again the barsk body, that I might run behind the Thassa warrior. The lope of a sure-footed animal in this maze of rock and fall would have been far swifter than our constrained walk. My impatience was a goad. I had to exert full control or I might have overridden her.

Now and then she glanced at me, and each time she looked quickly away again. It was as if something drew her eyes, searching ever for what was not there, and each time being met by loss. I thought I could guess what pulled and then repelled her.

"I am not Maquad."

"No. Eyes can deceive, they are the gateways for illusion. You are not Maquad. Yet am I glad in this hour you wear what was once his. Maelen is caught in coils not altogether of her spinning, the heart can betray the mind many times over."

I did not really understand her words, but it did not matter. For I had one bit of knowledge. I might be

Thassa only in outward appearance, yet I did not believe at this moment I could follow any other road, to any other end, than that which lay before me. Was I still Krip Vorlund, asked a doubting thought not far buried? As I had partaken of the nature of Jorth the barsk, sometimes losing man within the animal, so might I not also join with the residue of Maquad lingering in his husk? And if I actually returned to take on the body of Krip Vorlund once again—though that seemed remote now—would I be only Krip Vorlund thereafter?

"Why do they want Maelen? And how did they find you?"

The second question she answered first. "Not by chance—they trailed us. But whether they first came upon our tracks by chance and followed—that I do not know. As to why they want Maelen—that, too, is hard to read. They wish to lay upon her, as we heard, a measure of blame for what they have done. I think that they plan to use her somehow to win Oskold to them, or to open some door in the western lands where he may still be paramount lord. This much I can tell you: those who hold her have their orders to do just that, no more. He who comes will decide—"

Once more we climbed, and slipped, and climbed again where no trail ran, but where the kasi appeared able to pick footage. We were under the shadow of the peak she had indicated. Around us there was no rustling of brush, no sign any animal army marched with us, save that here and there a paw print left a sharp signature.

Merlay left her saddle pad. "The kasi can go no farther. We make our own road from here."

And a steep and perilous way that was. At times we had more holds for finger tips and toes, but still we fought for inches of advance. We rounded a rocky outcrop and so came to the other side of the rise. The snow had stopped, but it was followed by a still cold which bit at a man's lungs with every breath he drew. And we came together in a niche to look down into the purplish depths of the eastern foothills of Oskold's land.

Night was coming fast. I wished I had Jorth's eyes to read through shadows. The ground before us was as rough as that we had just covered. And to descent it in the dark promised trouble. But we had no time to linger. Merlay pointed.

"There!"

No tents or vans, but a fire, yes. It would appear that those there did not care if they attracted attention. I tried to pick out a spot on the slope where they could have stationed a picket to scout pursuit. Shadow slipped from shadow—mind-touch—This was Borba coming up to us.

"Come—" His head swung to indicate a path and we crept behind him. Thus we came down as silently as we could. And in that coming we passed a pool of dark. A hand, lax-fingered and very still, protruded from it, palm up and empty. Borba's lips wrinkled and he snarled as he passed that hand and what lay behind it.

We came off rock and into soil rooting small trees of a ragged timber line. From here we could not see the beacon of the campfire, must depend upon the small furred guide. I no longer possessed Jorth's sense of smell, but perhaps the Thassa were better equipped with noses than my own race. For I picked up whiffs of animal odor, enough to tell me that though we neither saw nor heard them, Mathan's force lay in waiting about us. Then a larger shape rose out of the ground at our feet and I caught the thought of the Thassa leader:

"A party comes to the camp. Hasten!"

We moved to the dark side of a rock. Beyond, the fire shot higher, gave more light, as it was fed energetically by two men. I counted eight in plain sight. They were all, to my eyes, like any sword-sworn I had seen in Yrjar. I could not read the emblems on their cloaks or surcoats.

"Whose?" I mind-beamed to Mathan.

"Oskold's there—there—there—" He indicated three. "The rest—I have not seen that device before."

The sound of a horn, sharp and clear, cut the small noises of the camp. There was silence for a second and then shouts of welcome.

"Maelen?"

"There!"

Merlay answered my question. What I had taken for a roll of sleep covering lay, unmoving, well into the firelight.

"They fear her—to look into her eyes," Merlay whispered. "So they have tied cloaks about her lest she turn them into animals. They have been told that she will do this, that we all shall do this."

I did not hear Mathan growl, but I felt the vibration through the fur-clad shoulder pressed close to mine.

"Can we get to her—" I had begun when another party tramped into the firelight. The flames glinted and flashed from ornamentation on cloak and helm. And he who led them was older than the rest.

"Oskold." Mathan's thought identified him.

Their voices carried, but the words were in the inland tongue and I did not understand. I tried to read the thoughts behind them. There was triumph, satisfaction, anger. Yes, emotions were easier to pick up than words.

One of the fire-feeders stooped and jerked at the bundle which was Maelen, pulling her upright. Meanwhile another stepped forward to grasp the covering about her head and shoulders and pull it loose. Her silver hair shook free, and then she raised her head with a toss which cleared that silver veil from her face; she stood head up and unbending to front Oskold.

"'Ware, lord, she will make you beast!" One of his companions laid hand on Oskold's arm to pull him back, the intensity of his thought readable to me.

Oskold laughed. His hand, covered with a glove reinforced across the knuckles with metal strips, swung up to strike Maelen full in the face. She crumpled. down.

So it was Oskold who gave us our signal. The raging fury which now boiled out of the dark, and the tree shadows leaped, tore, screamed, growled, shrieked in that moment after Maelen went down. I heard the cries of men, the tumult of the beasts, but I headed for Maelen.

I was no swordsman and my sword-knife was a poor weapon, but I reverted to Jorth's rage in those moments when flames became a red curtain in my mind, drowning thought, leaving me only one purpose in mind. This was as it had been when I had gone after Osokun and his men—

She was under my hand—still—no life in her, her face up to the sky, the red ruin that blow had wrought on flesh and bone made plain. And I crouched above her, snarling as any of the furred ones who fought about me.

As it had been with the outlaws who had killed Malec and taken our camp, so it was now with these. For there is a kind of horror in such warfare which the minds of men find impossible to comprehend. To have waves of animals break about them unnerved some from the start, fighting men though they were. Others rallied, killed, some standing their ground; others fought a rear-guard action to withdraw, always harassed, pulled down, overrun.

For me there was but one in that enemy company. And knife in hand, I made for him. In spite of the surprise of our attack, at least one of his guards had come to Oskold's side, fending off with his shield two rushes from a pair of venzese who sprang to snap and bounced back to wait another chance.

I tripped over a body and sprawled forward, almost into the heart of the fire. Then my hands, bracing me up again, closed on a beamer—something I had not expected to find there, but which fitted into my palm as familiarly as a long-worn glove. I did not even try to get to my knees; I lay and pressed the firing button of a weapon which had no right to be there.

The ray it threw was a thrust of eye-searing fire. No shield could stand against that, no, nor man either! I had wanted to let Oskold feel my hands upon him as he went down, but I took the means fate sent me and used the off-world arm. Once, twice— Oskold might be on the ground now but there were others of his following—There was a sputter and the ray died, its charge exhausted. I hurled it from me into the fire and crawled back to Maelen.

Above that fearful wound her eyes were now open and she saw me, knew me—of that I was sure. I caught her up and went back into the dark, to that rock where Merlay had been. I staggered a little when I reached that poor shred of cover, so I had to lean against the chill stone. Merlay was still there, but she did not touch what I held, only laid her hand upon my shoulder. A flow of strength was channeled so from her to me.

This was a battle, and it was fought, and men died and animals died, but for me it was a nightmare which I can not well remember. Only at last there was quiet, and we came once more to the fire. For it seems ours was the victory. Yet it might well be that it was also defeat—

I laid Maelen down on the robes Merlay spread to receive her. Still she looked at me and at Merlay, and at the animals who came to her, and last of all to the feline Mathan, who staggered into the fire shine with a wound in his side. But her thoughts did not come to me. Only her eyes told me she still lived.

Suddenly I could not look into them any longer, but got up and walked blindly away, stumbling among the dead. One followed me and sprang to catch my dangling hand between sharp teeth. I glanced down at Borba. A split ear dripped blood, but undaunted eyes met mine.

"Come."

Because nothing mattered now, I went as he wished and we thread among bushes until we came to where there was a line of picketed kasi. Someone moved ahead of me there, slowly, so slowly I thought he might be wounded. Borba hissed and pulled at my hand, urging me on. The figure, fumbling with a lead rein, swung around to face me. In this lack of light I could not see his face, but that he was a fugitive from the camp, I knew. I leaped for him. Under my weight he collapsed, though he struggled feebly. I struck an off-world blow, felt my slender Thassa hand go numb. But the one under me was still. I hooked fingers into his collar and pulled him with me into the firelit open.

"Krip Vorlund!"

It was not recognition but summons. I left my prisoner lying and went to the three who waited on me. Mathan lay with his head resting on Merlay's knee, and Maelen—I could not bring myself to look upon her.

But it was her mind-call which had brought me. I went down on my knees and took her two hands into mine. They gave me back no pressure, no sign that

more than her eyes lived. Beside her something
moved with a whine. Vors—was it Vors or another
of the same breed crouched there?

Merlay stirred, Mathan raised his head. There was
firelight here, but over us hung the moon. And that
Third Ring which had been so bright, so sharply
defined when this whole mad venture began, was
now only a misty haze, soon to disappear.

"Moon!" A thought—a whisper of a whisper—
"Mathan—moon!"

Her hands were very cold in mine, there was
nothing which could ever warm them now. Suddenly
the glassia beside her cried out, a kind of keening.

Mathan's head rose higher. There was a rumble
from his throat, but it was no beast growl. Rather it
was singing, a singing which entered my head, my
blood, traveled through me. Then I heard Merlay
take up that song, which she could not initiate, but
which she could second. And Maelen's eyes held
mine, searched into me, somehow touched a part of
the body I wore which had never been open to Krip
Vorlund. So I believe I sang, too, though I am not
sure. We sat there in the fine haze of the fading moon
Ring and helped sing Maelen out of death into a new
life.

When I again looked with full consciousness
around me, the hands I held were those of a husk
which the spirit had deserted. And resting on my
arm, warm and living, was a small furred head. I
dropped the hands of death to gather close warmth
and life.

The prisoner I had taken by the kasi lines looked at

me when we brought back his senses to him, but did not know me. I knew him well, though, for there was little change in him since that afternoon when he had suggested my meeting with Maelen. Gaul Slafid.

He tried to make a bargain with those of us he believed to be Thassa. Such stupidity I did not understand, unless being made prisoner in such a fashion muddled his wits for a time. Then he mouthed threats, telling us what would happen to all the Thassa unless we instantly set him free and made abject terms with those behind him. And here, too, perhaps fears prompted his ravings. But we heard enough so that I might guess the rest.

Alcey had hit upon the beginnings of it. Yiktor had been closely studied for years by men who needed, as part of their plans, a primitive planet as a base and supply depot. And, playing politics, the Korburg Combine had waded into waters so deep they must aid these exploiters or drown.

The Thassa had been thought to constitute a threat, so a grand crusade against them had been planned. It had been planned to unite the lords under one leader into an army which could later be directed as the exploiters saw fit. But the ancient feuds and rivalries had not made this smooth working, and they chose to use Maelen's involvement with Osokun to whip up that crusade.

What would come of it all, who knew? But at this moment Gauk Slafid was one piece removed from the game board. And I believe the realization of that ate into him acidly, so he mumbled on and on, refusing to face the wreck of his own ambitions.

We took him back with us into that strange dead-lake valley in the hills. And there was all stood before the Old Ones. Slafid they wasted little time upon, giving him to me to take to the port to face the judgment of his own species, saying he was of my blood and mine the responsibility for him.

But then they came to the judging of Maelen under their own law. And I was not allowed to question, or to speak thereupon, for they let me know at once that I only abode there by their favor. When I rode from that place, a guard of Thassa going with me, I carried a furred one who was not Vors, but another.

For this was their judgment—she was to abide in the body given her freely by one who loved her, that her spirit have housing—to remain so until moon and stars drew a pattern in her favor, according to some obscure reckoning of their own. And while so she was to be with me, whom, they said, had been her victim—though to this I did not agree.

With Slafid, who had now lapsed into sullen silence, we came to Yrjar. There he talked again, to officers of the Patrol come at the message borne by the *Lydis*. So was that off-world conspiracy finished, at least as far as Yiktor was concerned. That planet left to lick its wounds and sort some order out of chaos.

I sat at last with Captain Foss and those from the *Lydis*. And I looked past them to a mirror on the wall of the counsul's inner chamber. Therein I saw a Thassa. Inside that body, though I might be altered a little, I was still Krip Vorlund. Thassa ways were not mine. Not being truly of them I could not live their life. The would open their vans, their tents to me (Mathan, once more in human-guise, had asked me to join his clan), but among them I would be as a cripple stumping on one foot, using but one hand, seeing with but one eye.

All this I said to Foss, but the final decision lay with him and the others, according to our custom. For the casing which had brought Krip Vorlund to Yiktor was gone, cast into space when it had "died" weeks earlier. Now I waited to hear whether Krip Vorlund was indeed dead, or whether he would be allowed to return to life.

"Free Trader," Foss mused. "I have seen many things traded in my time, and on many worlds, but this is the first time I have seen an exchange of bodies. You say these Thassa look upon their outward flesh and bones as we would upon a suit of clothing, to be changed when the need arises. Does that also stand for you?"

I shook my head. "My own body, yes—but no other. I am Thassa to look upon, not Thassa in powers. I will remain as you now see me."

"Good enough!" Lidj brought his hand down in a mighty blow on the top of the table between us. "You pulled your weight before. Standing in another body will not change that. Are we agreed?"

He glanced at Foss, at the rest of them. And I read their verdict before they spoke it. Inwardly, I wondered if I had done right in asking to return. In me somewhere lay a small part of Jorth, and of Maquad. I perhaps wore more than just the body. But if they thought me Krip Vorlund, I would try to be him again fully. And, looking out upon the port and the waiting *Lydis*, I knew I must throw away all doubts. Jorth and Maquad were less than nothing beside what was waiting out there for me. I was Krip Vorlund, Trader, and that was all—it must be all!

Yet more than just another body did I take out of Yiktor. A small furred person shared my cabin and my thoughts. Many times I do not see her as she is, but as she was. She came by free choice and the will of the Thassa.

Time stretches far between the stars, and fortune makes many turns for good or ill. There are treasures and treasures. Perhaps one shall fall into our hands and paws. And we shall have our ship, and our company of little people to travel the trails of space. Who can tell? I am Krip Vorlund of the *Lydis*, and already they forget that I look different. But I do not forget who lies beneath the skin of Vors and will walk two-footed someday. We shall both see Yiktor again—and if it lies then under Three-Ringed Sotrath—who can foresee what may happen?

ANDRE NORTON, one of Ace Books' most respected and prolific authors—with over forty books and millions of copies in print—is world renowned for her uncanny ability to create tightly plotted action stories based on her extensive readings in travel, archeology, anthropology, natural history, folklore and psycho-esper research. With classic understatement, belied by the enthusiastic critical reception of all her books, she has described herself as ". . . rather a very staid teller of old fashioned stories . . ."

Miss Norton began her literary career as an editor for her high school paper and quickly progressed to writing, publishing her first book before the age of twenty-one. After graduating from Western University, and working for the Library of Congress for a number of years, she began her writing career in earnest, consistently producing science fiction novels of the highest quality.

Miss Norton presently resides in Florida under the careful management of her feline associates.

ANDRE NORTON

"Nobody can top Miss Norton when it comes to swashbuckling science fiction adventure stories." —*St. Louis Globe-Democrat*

07897	**Breed to Come**	$1.95
14236	**The Defiant Agents**	$1.95
22376	**The Eye of the Monster**	$1.95
24621	**Forerunner Foray**	$2.25
66835	**Plague Ship**	$1.95
78194	**Star Hunter/Voodoo Planet**	$1.95
81253	**The Time Traders**	$1.95

Available wherever paperbacks are sold or use this coupon.

ACE SCIENCE FICTION
P.O. Box 400, Kirkwood, N.Y. 13795

Please send me the titles checked above. I enclose _____ .
Include 75¢ for postage and handling if one book is ordered; 50¢ per book for two to five. If six or more are ordered, postage is free. California, Illinois, New York and Tennessee residents please add sales tax.

NAME_____

ADDRESS_____

CITY_____STATE_____ZIP_____

S-03

ANDRE NORTON

Witch World Series

Enter the Witch World for a feast of
adventure and enchantment, magic and
sorcery.

89705	**Witch World**	$1.95
87875	**Web of the Witch World**	$1.95
80805	**Three Against the Witch World**	$1.95
87323	**Warlock of the Witch World**	$1.95
77555	**Sorceress of the Witch World**	$1.95
94254	**Year of the Unicorn**	$1.95
82356	**Trey of Swords**	$1.95
95490	**Zarsthor's Bane** (illustrated)	$1.95

Available wherever paperbacks are sold or use this coupon.

⬛ **ACE SCIENCE FICTION**
P.O. Box 400, Kirkwood, N.Y. 13795

Please send me the titles checked above. I enclose _____.
Include 75¢ for postage and handling if one book is ordered; 50¢ per
book for two to five. If six or more are ordered; postage is free. California, Illinois, New York and Tennessee residents please add sales tax.

NAME_____

ADDRESS_____

CITY_____STATE_____ZIP_____

S-04

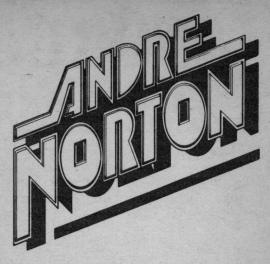

Classic stories by America's most distinguished and successful author of science fiction and fantasy.

☐ 12314	**CROSSROADS OF TIME**	$1.95
☐ 33704	**HIGH SORCERY**	$1.95
☐ 37292	**IRON CAGE**	$2.25
☐ 45001	**KNAVE OF DREAMS**	$1.95
☐ 47441	**LAVENDER GREEN MAGIC**	$1.95
☐ 43675	**KEY OUT OF TIME**	$2.25
☐ 67556	**POSTMARKED THE STARS**	$1.25
☐ 69684	**QUEST CROSSTIME**	$2.50
☐ 71100	**RED HART MAGIC**	$1.95
☐ 78015	**STAR BORN**	$1.95

ACE SCIENCE FICTION   S-02
P.O. Box 400, Kirkwood, N.Y. 13795

Please send me the titles checked above. I enclose _____.
Include 75¢ for postage and handling if one book is ordered; 50¢ per
book for two to five. If six or more are ordered, postage is free. California, Illinois, New York and Tennessee residents please add sales tax.

NAME_____

ADDRESS_____ _____

CITY_____ STATE_____ ZIP_____